THE KING OF FROST AND SHADOWS

FATED TO DARKNESS
BOOK 1

JEN L. GREY

NAME GLOSSARY

Lira (LEE-rah)
Tavish (TAH-vish)
Eiric (AY-rik)
Faelan (FAY-lan)
Finnian (FIN-ee-an)
Caelan (KAY-lan)
Eldrin (EL-drin)
Lorne (LORN)
Moria (MOHR-ee-ah)
Torcall (TOR-kahl)
Finola (fi-NO-lah)
Rona (ROH-nah)
Dougal (DOO-gal)
Malikor (MAL-ih-kor)
Moor (MOOR)
Struan (STROO-an)
Pyralis (pie-RAL-is)

GENERAL GLOSSARY

Ardanos (ard-AN-ohss) – Realm Name

Aetherglen (AY-thur-glen) – Unseelie and Seelie joined kingdom

Cuil Dorcha (COOL DOR-kha) - Unseelie Kingdom

Dunscaith (DOON-skah) – Unseelie Castle

Gleann Solas (GLYAN SO-las) – Seelie Kingdom

Caisteal Solais (KASH-tul SO-lash) – Seelie Castle

Aelwen – (A-el-wen) - River in Seelie Kingdom

Tìr na Dràgon (CHEER na DRAY-gon) – Dragon Kingdom

Cù-sìth (koo-shee) – Wolf-like Unseelie creature

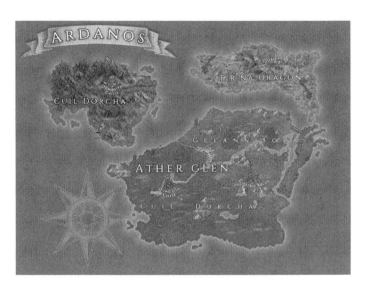

The lantern in my hand flickered as I tiptoed through the castle's dark secret passageway. I'd learned that Tavish, the Unseelie prince and my friend, was doing poorly, and I needed to see him. I didn't understand why Father wanted to hide this from me, and I didn't know where Tavish's parents were, but he shouldn't be alone.

He'd do the same for me if our roles were reversed.

When Father hadn't come to wish me good night with Mother, my pulse had started racing. The last time he hadn't shown, I'd learned the next day I'd been betrothed to the dragon prince, Pyralis, and that the Unseelie were no longer our acquaintances.

Yet again, none of it made sense to me, but I supposed that was to be expected. I was only ten years old.

I'd always assumed I'd be promised to Tavish. My parents and I and the Unseelie royals met twice a year so the ruling fae families could spend time together. Though the relationship between the two kingdoms had always been uneasy, it was nothing compared to our fraught relationship with the dragons.

When I pressed her for answers, Mother had let it slip that Tavish was here in the holding cells. Then she'd asked me not to let Father know she'd told me. He didn't want me to know, likely because he knew I'd do this.

Cobwebs hung in the corners of the stone walls, and I tried to control my breathing. I hated how dusty it smelled in here, and I avoided glancing at the floor. I'd walked the corridor twice a year since I'd turned four, learning its twists and turns in case something ever happened and I needed to escape. Father's intent hadn't been for me to use it to sneak around behind his wings.

An animal scurried by my feet, and my heart hammered, pounding against my ribs. I closed my eyes and tried not to scream. Maybe I should've waited until morning to visit Tavish, but the weird expression on Mother's face and the way her vibrant red wings had hugged her body had my chest feeling tight, like I couldn't breathe. I'd never seen her forehead with lines before. Between that and Tavish being in a holding cell, I'd realized things in the Seelie Court were worse than Father had let on ... bad enough that he'd promised me to a *dragon*.

When the creature had scurried far enough away, I took two more steps and turned right where the door would be. I lifted the lantern higher, my arm shaking with fatigue from how long I'd been carrying it around. The holding cells were as far away as you could get from the royal bedrooms and a place that an attacker would least expect us to flee to. That was one reason the holding cells were rarely used, and only for a partial day when they were—to keep the cells free each night in case the dragons decided to attack. The last we'd heard, their kingdom's resources were strained, so they were searching for another land to move to.

Gritty stone rubbed against my fingertips. I'd never

opened the door before—Father always handled it—but I'd watched him closely enough to find the lever in the bottom corner.

I squatted, my pale-blue silk nightgown brushing the smooth floor, and then flinched, realizing I'd need to change when this was over, or someone would notice the dirt. Exhaling, my aqua wings fluttered behind me, revealing my nerves. Luckily, I was alone, though I could still hear my father's voice echoing in my head. *Lira, as the future Seelie queen, you can't let others see your emotions. You must always be confident and strong.*

Easy for him to say. He'd been nine hundred years old when they'd finally been blessed with an heir.

My finger reached a divot, and something sharp pricked my finger. I jerked back and stuck my finger into my mouth. The sweet honey taste of my blood hit my tongue as I tried to ease the sting ... and the stone wall faintly creaked open.

A groan sounded from the darkened room, and I edged inside, allowing the lantern to cast a warm glow.

I froze.

The boy I remembered from not too long ago couldn't possibly be the fourteen-year-old before me.

His face was paler than normal—which spoke volumes for the Prince of Darkness, Frost, and Nightmares— reminding me of the snow I'd seen a handful of times when we'd traveled to the Unseelie castle. His onyx wings enveloped him like a barrier, and I noticed a large pool of black blood underneath his right side.

I rushed to him, forgetting to be quiet. This broken figure was a shell of the boy from my memories, a boy who used to chase me through the woods and clouds. I dropped beside him, making sure I didn't kneel in his blood and placed the lantern next to me. I took in the sizable wound in his side and gasped. The skin looked jagged as if torn by a dagger, and I could see tissue between the rushes of blood trickling from him.

He grimaced like the light bothered him, which it probably did since he wielded darkness.

I had so many questions, but that didn't matter. In his state, he couldn't respond. I scanned him, noting no signs of herbs or bandages. Why hadn't a healer come, and why didn't he at least have a cot to sleep on? It was as if Father didn't care that he could die.

I took his hand in mine. It felt like ice ... colder than I remembered. The contrast between my sun-kissed skin and his snowy complexion reminded me again of how different we were.

One thing was certain, he could die.

At the thought, something inside me sparked—a magic that felt different from the cool, refreshing kind I used when wielding water. This sensation felt warm and comforting, and it pulsed from the spot inside me next to my water magic.

My skin buzzed where we touched, and the warm magic funneled toward our connection, my power flowing into him.

I tensed. Unless a fae was an experienced healer, we only shared magic if we found our mate. If my parents learned what I'd done, I'd be in more trouble than I could comprehend. Sharing a piece of myself like this would make me vulnerable, but before I could pull away, his wound began to shrink.

Head tilting back, I didn't understand what was happening. Impossibly, I *was* healing him. The last fae who could heal injuries through touch had lived thousands of years ago, and there hadn't been one since. We now relied on healers with earth magic to know which herbs and plants would help people heal faster.

Yet, I couldn't deny what was happening in front of my eyes as the wound stopped bleeding and closed completely.

Something heavy weighed on my body.

His eyelids fluttered but remained closed. I had to believe that if I continued to use this new magic, I'd heal him all the way. Yet, the magic inside me weakened, and my head lolled sideways as fatigue settled over me.

I blinked several times, forcing my eyes to stay open.

Shuffling outside the main door caught my attention. My mouth dried. If the guards came in here, they'd catch me.

Then one of them said, "Watch out! There's—"

His words ended in a gurgle, and the door was flung open.

An Unseelie man I'd never seen before blocked the doorway. Shadows curled around his body, hiding him from anyone behind him. He had long, white hair and white eyes.

When those eyes focused on me, he sneered and marched toward us. "What are you doing to my cousin?"

I peered behind him and saw a guard bleeding out on the floor. Fear strangled me. Even though I needed to move, I went still as a statue. Not even my wings spread out behind me.

The air brimmed with tension, and he charged me.

"I'm heal—" I started, but he shoved me away from Tavish.

I shrieked, but the back of my head hit the floor, cutting short my cry. My vision hazed just as the man picked up Tavish's unconscious body. The last thing I saw was him blanketing them both in shadows.

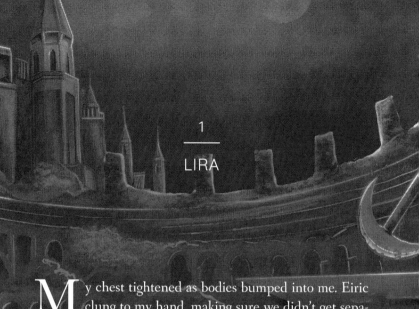

My chest tightened as bodies bumped into me. Eiric clung to my hand, making sure we didn't get separated among the masses, adding to my wariness. I couldn't shake the feeling that we should head home and leave this overcrowded New Year's Eve party. The air had become electric since we'd joined the crowd for the New Year's countdown, but now it felt different ... like danger was more imminent. Hard to believe because I'd been on edge after waking from my recurring nightmare this morning.

"Dammit, Lira," Eiric said loudly over the noise of the jazz music. "I can't believe you talked me into coming to the City Market on New Year's Eve! We're just asking for drunk people to spill their drinks on us or, worse, vomit all over us."

Yeah, I couldn't believe it either. Earlier, while people-watching from a bench three blocks away, the idea had seemed perfect. Now, the urge to flee damn near overpowered me. Everywhere I looked, I saw dark-slate eyes watching me.

A shiver shot down my spine at the vivid image in my

mind. Something made me want to see the person they belonged to, but he was always hidden by shadows and darkness. Only his eyes were visible to me.

I'd had the same nightmare every night for as long as I could remember. Though, through the years, the eyes had become crystal clear, so much so that I could have drawn them perfectly if I'd had the talent.

I'd hoped to calm the restlessness inside me by getting out and around people in the fresh air, but the scents were definitely *not* refreshing. I wanted to jump into the ocean or take a shower because I was certain I smelled like body odor as well.

Despite the faint chill of late December in Savannah, with all of us bunched together, it felt like it was at least seventy degrees out here, and we were still on the outskirts of the grassy lawn, far away from the stage.

"Look, E." I paused behind a group of guys who were leering at the women in front of them and turned toward my best friend, who also happened to be my sister. I hated to admit that I'd made yet another bad decision, but my discomfort trumped my pride ... for the most part. "If you want to go, I guess—"

"Oh no you don't." She arched a perfectly sculpted brow and shook her head, her short, tight curls barely moving in two pigtails piled on top of her head. "You're not blaming this one on me." The glitter sparkled on her dark skin as if she were magical. "Since you're willing to leave 'for me,' I'm not taking you up on it." Her emerald eyes twinkled with glee. She'd purposely worn a long-sleeved shirt the same green color, which wasn't surprising. She favored shades of green.

I lifted my head and pushed back a few of the long

blonde curls stuck to my face. I wrinkled my nose from a combination of the smells and her calling my bluff.

The way she smirked should've made me angry with her, but instead, I snorted and said, "*Wow*. Some sister you are."

Something hit me in the back, pushing me forward into the tallest guy in the group of men.

My shoulder hit Tall Guy, and he jerked forward.

"What the fuck?" the guy said angrily.

Eiric grabbed my arm and steadied me so I didn't hit the ground and get trampled. She glared at the two women who'd run into me and took a few steps back, pushing them away with her butt.

Tall Guy spun toward me. "You made me spill my—" His bloodshot eyes landed on me, and the anger twisting his face smoothed into a grin. "Damn. I mean, are you okay?"

Ew.

Standing a couple of inches taller than my five-foot-ten frame and buff, the guy wasn't bad-looking. If he'd been sober, he'd have been attractive to most women. Looking at him closely, I realized he might be the tight end on Savannah State College's football team. And boy, if I was right, he had a reputation as a womanizer.

Not that it mattered. The issue was still the same.

I'd never found anyone I was interested in—male or female—and clearly, that wouldn't change tonight, though I sort of wished I could find someone I was into.

"I'm fine," I said, answering the question he'd probably forgotten he'd asked a few seconds ago. "Sorry about running into you. I hate that I ruined one of the many drinks you've clearly overindulged in tonight."

Eiric sighed, but the corners of her mouth turned upward. She liked to tell me that my mouth got me into as much trouble as out of it, which meant I shouldn't say half the things I thought. However, she could never hide her amusement from me.

"It's fine." He threw an arm around my shoulders and pulled me to his side, his stale alcohol breath hitting my face.

I wanted to gag.

"Come with me, and I'll get you a drink too." He winked, lowering his head so that his scruff brushed my temple. He tried to lead me away from Eiric, so I dug my white tennis shoes into the grass.

The way he leered at me told me everything. My stomach gurgled, and I regretted coming here. It was still thirty minutes till midnight.

"Actually, I don't drink." That wasn't true. I had in the past, but nothing had ever happened. Eiric and I had watched a ton of people get drunk and tipsy, but we'd never gotten a buzz, not even after splitting a gigantic bottle of tequila between us.

"Oh." His forehead lined as if he'd heard the world's most complex math equation. "That's fine. You can keep me company while I get a new brewski."

Not rolling my eyes physically hurt me. How did this guy get any women? Yet I was certain he'd slept with numerous girls on campus. I felt bad for every one of them, knowing there was no way he could possibly be a good lay. "No, I'm good."

"Please?" He pouted and tugged on me again.

Eiric stepped up next to me, her face stoic with a look that could make any grown man feel like a child. My sister placed her hands on her hips, ready to give Tall Guy a lesson in etiquette. But that wasn't all. She was preparing.

Our parents had taught us as children how to defend

ourselves, and we never left home without protection, especially on nights like this.

We each had a knife strapped to our ankle—which was why we favored boot-cut jeans—and a pocketknife in our right pocket since we were both right-handed. We had easy access to a weapon if we needed quick protection.

"My sister said no." Eiric glared. "So let her go."

Tall Guy pretended she hadn't spoken, keeping his gaze locked on me.

Something inside me suddenly *tugged*, and the hair on the nape of my neck stood in warning. My skin crawled at the unsettling sensation, one I only ever experienced in my nightmares.

"There you two are," a deep voice with a faint accent boomed from the edge of the crowd where Tall Guy had been trying to take me. Even though there was no way this man was talking to us, my eyes homed in on him like he was a glass of water I desperately needed.

And what I found shattered me.

Gray eyes the color of storm clouds met mine, causing my heart to quicken. They were so familiar, yet I couldn't place them. Still, they spoke to something deep inside me.

He slid gracefully toward us through the groups of people, and my palms became sweaty, which was ridiculous. He wasn't looking for me.

But I wanted him to be.

"Don't be so uptight," Tall Guy shot back at my sister. "You're hot too. One of my boys will gladly take your attention, but blondie here owes me a drink."

I swallowed as Sexy Man scowled. His pale complexion reflected the various lights from the stage, adding more allure to his devastating good looks.

"I hate to inform you, but *blondie* here is with *me*." Sexy

Man's dark hair fell into his eyes as he reached out and took my hand then pulled me away from Tall Guy and toward him.

My skin buzzed where he touched me, and my legs moved with ease. I didn't realize what I was doing until I was nestled into Sexy Guy's side with his arm around my waist. Between the way my body reacted to him and his unique scent—a mixture of wet earth, jasmine, musk, and amber—I had to fight to keep myself from burying my nose in his shirt.

Eiric tilted her head, taking in the newcomer. Her hand lowered to her pocket, readying to take out the knife at the first sign of distress.

I wasn't sure what she saw in Sexy Man that made her more uneasy than Tall Guy, yet it was sort of funny that the one I'd labeled Tall Guy was at least two inches shorter than the newcomer.

Tall Guy gritted his teeth as he noted my relaxed posture. "She's your girl?"

Sexy Man chuckled darkly. "The one I've been searching for almost half my life."

My stomach somersaulted, and my cheeks hurt from how huge I was smiling. Great. If Sexy Man was interested in me, I was definitely not playing it cool. I finally felt something for someone! Though the sensation was startling. Being next to him felt *right* ... and I never wanted to be apart from him again.

"Come on, man," one of Tall Guy's buddies said and clapped his back. "We all need a refill and a girl to kiss at midnight."

Eiric gestured between the two guys and said, "If all else fails, you could kiss one another." She shrugged and moved to my other side. She gave Sexy Man a quick glance then focused back on Tall Guy.

"If you're so worried about us finding someone, you can kiss me, Green Eyes." Tall Guy grinned and winked at her.

"I'll pass." Her nose wrinkled, making her disdain clear. "I'm sure you can find someone as drunk as you. You'll be fine."

Sexy Man's hand tightened on my waist as he glanced from Eiric back to me. He nodded to the left, which would take us farther from the crowd. "Are you ladies ready to go, or would you rather stay in *this*?" His body stiffened, conveying he was as uncomfortable as Eiric and I were.

"Let's go." I didn't give a damn if Eiric gloated. I wanted to get away from the crowd. I'd heard on campus that this was one of the best places to go for New Year's, but it wasn't for Eiric and me. We both preferred hiking, swimming, and gardening to being around drunk people. When I'd suggested we go, she'd asked me if I'd lost my damn mind, and our parents hadn't been thrilled, but what could they do? I was twenty-two, and Eiric was twenty-one. We were both of legal drinking age, and we lived at home to save costs while I attended Savannah State College to study environmental science and Eiric went to Georgia Southern for her geology degree.

Sexy Man led me out of the crowd with Eiric on our heels. He moved fast, but surprisingly, I had no issues keeping up with his pace. We dodged people who'd been drinking and hanging out on the roads of the oldest section of Savannah until we made our way to Telfair Square.

When the crowd thinned, Sexy Man released his hold but stayed beside me. Eiric cut her eyes at me, and I could hear the unasked question—*What's the plan?*

The thought of heading home and leaving this man had

my heart squeezing in discomfort. And it'd be rude to abandon someone who'd rescued me, right? Not that Eiric and I couldn't have handled the situation on our own, but still ... he'd been considerate and heroic. Speaking of which, I hadn't said another word to him since we'd left. How rude of me.

My tongue felt thick and heavy, and I wondered if I was getting sick.

After much concentration, I cleared my throat and rubbed my hands together, already missing the way my body fit perfectly against his. "Thanks for that back there. I'm sorry if we ruined your night. I'm sure you were meeting a girl or something." My voice damn near cracked on that last part as I realized how it could be taken.

Eiric smirked, and my blood ran cold. She must have figured out that I had a thing for the man. She'd had sex with dozens of guys and a few women, whereas I couldn't fathom even kissing anyone. It had never appealed to me, so seeing me like this had her grinning widely. I'd kill her if she didn't stop since he could see both of us.

"When I saw you, no one else mattered." Sexy Man winked, turning his attention to me. "But don't fret. No one will miss me. I didn't have set plans."

Warmth spread through my chest. He didn't speak like most people our age, and I found that fascinating. "My name's Lira." I motioned to my sister. "This is Eiric."

"Lovely names. They sound as if they're from another world." He bowed faintly. "I'm Tavish."

Head tilting back, Eiric furrowed her brows. "That's unique. How did your parents come up with that?"

"It's a family name, and we aren't from anywhere close to here." His irises darkened, and I missed a step.

They reminded me of the eyes from my nightmares, but

they weren't dark enough ... and, most importantly, I was awake.

What the hell was wrong with me?

It must have been the stress from being close to completing my Bachelor of Science in Environmental Science in May and having to find a job.

We headed into the section of Telfair Square with a brick path and trees everywhere, toward where we'd parked our car, but I wasn't ready to go yet. I glanced at my watch. It was only five minutes to midnight. If I was ever going to kiss someone, I'd love for it to be Tavish before he disappeared from my life.

A few people loitered around, and I could still hear the music from the City Market.

"E, is that you?" a woman called, and I looked toward where the path split and circled some bushes with three benches spaced around the grass. She waved my sister down from thirty feet away. "Come ring in the New Year with us!"

My sister smiled but shook her head, ready to turn the woman down to stay with me. She was protective of me like that, and I loved her for it usually, but not tonight.

I touched her hand and smiled. "Go hang out with them for a minute."

She stiffened and looked from me to Tavish. "I thought we were going home."

"We are, but in four minutes, it'll be midnight. I'm sure we can wait that long." I stared into her eyes, wanting her to get the message. *Give me a few minutes alone with Tavish.*

"I can stay with her." Tavish smiled, becoming more breathtaking. "No one else will talk to her or touch her while you're gone."

Eiric grumbled, "That's what I'm worried about."

I reached out and squeezed her hand, urging her to go. It would be four minutes. Nothing could possibly go wrong in that short amount of time.

"Fine." She huffed, relenting, then leaned toward me and whispered, "You owe me. You better kiss him, dammit, and don't disappear on me." Then she said out loud, "I'll be right back."

Tavish moved closer to me, taking my hand again, and when my sister reached her friends, he tugged me off the brick path and under a huge southern oak tree. He pressed my back against the bark and grinned.

"It's dangerous to go off with strangers," he whispered as he touched my chin, his thumb pulling down my bottom lip.

He tasted faintly of winter air and the night, and my body warmed for more of him. I breathed, "After what you did, I believe I'm safe with you."

His lips grazed mine, and if I thought my skin had buzzed when he'd touched me, now I jolted ... and it wasn't even a full kiss. I couldn't imagine what I'd feel next.

He placed a hand over my head, trapping me.

I licked my lips, eager for his kiss.

Instead, he chuckled. "Oh, sprite, I'm the one you should fear the most." His eyes darkened to a deep slate ... the very eyes that haunted my nightmares.

The tree behind me disappeared, and I fell.

Iridescent swirls circled my body as I tried grasping something. But each time, my hands came up empty.

What the *fuck*?

The swirls vanished, but I continued to drop. Cold air wrapped around me, and my hair blew into my face. A strangled scream caught in my throat as I realized *this* was the moment I died.

That was what I got for hoping for a fucking New Year's kiss.

Now I understood what true terror felt like.

My hair whipped my face, stinging my eyes, but I saw I wasn't the only one falling. Tavish was right above me, dropping faster and catching up with me. Even though he was also tumbling to his death, he had a huge grin on his face.

His comment that I should fear him the most replayed in my mind like a tornado siren, but the red flag had come way too late.

"What's wrong, sprite?" He laughed, reveling in the fall. "You scared of a little drop?"

Of course, the first guy I was attracted to would happily

watch us crash to our deaths. Now I wanted to go back to not feeling a damn thing for anyone.

I'd at least fucking die with dignity.

I spun so my back was to him, expecting to see the ground I'd crash into, but we seemed to be tumbling into an abyss. My stomach lunged into my throat, and I wanted to vomit. The anticipation of death had to be worse than the real thing. At this speed, death would be quick and painless.

Then hope sprang into my chest, clenching my heart.

Maybe this was a dream.

The same eyes I dreamed of each night and falling infinitely like this couldn't be real life. I just needed to wake up.

I pinched myself, and pain shot up my arm.

Worse, I was still falling.

"Almost there, sprite," Tavish teased as he caught up to me and fell beside me.

We tumbled toward *something*, but only one of us was fearing for our lives.

The wind turned cold, and a dark blob appeared below us, with glowing red places surrounded by what appeared to be water.

My heart raced as the wind pressed against my chest. I struggled to breathe, and my ears popped from the altitude change.

"I must admit, this moment is more exhilarating than I expected." His gaze remained locked on me like my fear made dying worth it. "All these years, yet your horrified look is nothing like what I anticipated."

"Are you serious?" I yelled, trying to glare at him.

I hated that, despite the morbid joy written across every inch of his cold face, he had become more breathtaking since I ... well ... fell. With my back against the trunk of a huge-ass oak tree, I hadn't seen what had happened to me. "This is the first time we've met, so what the fuck are you talking about?"

The land underneath us grew larger, and I could see sharp, jagged, mountainous cliffs, numerous volcanos, and dry, cracked ground peeking through darkness and fog. I feared one of the sharp tips would deliver my death.

"Ah, we've met before." He winked. "In fact, we spent much time together when we were younger."

The hairs on the nape of my neck lifted, and I wasn't sure if it was from that gesture or the below-freezing air. "I'd remember you. That's not possible."

"Don't worry, sprite. You'll remember soon."

I had no idea why he kept calling me by the name of a soda, but dammit, I wouldn't remember anything after we hit the ground.

Something exploded from his back, and before I could comprehend what I saw, he'd closed the distance between us, wrapping his arms around my waist and holding me against his chest.

My body jerked with his as our descent slowed, and understanding crashed into me.

He had *wings*.

I blinked, taking in his massive wingspan. The leathery onyx wings glistened magically, reminding me of the glitter on Eiric's cheeks.

And as if that wasn't bad enough, everywhere that my body pressed against his buzzed, feeling way too nice and chasing the cold away, his presence comforting me.

It sure as hell shouldn't do that.

I placed my hands against his chest to get away from him. The last thing I wanted was to feel safe with a man who wanted me dead. "Let me *go*."

He laughed, his chest rumbling against mine. The sound was deep and genuine and had my stomach doing flips all over again. "Are you saying you'd rather fall to your death than have me hold you?"

Was I? That did seem rather extreme. "Yes. Yes, I am. Let me go so I can get my suffering over with, short and sweet." There was no telling what his sadistic ass had planned for me.

"Aw. Where's the fun in that?" His arms tightened, keeping me in place. "I have plans for you. Your parents will answer for their crimes against mine."

The fight left me, and I tensed, more confused than ever. "My *parents*? My dad's a security guard, and Mom works for an optometrist." There wasn't a damn thing they could have possibly done to this man ... a man who had wings. Maybe sleep deprivation had caught up to me.

He laughed again, dark and hateful. "If that were true, you wouldn't be here with me."

A lump formed in my throat. Did he mean my birth parents? My parents had adopted me when I was ten years old, and I couldn't remember anything from before I moved in with them. It was as if the first ten years of my life didn't exist, and when I was younger, I'd wanted to know why. As I got older, I decided that the best thing for me was to let those memories remain forgotten. My mind had to be protecting me from something.

Clearly, that was the case, but now I wished I'd let the therapist my parents had sent me to look for those answers. Maybe then I'd understand why this guy hated me enough to save me one moment and kidnap the next.

"If my parents hurt them, why do you need me?" I lifted my chin, forcing myself to meet his eyes and ignoring the way the land underneath us moved swiftly as he flew ... somewhere.

"You're going to break them, sprite." His slate eyes met mine, all warmth gone. "You're going to bring them to their knees."

I snorted, the sound like sandpaper against my throat. "If you think my sperm and egg donors care about me, you're wrong. They gave me up when I was ten, and I haven't heard a word from them since. I don't even remember them. Your best bet is to take me back home or just kill me and get it over with."

"Oh, death isn't in your imminent future. That fate would be too easy."

Terror dug its sharp claws into my chest, and even though the fall was no longer pressing the air out of me, I still couldn't breathe. If this *wasn't* a nightmare, I could only imagine the terror and panic Eiric and our parents would experience when she came to find me after midnight.

Eiric would blame herself for my disappearance even though it wasn't her fault. I'd encouraged her to leave me alone with him. But I had no doubt she'd carry the burden for the rest of her life.

Maybe that was for the best. Would he have tried to take her, too, if she hadn't left to visit with her friends? I'd rather she live with that guilt than be part of whatever hell would be my future.

Something cold hit my cheek, pulling me back to the present. I glanced up to see bits of snow falling from the sky through thick, stormy clouds and gasped.

We'd been in Savannah moments ago, and it wasn't nearly cold enough for snow.

Where the hell were we?

"Ever seen snow before?" Tavish asked. His breath warmed my ear.

Goose bumps pebbled my skin, but they had to be from the snow. Not *him*. The bastard.

"Yes." I refused to tell him I'd only seen it once, and it hadn't even been a dusting. The jackass didn't deserve to know anything about me.

"You don't seem to enjoy it. That's unfortunate." He nodded to his right. "There's snow here year-round and not warmth like you're used to."

I flinched and turned my head to see what he meant. My eyes widened.

A gigantic castle as dark as the sky towered on a jagged mountain peak. It didn't seem to have a single light on within, though I caught a few glimmers in the houses nestled at the bottom of the slope. They were made of the same dark material and continued down the land near the edge of the water that crashed against the shoreline.

Snow covered the ground, and a steady flow drifted from the sky.

No one stood on the streets, giving the town an eerie vibe. I'd never seen or heard of this place before. "Where are we?" If I got a location, maybe I could escape and get back home.

"Somewhere you'll never leave." He sneered. "Unless I allow it."

Wow. He was confident and cocky. I'd give him that. "Then you won't be afraid to tell me the location." I arched a brow, trying to come off as confident as him, though I didn't feel that way at all. I was truly at his mercy, and I hated that.

Eiric had told me countless times that always thinking the best of people would get me into a shitload of trouble.

She must have fortune-telling abilities because if she could see how far I'd fallen, she'd say she told me so.

"Are you sure you want the answer to that query?" He tilted his head. "I don't want to overload that pretty head of yours too much in one night. I can't have you breaking down until I permit it."

My stomach almost fluttered at his compliment, but I shut that shit down. I refused to feel any more attraction to this pompous ass. "Try me."

"You asked for it." He lowered us toward the buildings. "Welcome to the new Unseelie lands."

I snorted. "Unseelie, as in *fae*?" I wanted to dismiss his words as a joke, but he had wings, and I'd fallen *through* a tree. All of that defied the physics of Earth.

"Of course fae." He smiled ominously. "That was an asinine question."

His gruff words hurt, but I straightened my back, refusing to let him see it. The movement pressed my chest into his more, increasing the pleasant buzzing of my body, which was hugely problematic. I didn't want to feel *any* sort of nice feelings toward him.

I swallowed, not wanting to aggravate him more. I was his prisoner for now, whether I liked it or not.

Forcing my attention away from him, I turned back to the castle and noticed a man standing in the darkness of each open window. They wore dark armor and also had wings, each pair a different shade of gray, from very dark to nearly white.

Tavish flew to the far end of the castle, snow falling in his hair and on my face. The white flecks contrasted with his dark hair and nearly blended in with the paleness of his face.

He flew us in through a low window while the guard

moved aside to allow us entrance. When Tavish landed, he released me and took several steps back like he couldn't get away from me fast enough.

Unfortunately for me, my traitorous body wanted to chase after him. I already missed the buzzing from his touch, and I needed another fix, like a drug addict. I made sure my feet stayed planted and glanced around the room for exits.

Darkness clung to me and soaked into my bones, chilling me. I didn't want to stay here.

All I could see was a long-ass hallway, but every ten feet, lanterns radiated dim light.

"Your Majesty." The man bowed, dark-blue hair hanging over his shoulders. "I see you found the—"

"Woman," Tavish interjected, his irises darkening to match his wings. "Yes, I have. Do you have the room ready for her?"

Your *Majesty. Oh my goodness, please tell me I heard him wrong.* I didn't need some powerful fae royal wanting to torture me.

The guard straightened, his golden eyes meeting mine. He nodded. "It's prepared as you requested."

"Good." Tavish lowered his wings and pulled them close to his back. "Come, Lira. It's time to show you your new home."

There were so many things I wanted to say, but I kept my mouth shut. I had no clue how to get out of here or what Tavish wanted from me. I needed time to form a plan before I said or did something foolish and made my situation worse.

Tavish strode down the hallway, not bothering to check whether I followed, but his guard growled at me when I didn't move, so I begrudgingly obliged.

After a few steps, faint light from a nearby room caught my eye, and Tavish stopped at the open barred-gate doorway. He turned to me and gestured inside. "Welcome."

When I glanced in, I wanted to cry. The room was dark except for one light right over a small, thin bed pressed against the stone wall. A fuzzy blanket lay on it, but no pillow and a bucket sat in the corner. It looked worse than a prison cell in my world.

"What's wrong, sprite?" He smirked. "Not to your liking? I thought keeping you in a holding cell would bring things full circle."

I wanted to scream that I didn't understand, but he already knew that. My confusion was getting him off, and I refused to give him any more pleasure. The urge to flip him off surged through me, but I gritted my teeth and said, "It's fine, *nightmare*."

His head tilted back, and he grinned. Those irises lightened to a stormy gray as if he had let a little light in. "Then off to it. And if you use the bucket, you get to empty it in the morning."

My stomach dropped. The bucket was for the bathroom. *Lovely.* I'd rather sleep with a full bladder than use it, especially as any guard could see through the barred door while I was relieving myself, which must have been his intention. He wanted to humiliate me. "Noted. Thanks."

His head tilted back. "I'll let you have that one because you don't remember not to thank a fae. Next time, I won't be so kind, and you will owe me." He stalked out of the room and shut the gate with a clang. He didn't look back as he walked away.

Shit. I'd have to break that habit fast. And even worse, I felt terribly alone when he was gone, even though I was safer with some distance between us.

I walked to the bed and lay down on it. I could've sworn they'd placed rocks underneath the mattress. I wouldn't be surprised if they had.

I turned to face the stone wall, not wanting any guard to see me come undone. Placing my arms under my head for a pillow, I let my tears break free and stream down my face. Pressure built in my chest as a sob tried to escape, but I refused to let anyone hear my breakdown.

Instead, I swallowed the noise and closed my eyes, picturing Eiric's and our parents' faces. I pretended to be home, safe in my bed, with the calming sound of the ocean playing in my earbuds to help me drift off to sleep.

Soon, the darkness took me.

———

A BOISTEROUS LAUGH startled me from my sleep. I spun around, despite my back and head killing me, to find a menacing man opening the door to my cell and barging in, the blue-haired guard from last night right behind him.

"So this is the thornling," the tall, muscular man with white wings said as he reached down and grabbed me by the neck with one hand. His eyes were as white as his wings, and a deep scar marred his cheek.

I tried to push his hand away, but his hold tightened, cutting off my air supply.

"That's what King Tavish said." The blue-haired guard nodded. "She was crying all night, and it was damn exhausting."

"Sounds like we need to toughen her up." He smirked. "I'm more than willing, seeing as her people gave me this." With his free hand, he caressed the scar. "Time to return the favor."

He lifted me up by my neck, and I choked, my ears ringing. My heart raced as I realized this man wasn't as controlled as Tavish. Still trying to pry his fingers from my neck with my other hand, I reached for my dagger, but I couldn't get to it.

With his free hand, White Eyes drew a sword. "I'm thinking I should cut her from cheek to neck. It only seems fair that her scars be worse."

As the edges of my vision darkened, I could only think of one thing I could do. I drew back my foot ... and kicked the guy in the crotch.

My toes met metal, and I felt something snap.

3

TAVISH

Eight hours and thirty-two minutes had passed since I'd left Lira in the holding cell. The fact that I was aware of each passing minute was driving me mad.

For twelve years following her disappearance from Ardanos, I'd been obsessed with hardening my heart more than the icy land outside of Dunscaith Castle ... and locating her. I pushed the midnight-blue covers from my body and placed my bare feet on the smooth, cool floor. Normally, the cold didn't bother me, but this morning, the chill caused a faint shiver.

How strange.

Granted, upon seeing her last night on Earth with some rancid human all over her, something had shifted in me. Something more hungry for violence than normal.

I glanced out the wall of windows across from my bed, darkness still blanketing the sky despite the sun's ascent. I normally allowed the sky to lighten to twilight during the day, but I wasn't in the mood for anything but dreary darkness to match the turmoil inside me.

Images of Lira as a girl flashed through my mind. I'd always found her cute, but now ... now she was—

I halted my thoughts.

Her beauty didn't mean a blasted thing to me. I'd brought her here for one thing only.

Vengeance.

She was a pawn in my game of chess with the Seelie king and queen. Nothing more than that. The Seelie royals had killed my parents and taken me to their kingdom to die so that my people would be ruined. They'd even betrothed Lira to the wildling dragon prince, Pyralis, even though she'd always been marked as my future wife, meant to rule by my side.

Destroying her was part one of my plan to take back what was rightfully ours. I would make her parents bow to me and destroy their alliance with the dragons. After all, the Seelie betraying their own kind had been bad enough, but promising the Seelie princess to a scaley, fire-breathing destroyer had made their betrayal even worse.

Those sunscorched traitors had taken everything from me—even the boy I used to be. I wouldn't allow my people to stay here on this dragon-decimated island to starve to death.

A knock on the door brought me back to reality.

"Tavish," a familiar voice called out.

My cousin, the man who'd risked his life to rescue me from the Seelie palace dungeon. If it hadn't been for him, I would've died, and the Unseelie royal line would have ended, weakening my people further. Though we'd had our severe disagreements since the night I'd lost my parents, he'd become like a second father to me.

"Come in." I flexed my wings, stretching them from my back. Outside the window, a group of men headed toward the rocky embankment with satchels on their backs and fishing rods to catch food from the ocean.

The oversized double doors opened, and Eldrin stepped inside then shut them behind him. "I was surprised you didn't alert me when you came back with the thornling." His long white hair was tied in a ponytail. With how dark I'd kept the sky, there wasn't enough light to make his eyes look silver, and they appeared gray like mine.

I didn't bother answering. He hadn't asked a question, and even though he was the one person I trusted more than life, I didn't feel like dancing around a lie. Being fae was a curse at times.

I snagged the black tunic from my night table and slid it over my head. It smelled of Lira's magic—wild roses, moonlight mist, and vanilla. Her scent was more potent than I remembered despite the suppression of her fae side.

No wonder she had dominated my thoughts last night ... so much so that I couldn't risk entering her dreams for fear I would go to her. My plan had been to continue to demoralize her until she realized she couldn't escape me, even in her dreams, but after seeing her in person, I feared it might backfire on me.

"I know the girl is here, so why aren't you more joyful?" Eldrin strolled across the room past my bed and took a seat at the small rectangular table my chessboard sat upon, his back to the open window.

Gritting my teeth, I took a shallow breath. "She's innocent. I take no joy in doing this to her. It's merely something I must do for my people so we can reclaim our rightful land instead of staying exiled in this dreadful place." I lifted the black belt that held what had been my father's sword, which I'd claimed as my own upon my return. The dark sword with its white-edged tip was unusual and not something from the Unseelie land, which made it impervious to our magic. I placed it around my waist. I didn't go anywhere without it ... unless I had to go to Earth, which had happened only twice to date.

Eldrin shook his head and turned to the chessboard, moving his fae guard two spots over. "She isn't *innocent*, Tavish. She's a blasted thornling. Her parents *killed* yours and wanted you to die."

Internally, I flinched, but on the outside, I didn't budge. Showing emotion was a weakness, something I had learned the hard way when I failed my people. "That wasn't by her hands." I hated feeling this way, and last night, it had hurt to see her fear as she'd tumbled toward what she'd thought was her death. I'd waited so long to catch her, needing to prove to myself that her fear and distress wouldn't affect me.

And I'd hated every second of it, though I'd forced myself to appear heartless. After all, while at one time we might have been cordial, we were now mortal enemies. I had to keep my reasons for taking her at the forefront of my mind.

"Tavish, do you remember the last time you didn't listen to me?" Eldrin leaned back in his seat, gesturing to the spot across from him. "And what you had to do to get the people to *not* rebel against you? If you'd listened—"

"I know what I have to do." I hated it when he spoke down to me like this, and I only tolerated it in private. He had our people's best interests and mine at heart. "I created the gauntlet." A necessary means to keep traitors in check.

"Exactly." He placed his hand firmly on the table, causing the chess pieces to tremble. "That girl is not inno-cent, and when she remembers everything, she'll be like all the others. We need to break her before she regains her magic."

I slid on my boots and rolled my shoulders. He was right. I couldn't let my boyish memories influence the man I was now. "Which is why I'm heading down to the prison to see her." My heart jolted for a second, and I pulled my wings tightly around me. That had to be yet another strange side effect of being on Earth, like the buzzing when we'd touched.

He smirked. "Very well. Should I come with you?"

I opened my mouth to say no, but I realized that his company would remind me of everything I already knew. "Of course."

We headed out of my bedroom and down the hallway toward the prison. Unlike the Seelie fae, I kept my bedroom on the same side of the castle as the prisoners; I didn't want my people to believe I feared those imprisoned here. To maintain control at such a tender age, I'd been forced to be fearless … or pretend to be.

Eldrin kept pace with me, our feet echoing against the floor, though we could easily fly or tread lightly. But I enjoyed the prisoners hearing our presence, their fear a small benefit of having to keep them fed and somewhat clean while they stayed here. Each imprisoned fae had committed either a crime against an innocent or against me, one that wasn't severe enough for me to kill them on sight. As a reminder to my people, once a month, the guards would drag the prisoners outside to remind our people of what would happen if they broke my laws, which were quite simple.

As we made the sharp turn that would lead me to Lira, I heard Malikor's deep, angry voice threatening her. Without thought, my wings flapped and sped me forward. Desperation to reach her before something horrible happened set in.

A sickening *pop* came from the room, and Faelan

winced from his spot in the hallway. His head turned my way, and he froze.

I shoved him out of the way, entering the cell to find Malikor's back to me and Lira lifted up by her throat, her face flushed. Hot rage thawed my icy blood. I removed the sword from my hip, knowing the perfect spot to hurt any fae.

Lira whimpered, and tears filled her eyes.

"You don't think we know to guard our cocks?" Malikor snorted.

I swung my sword and sliced off his left wing, close to the base of his armor. The wing hit the floor with a thud as black blood gushed from his wound.

He dropped Lira, and I darted around him and wrapped my free arm around her waist before she could crash to the floor. Everywhere my arm touched her, even through her strange clothing, tingles erupted between us. My breath caught at the sudden barrage of weird sensations.

"My wing!" Malikor exclaimed. His face blanched as his right wing fluttered to help him keep his balance now that one side of him was significantly heavier than the other.

Lira's body leaned into mine, catching me off guard. She should have known better than to trust me like that. She was here because of me.

However, that was her problem, not mine, so I lowered her to the cot.

"You cut off my wing because of a blasted sunscorched?" Malikor yelled, his nostrils flaring.

I kicked him in the chest. He flew back several feet into the hallway and crashed into the wall.

No one spoke to their king in that manner.

No one.

Not even *Eldrin*.

Malikor groaned and sagged forward, blood puddling underneath him.

I stalked slowly toward him, anger tightening my chest. "She's in a prison cell with no recollection of who or what she is. She has no means to protect herself, and you swooped into her cell to choke her and cut her. What sort of blasted coward are you? You know the *rules*. They aren't hard to remember because they're that simple."

Behind me, Lira whimpered and gasped. Each tormented noise she made pushed me farther along the edge of control.

"She's not one of us." Malikor's breathing quickened. "She's our enemy. You brought her here—"

"*I* brought her here." I could feel the darkness inside me surging forward. "Not *you*. She's *mine* to do with as *I* like. Not yours."

Eldrin and Faelan stood together on the other side of the cell, watching me. Eldrin's expression remained stoic, but the way the skin around his eyes tightened informed me he didn't like this confrontation. Whether it was from my actions or Malikor's didn't matter. I made the laws for my people.

"There's only one way to make this right." I pressed my boot into his chest and lifted the sword, holding it level with his eye.

"My King," he rasped. "You've cut off my *wing*."

"For abusing your position as a guard." I dug the tip of the sword into the top of his cheek, going deep so he had matching scars on both sides of his face. I'd learned at fourteen that I couldn't be merciful. People mistook kindness and empathy for weakness. Unseelie fae understood only fear and violence.

He screamed, the sound getting louder as I dragged the blade all the way down to his neck. I didn't worry about killing him; if he died from this, so be it.

"And that is for attacking a woman in a cell who had no way to defend herself," I rasped, allowing frost to lace each word.

Lira's breathing slowed, and her whimpers sounded muffled as if she were covering her mouth or face. I hated that I was so attuned to her, but she was important to the kingdom. That had to be the reason.

Malikor fumbled onto his knees, his hands covering his cheek as black blood slid between his fingers.

I spun and headed back into the holding cell, my focus locked on the sizable white wing that lay on the ground, blood oozing out of the muscle that had held it. I lifted the wing and used the skin to clean the blood from my blade.

Lira gagged, and Malikor's bottom lip quivered.

When I glanced at Faelan, he swallowed hard, while Eldrin could've passed as bored. However, I could see the gleaming approval in his eye. He loved it when I embraced my ruthlessness. He believed it strengthened the crown.

I smirked, continuing to play the part. "Faelan, take Malikor to his chambers. If he survives until morning, he gets to clean out the prisoners' buckets."

"My King." Faelan grimaced. "Should I not take him to a healer first, or do you prefer that I send one to his room for treatment?"

"He isn't allowed to be treated," I growled. The mere sentiment of him receiving healing when I'd bestowed the same level of punishment on him as he'd wanted to give *her* with no aid didn't settle well with me. "He broke the law, same as any other prisoner here. His only saving grace is that he's been loyal until now. If he survives, he'll join the prisoners. If he doesn't, I won't mourn his death. But this is his *one* chance." I looked at him. "Do one more thing wrong, and I'll stab you in the heart myself."

Everyone knew I would follow through on those words. I'd proven it numerous times over the years.

"Do you understand?" I squatted and placed my blade over my knee then held up the hand holding his white wing, now coated in his blood. Another visual to remind him of what he'd done.

Malikor kept his gaze trained on the floor, but he whispered, "Yes, Your Majesty." Black blood dribbled into his mouth from the wound.

"Good." I dropped the wing and kicked it. "When you come back, Faelan, clean this up."

He nodded. "Yes, Your Majesty." He then helped Malikor down the path toward the guards' quarters.

I turned toward Lira.

She was breathing erratically, and her face had turned faintly green. Unfortunately, that wasn't a bad color on her.

"Though I enjoyed the show, I'm not sure that other guards won't try to harm her." Eldrin leaned against the doorframe, tilting his head as he watched Lira. "Unseelie hate thornlings. They just won't be so obvious about it."

My stomach hardened strangely. I couldn't deny he was right, and the way Lira kept glancing at the wing and blood made me certain that they bothered her.

How peculiar.

If I were her, I'd be thrilled that my attacker had been punished. He'd bled for his wrongdoing.

But that didn't solve the actual problem. And there was only one solution.

I grabbed her hands, and she fought me through the

buzz that sprang up between us again. She tried to tug herself free from my grasp.

Good. I liked seeing her fight and not look so defeated. Her challenging me would be the best way for me to break her ... and destroy her.

Tightening my hold and ignoring the unwelcome sensation where our skin touched, I forced her to her feet. She leaned away and tried to step back but stumbled.

What the hell was her problem?

She removed something from her pants pocket and opened it up, revealing the smallest dagger in the world.

"Let me go, or I'll hurt you," she seethed.

Then the strangest thing happened.

I gritted my teeth from the agony throbbing in my right toe and swallowed the bile rising from the brutality and gore around me. I wanted to keep the hand holding my pocketknife steady.

The world stopped as Tavish blinked at me before throwing his head back and laughing. His cold features warmed, and a different sort of knot twisted in my stomach. The sound of his laugh soothed something inside me, like swimming in cool water on a hot summer's day.

How could I feel something other than horror with a man's chopped-off wing and *black* blood puddled around me? Yet the very man who'd created the gore made me feel something inside that I didn't want to analyze. I hated that I couldn't overlook the fact that he'd done *all* this to protect *me*. Had he not intervened, I'd be in a world of hurt, if not dead.

He straightened, his irises turning a light gray reminiscent of twilight. "Sprite, do you truly believe this child's toy can harm me?"

My stupid stomach fluttered again, and I remembered

something the wise Halsey once referenced in one of her songs, she sang about red flags feeling like butterflies. I understood the lyrics perfectly now, and even though he'd used that nickname in a condescending way before, it didn't feel like that now ... or I wanted to believe that was the case.

"Tavish," Eldrin snapped.

Darkness rolled back into Tavish's eyes, and his features turned stony again. The man who both intrigued and terrified me fell back into place and I appreciated my internal temperature returning to normal.

"That is *King* Tavish, even to you," he snapped. "Or should I remind you again?" He arched a brow at the white-haired man.

The man flinched and rubbed a spot on the right side of his chest. "No need, *My King.*"

With the way Tavish held himself so rigidly, I was certain the man I'd seen just moments ago had been a figment of my imagination. When he turned his attention back to me, I wanted to disappear into the darkness, which made me clench my jaw tighter, determined not to let him see that he did, in fact, make me uncomfortable.

Dad had told me that any sign of fear made predators want to hunt and break their prey more. They'd signed me up for many self-defense classes, including kickboxing, and we'd sparred in the backyard most weekends. Each time, we'd chanted the same mantra at the beginning and end: *Show no fear and do what you need to in order to survive.*

"I severely injured and possibly killed one of my best guards because he hurt you and wanted to do more." He sheathed his sword back at his side like he wasn't threatened by me at all. "And this is the thanks I get. Did they not teach you manners on Earth?"

My mind swirled, making me dizzy. "You want me to

thank you for kidnapping me, taking me away from my family, allowing me to believe I was falling to my death, and locking me in a room where I can't even piss in privacy and am surrounded by men who want to hurt me, including *yourself?"*

Damn. Had I known this was my future, I'd have gladly stayed home for New Year's and hidden under my covers. I wanted a redo and to get away from all the craziness.

"Oh, it's not just the guards." Tavish smirked and crossed his arms. His biceps bulged even under his shirt. "It's every person in Cuil Dorcha."

"Cuil Dorcha?" I parroted, not lowering my hand. I refused to admit defeat with my pocketknife. I had no clue why. I needed to either wake up from this nightmare or find a way to escape and get back home. The main problem I faced—if this wasn't a dream—was getting back to whatever portal, magic, transporter, or beam I'd gone through to get here, and it had been high in the sky.

"Oh, dear Fate." The white-haired man rolled his eyes. "This is more pathetic than I expected."

"*Quiet,*" Tavish growled. "Eldrin, do I need to teach you how you are to talk to her?"

My breath caught, and that strange pleasurable pressure returned.

"She is *mine* to break in whatever time and way I choose," he said and stepped toward me.

Stomach dropping, I inhaled, needing my head to remain clear. One minute, he was protecting me, and the next, he made it clear he wasn't doing it from a place of caring.

"Cuil Dorcha is the name of my kingdom." Tavish leaned back, his dark wings folding tight into his back, blending in with his shirt. Darkness clung to him more than it had yesterday, which shouldn't have been possible.

Of course he was a *king*. This was his kingdom. The memory of the dark houses with barely any light sent a chill down my back.

"Put down the toy before my patience is gone." He tapped a foot on the floor, the tip of his black boot hitting the edge of the puddle of blood. He didn't even blink, as if the blood and mangled wing weren't anything out of the ordinary.

Bile churned and burned my throat. What sort of man ... fae ... fae man was I dealing with? Worse, he was in charge, so he could do any damn thing he wanted to me. I couldn't hide my flinch.

He smirked. "Excellent. You're beginning to comprehend your dire situation." His face tightened, making his rugged appearance more pronounced.

I swallowed, hating that I'd shown weakness.

I'd been so heartbroken and distraught last night that my shock had worn off. If I didn't find a way out of here quickly, I could very well wish I were dead.

Even though everything inside me wanted to strike out at Tavish, I forced myself to lower the pocketknife. If I wanted a chance to escape, I needed to stop antagonizing him. I needed him to believe I would be complacent. I placed the weapon back in my pocket, expecting him to demand I turn it over.

Instead, the corners of his lips tilted upward.

Lifting my chin, I puffed out my chest. "You won't even ask for my weapon."

He chuckled. "Sprite, that toy wouldn't harm anyone here. Everyone in this castle and our town is trained in combat. If you managed to injure someone or kill them with that icepick, then the person will have deserved it."

The air expelled from my lungs in one swoop. The more I learned, the heavier my body felt. That didn't change what needed to be done. I had to get the hell out of here. I'd just have to be careful of the townspeople as well.

"That includes the children." Eldrin placed his fingers through the bars of the door. "In case you decide to attack a child who might visit you here from time to time, as they're trained to keep the prisoners in line."

"Children?" I squeaked.

Tavish scowled. "Children begin training as soon as they learn how to fly. We need to be prepared in case your people attack us again."

"*My* people." I gestured to my back. "I don't have wings. And if mine were chopped off—" I winced, refusing to look at the separated wing again. "—I have no doubt I'd remember that."

"Are you sure you have the right girl?" Eldrin wrinkled his nose. "She lived in Gleann Solas for the first ten years of her life. This woman acts entirely human."

Ten years.

My skin crawled, and I sucked in a shaky breath.

No. It had to be a coincidence. I'd remember if I'd lived in a different world.

"She's the right woman. Those eyes are the same exact shade of blue I remember." Tavish sneered, and despite the dangerous edge to his face, he could easily pass for a god in one of the folklore books I liked to read, trying to find answers about the eyes in my dreams.

He scoffed. "I have no doubt it's her. Smell her. She smells of Seelie even after being in the human world for twelve years. And I could never forget those eyes."

The words sent goose bumps all over my body, but I refused to acknowledge it. I averted my gaze, not wanting to look at him, but I grimaced when my attention landed on the blood and the wing again. The white skin on the wing was turning a light gray and wrinkling.

Once again, there was no way I'd forget someone like *him*. "When did we know each other?"

"When we were both younger, but don't hurt yourself trying to recall. The memories will come back soon enough. Now, come on," Tavish said without the usual growl. "Let's take you somewhere else."

A sour taste filled my mouth, and I wanted to gag all over again. My throat was still raw from the way the bastard had choked me, but that was the least of my problems.

Eldrin rubbed his hands together. "Ah, yes. We should put her with the rest of the prisoners."

I shook my head, my ears pounding. If the guard was willing to hurt me like that, I didn't want to imagine what the prisoners would do if they got their hands on me.

Although ... why had Tavish intervened unless the reason was that the guard hadn't had permission to hurt me?

"I have other plans for her." Tavish stepped into the space between Eldrin and me. Then he added, "Which I need to handle with her *alone*."

Eldrin tucked a piece of his long white hair behind his ear, and I had to swallow a gasp.

Tavish's hair wasn't as long as the rest of the men's I'd seen here, but it was shaggy and hung over his ears, so I hadn't noticed them. But when Eldrin moved his hair, I'd seen that the tips of his ears were pointed like the images of fae in folklore books.

Fairy tales and folklore had always intrigued me, but I'd never imagined any of it was true. The more I saw here, however, the more I couldn't deny that some parts of the books were right.

"Very well, *My King*." Eldrin leaned to the side to study me once more. "All I ask is that I get a turn in punishing her for what she did to your father. You know how close I was to my favorite uncle."

This weasel wasn't merely Tavish's advisor; he was family, and if he was the only family member Tavish had, he would be next in line for the throne. I wasn't sure how it worked in this world, but on Earth, that was a big deal.

"No one but I will touch her." Tavish leaned forward, towering over the man. "Do I make myself clear? Not you, not the guards, and no prisoners. Anyone foolish enough to try to harm her in any way again will die by my sword. There won't be any chance of living like I afforded Malikor."

A muscle in Eldrin's jaw twitched, but after a moment, he bowed his head. "Of course, My King." Then he stepped out of the way so that Tavish could leave.

Tavish turned toward me and grasped my wrist.

My skin buzzed. The sensation was comforting and warm, making me want to trust him. Not only that, but my chest tugged toward him, urging me to close the distance between us.

I maintained enough control to stop myself from doing something foolish.

He gently pulled me to follow him, so I obliged, but when I put pressure on my right foot, pain shot through it, and my knee gave out. I groaned as I stumbled, but Tavish moved quickly, wrapping an arm around my waist to steady me.

Our faces were mere inches apart, and his scent filled my nose, making me dizzy. I didn't understand how I could have such a reaction to him when he meant me harm.

"I should've killed him." His arm tightened around me.

My mouth went dry, and I remained silent. I wasn't sure what to say to that, but the threat didn't bother me like it should have. A part of me almost liked it. That must be because of all the unprocessed trauma I'd gone through.

He bent and lifted me into his arms like a princess, and my body damn near imploded.

I managed to swallow around the lump in my throat. "I can walk. It might just take me a minute."

"We have somewhere to be, and we're already behind schedule." He gracefully breezed through the door and turned down the hallway. His wings expanded, and soon we were flying.

The cold air of the castle blew in my face, but I kept myself turned forward, wanting to remember everything we went by and not wanting to smell him any more than I had to.

The hallway was dark, and when we passed a window, the sky looked dark and stormy, but I noticed people strolling below the castle. "What time is it?" Though I hadn't slept well, I'd thought I'd gotten at least a couple of hours of rest. Granted, I didn't understand how time worked here.

"It's morning. Time works similar to Earth here."

That was super helpful. "When does the sun come out?" I'd love to get a better idea of the land that surrounded the castle while I could.

"It doesn't," he replied curtly. "We live in darkness and snow."

My lungs seized. To never have sunlight or warmth

sounded like a horrible existence. Further proof that I wasn't meant to live here.

The dark castle was gorgeous, though simple. There weren't a ton of items decorating the place, giving it a sterile but clean feel. He flew me by a few doors and stopped at one on the right. He landed but didn't put me down, then opened the door.

The room was massive, with a gorgeous dark chandelier hanging from the middle of the high ceiling.

A loud, threatening growl forced my attention to a fae man dressed in dark armor with what appeared to be the biggest wolf in existence next to him. It was the size of a cow. The wolf seemed to have black fur, but even in the darkness, the ends glinted a dark green. Its eyes glowed green, reminding me of a traffic light. The fur on its neck rose, and its eyes locked with mine while it bared its teeth and drooled.

"If this is what being a female prisoner is like around here," a man sitting on a nearby couch said, "I need to find one like her that I can carry around." The man wore a gray tunic, and his ash-blond hair hung in his face. The sides were cut short, revealing his pointed ears with dark earrings looped in both.

"Now's not the time, Finnian," Tavish rasped as he folded his wings behind him. He strolled over to the wolf and guard. "Let's get this over with."

Fear clawed at my chest, and I couldn't turn my gaze away from the angry animal.

The closer we came, the more the wolf drooled and snarled. Its green eyes glowed brighter as it edged forward toward me.

Tavish lifted a hand. "Not yet, Nightbane."

The creature stopped, but the snarls morphed into a deep rumble.

When we were a few feet away, Tavish lowered me to the floor.

Every ounce of me wanted to cling to him and beg him not to. I didn't know what the plan was, but I was certain I didn't want to be near the scary wolf. My heart hammered against my ribs like it wanted to escape.

"Don't worry," Tavish said in a cold voice. "This won't take long."

He disappeared from my side and commanded, "Nightbane, come."

The creature hunkered down and snapped as it moved toward me.

Each step closer Nightbane took had more dread pooling in my stomach. I stumbled toward Tavish before I could stop myself, and my ankle gave out.

He'd saved me a few times now, and my instinct told me to stay close to him. But he was also the reason I was in this mess.

Bastard.

Nightbane's eyes glowed brighter, making them creepier and reminding me of the hue around the moon during a total solar eclipse. He lunged, his sizable paws pushing firmly on my chest.

The beast weighed more than me, and before I realized what was happening, Nightbane had me falling onto my back. I gritted my teeth, bracing for the inevitable impact and pain.

Strong arms circled my waist just as Tavish grumbled, "Blighted abyss. The worst decision you could make is trying to run away from a cù-sìth."

He pulled me up, my skin buzzing where his arms touched me and heat flaring through me as my back settled against his muscular chest. He took the brunt of both my weight and Nightbane's, though the animal's paws kept digging into me while it towered over me.

Drool hit my cheeks, and I swallowed to prevent myself from vomiting. I had to get out of this, but *how*?

"Calm down," Tavish gritted. "It will be more efficient if you allow him to do his job. You're irritating him, which will make this far more challenging than it needs to be and hurt worse than necessary."

Did the sexy buffoon just tell me to die without a fight?

Fuck no.

Nightbane lowered his huge face to my neck, his mouth still open, while Tavish tightened his arms around me to hold me in place.

I refused to die without a fight. I didn't care if he was king of the world in this universe.

Jerking my chin down, I caught the wolf's snout between my head and neck. Nightbane flinched back, freeing himself from my hold. Then he opened his mouth, and a terrifying noise like nothing I'd ever heard before expelled from what could only be his soul.

Now I understood what Tavish had meant. Still, I lifted my knees toward my chest, hoping like hell Tavish wouldn't let me go.

"Lira—" Tavish warned, tightening his arms to the point that my ribs ached. "Don't—"

I used as much strength as I could muster to shove my feet into the mutt's lower belly and get him off me. My right ankle throbbed, and my legs gave out. The huge beast merely stood on its hind legs and moved mere inches from me, and I doubted anyone here would believe that I'd prac-ticed self-defense at least four times a week since I was ten, given how pathetic the kick had been.

Regardless, it was enough for Nightbane's demeanor to snap. A threatening growl rumbled from deep within, and his putrid breath hit my face. His eyes shone bright like green lasers as the fur on the nape of his neck rose even higher.

If the wolf dog had been angry before, he was furious now.

"Does she want to die?" Finnian chuckled. "Because it sure seems that way. I get she's Seelie, but—"

Nightbane jumped.

This was it ... the moment I died.

My body shifted so that I faced the floor and dropped. I hit the tile floor, but it wasn't a hard impact until a gigantic body landed on top of me. My body buzzed as Tavish tensed, protecting me.

The air left my lungs as his weight bore down on me.

"Nightbane!" Tavish roared.

The wolf whimpered and whined heartbreakingly.

Tavish's weight vanished off me, and I could take a breath.

"You weren't instructed to attack," Tavish said sternly.

"Your Majesty," the armored man who was with Nightbane croaked. "She's a Seelie and a prisoner—"

I spun around to find Nightbane cowering and pawing at the floor, his once ferocious face looking more like that of a scared puppy than a grown wolf.

"Did I ask for your opinion?" Tavish interjected. His wings spread out, blocking me. "What is the punishment for providing something I clearly don't want?"

I scanned what I could see of the room around his wings, noting Finnian sat at the edge of the couch. His light-blue eyes weren't locked on the debacle but instead on me.

He tilted his head as if I were a puzzle he couldn't piece together.

When our gazes locked, he didn't even pretend to be ashamed and continued to stare at me. I inhaled sharply.

Nightbane yelped, pulling my attention back to him. Tavish stepped closer to the animal, spreading his wings out until I couldn't see the wolf anymore. Shadows swirled around him, floating across his skin and body. A few edges darkened to the color of night ... to the color of the sky outside, as if it might be dark because of him.

I shivered. That was crazy.

My heart skipped a beat like it was trying to answer the question, but I ignored it. Accepting that I'd been taken into an alternate reality, or whatever this was and that these people had wings was hard enough, never mind accepting that this man could control the night. And if he could, I didn't want to think about what that meant.

The wolfish animal closed its eyes, no longer seeming menacing. In fact, my heart ached, wanting to ease its pain.

"What are you doing to him?" I asked and limped ungracefully up to Tavish.

I hated that standing next to him didn't bother me the way it should have. Even though I didn't like him, I knew he wouldn't let anyone else hurt me ... but the *anyone else* gave me the largest pause. He'd made it clear that he was the only one allowed to hurt me, and that should have made me nervous, especially after seeing what he was capable of not even an hour ago, but until the time came to escape, my smartest move was to stay close to him for protection until I could bear weight on my right foot.

"Punishing him." Tavish's eyes were dark, the same color as when he haunted my dreams, and darkness clung to him, his shirt blending in with the air around him.

I feared what he was doing to the animal, and before I could consider my actions, I kneeled next to Nightbane. Not that the poor wolf could do anything even if he'd wanted to, not in the state he was in.

The reality of my situation crashed down on me harder. Whatever Tavish was, he wasn't a man, and he didn't hesitate to hurt anything he deemed a threat, which included me.

"I think he learned his lesson." I tried to keep my voice level despite my heart pounding against my ribs, yet my voice still rose, revealing my fear and heartbreak for the animal.

Tavish's head snapped toward me, and he blinked. "Are you defending an animal that wanted to kill you?"

I flinched. He had a point, but if Tavish had tormented Nightbane like this since he was a pup, no wonder he was so angry and afraid. I had my own trauma from nightmares of the man standing before me. On so many nights, I'd climbed into Eiric's bed to be close to someone, yet Tavish's eyes had still terrified me.

Eiric.

My chest throbbed.

"Maybe too much time on Earth makes fae stupid," Finnian suggested, strolling to the other side of Tavish. "She's Seelie so that already puts her at a disadvantage with intelligence, but *this* is a level of foolish I've never observed before."

I rolled my eyes. "I'm pretty sure I'd remember if I were *Seelie*."

"What he means is that when fae stay on Earth too long, they forget their life here." Tavish's irises lightened to a stormy cloud.

Nightbane stopped whimpering but continued to breathe heavily.

"Maybe it messes with their minds more than we realized. This is the longest a fae has ever gone to Earth and returned." Finnian grinned. "I'm sort of intrigued about what would've happened if she'd stayed longer."

The guard cleared his throat. "Your Majesty, what would you like us to do? Nightbane still hasn't gotten enough of her scent."

I looked at the guard, noting his dark hair with frosted tips peeking out from under his helmet.

"He needs her scent to keep track of her like the other prisoners." The guard's face twisted into disgust as he looked at me. "She seems to enjoy causing trouble."

"That she does," Tavish muttered. "I fear more so than Finnian."

Nightbane's eyes opened. They were a dark emerald close to the color of the tips of his fur. He turned his head toward me and bared his teeth, but nothing more.

I scooted away from him. Though he didn't appear as menacing, I didn't want to be an easy target if he decided to attack me again.

"This would go a whole lot quicker if you would allow him to smell you." Tavish's wings rippled. "Then we can take you somewhere else. I have things to accomplish today other than babysitting you."

My stomach knotted. The thought of being away from him and going back into the holding cell where more guards could attack me wasn't high on my bucket list. Still, if it got this menacing animal away from me and prevented Tavish from torturing the wolflike creature more, I was all for it. Unless ... "Is he going to bite me? Is that how he gets my scent?"

Tavish pinched the bridge of his nose.

Finnian patted him on the back and answered, "He doesn't like being touched, but the best way for him to get your scent is for you to put your hand on his nose. It makes him feel vulnerable, which is why he's all growly. Something I expected Tavish to warn you about."

"Why would I?" Tavish straightened his shoulders. "If she wants to be attacked, so be it."

I couldn't help but notice that he'd flinched.

"Yet you protected her from him," Finnian countered with an arched brow, glancing between us.

"She won't make the same mistake twice, or she'll deserve it." Tavish pointed at Nightbane.

Finnian struck me as genuine, so I decided to trust him ... more so than Tavish. I inhaled to center myself then reached my hand out to the animal.

Nightbane growled, his eyes turning a lighter, glowing green once more. The closer my hand got, the more threatening the noises he made.

Pulse racing, I closed my eyes, not wanting to see him bite me as I touched his nose. I expected it to feel like a dog's, wet and cold, but it felt warm, his hot breath reminding me of a fire, yet inside, he felt frigid and empty.

I wasn't sure how I knew that just from touching him.

Something sparked inside me as Nightbane inhaled deeply. The noises temporarily disappeared as a faint thrum pulsed through me. The pulse seemed to brush under my skin and travel to the hand that touched him, but it didn't feel foreign—it felt like part of me.

Great. I had lost my mind. Yet the thought comforted me. If I was crazy, all of this would make sense.

"That's adequate." The guard came over to the animal. "He has her scent now."

Nightbane pressed his head into my hand, so I slid it beyond his nose and opened my eyes to find his locked on my face. His irises had returned to a darker green, and his mouth was closed.

"You can lower your hand, Lira," Tavish said tightly. "Before he attacks you again."

The three men watched me, each with a different expression. The guard scowled like he wanted to hurt me while Tavish held his wings firmly behind him, his arms crossed. I wasn't sure if he wanted to eat me or sacrifice me. It was as if he was trying to decide which would seal my fate when it was time.

Finnian smirked like I'd been brought here to entertain him, and somehow, that worried me more than the other two because I had no clue about his intentions.

"Lowering your hand means you don't have to touch Nightbane anymore." Finnian raised his arm like mine was, then lowered it as if I couldn't comprehend his words.

Jackass, but in a way, he reminded me of Eiric.

Not wanting to be the center of attention anymore, I started to lower my hand, but Nightbane whimpered and moved closer so I would remain touching him.

The strange feeling sputtered inside me as if the sensation were warming Nightbane from within.

"She's doing something to him." The guard rushed over and shoved me toward Tavish and Finnian.

I tried to stop my fall and hit my funny bone. Sharp pain sprang up my arm, and my body jerked. Nightbane snarled and moved in front of me.

"You stupid, sun—" the guard started, but Tavish removed his sword from his side and pressed it against the man's throat just above the armor. The guard's eyes widened as blood trickled down his neck.

Tavish's nostrils flared. "You harmed her."

I gritted my teeth, trying not to let the guard know he'd hurt me, but I stopped the tears from filling my eyes. My vision blurred, and I blinked rapidly to hold them back.

"She was doing something to Nightbane," the guard spoke slowly. "He's never acted like this before, and you know how hard it is to find a cù-sìth."

"Do not touch her." Tavish pressed deeper, the blood running faster down the guard's throat. "Why don't any of you understand?" Rage laced his voice, making it deep and raspy.

My body warmed, and I sat upright. Nightbane was still hunkered in front of me and growling, blocking the guard from reaching me.

I didn't need to see his eyes to know they were glowing.

"Your Majesty, she's a prisoner. You've never protected one before, and—" The guard leaned back.

Tavish countered the move, pressing the edge of his sword deeper into the guard's throat. Tavish spoke so low that the hairs on my arm stood upright. "She is the Seelie princess and the very person who will bring the Seelie to their knees. *I* determine if and when she's hurt. Do I make myself clear? I'd hate to lose another guard today because you can't control yourself."

The guard nodded. "Yes, Your Majesty."

"Good." He lowered his sword and sheathed it. "One more mistake and you're dead. You aren't to touch her. Do you understand?"

Tavish bent down and picked me up in his arms. "Take Nightbane to the prison cells so he can patrol while they work."

My elbow ached, and my head pounded, yet the buzzing of our connection soothed me in a way I didn't want or need to understand. He turned, flinching ever so slightly like he was uncomfortable. Still, he didn't pause as he strode to the door. "Finnian, retrieve Caelan and meet me in my room in fifteen minutes."

"Of course, Your Majesty." Finnian bowed with the corners of his mouth tipped up as if to hide a grin.

Even though I wasn't safe with Tavish, not really, I dreaded heading back to the holding cell, but at least I still had my dagger. A guard wouldn't expect me to have that. Next time, I'd have to go for a neck or wing like Tavish had. My dagger had a short blade, but beggars couldn't be choosers, not with their lives at stake.

Tavish marched back toward the prison, his feet echoing against the floor. I'd expected him to fly again, but I wouldn't hurry him along.

My arms ached to wrap around his neck, but I kept them crossed firmly over my chest. I didn't need his touch to add more confusion to the mix.

When we reached the last door on the right, he stopped and opened it.

We walked into a gigantic room in which half the walls were windows overlooking the kingdom. A portion of the ceiling was glass as well. The largest bed I'd ever seen sat underneath the skylight, giving whoever might lie on it a clear view of the sky. I couldn't help but notice the twinkling stars and a blue aurora borealis. It was gorgeous.

"You'll be staying here with me," he said simply, setting me down and closing the door behind us. "You'd best behave and make sure you keep me happy."

I inhaled sharply. "Is that my punishment? You're going to force me to have sex with you?"

He froze, his irises again turning stormy, then stalked

toward me. I tried offsetting his advances, but my right foot gave out. Luckily, I was close to a wall.

Placing a hand on either side of me so that I was trapped between his arms, he lowered his face to mine, our foreheads touching. He then whispered, "There would be no forcing about it."

My damn traitorous body heated, though my head told me to escape his clutches. I stood there, my breathing ragged as I fought like hell not to put my lips on his. Being trapped between him and the wall had all sorts of irrational images playing in my head, and none of them would happen.

I lifted my chin, not realizing that would bring my lips closer to his. His breath hit my face, and every cell in my body burned. How could someone as sexy as him be so cruel and arrogant? Granted, if he hadn't been, there was no telling how far I might have fallen for him.

"Already desperate to kiss me, sprite?" He smirked and lowered his head closer.

Yeah, my dumb ass was, but thankfully, *my* head decided to scream louder ... barely. "I'm not going to kiss you," I muttered, though I hated how breathy my voice sounded. I hoped he couldn't hear the longing in it.

He leaned lower, his lips only millimeters from mine. "Who says I won't kiss you?" His voice was low and breathy too, and I had to clamp my hands together to prevent them from wrapping around his arm and my fingers from threading through his hair.

My lips jolted, remembering how it'd felt when our mouths had brushed not even a day ago. We hadn't truly kissed, but I wondered what it'd feel like, which had to be what he wanted.

To bait me and prove I was weak and moldable.

That I was pathetic.

That wouldn't happen.

I'd rather die than allow a man to treat me poorly.

I placed my hands on his chest, desperately attempting to ignore how muscular it felt. I could feel the curves without even trying, and I wondered what he'd look like without a shirt on.

I needed to show him that I wouldn't kiss him, not stand here like I wanted to devour him. If I struggled like this with him all broody and in clothes, I didn't want to think about how I'd react to him naked.

I definitely couldn't wonder about that.

He was my enemy, intent on destroying me on his own terms. He'd made it clear that he wanted the pleasure of breaking me. Still, I'd felt the buzzing between us even on Earth, and I wanted to know what he'd done to cause that reaction.

My head cleared, and I shoved him off me.

He stumbled back a few steps, spreading out his wings to catch his balance.

I growled, "I won't let you kiss me."

He grimaced and flinched, tucking his wings behind him.

My heart dropped into my stomach. "Are you hurt?" If protecting me from Nightbane had hurt him, I didn't want to consider what the wolfy beast would've done to me.

"Nothing you should concern yourself with." His face smoothed back into a scowl while his irises returned to their dark color.

"If you got injured because of me, I want to know." I moved, limping on my foot. My toes still throbbed, but I managed to put more weight on my heel.

As I moved, I noticed a small cut in his skin. Blood trickled down his wings.

A knot formed in my stomach. "Nightbane injured you." The muscles in his wings were like the rest of his body —strong and defined.

"It's nothing." He waved a hand, folding his wings into his back so they disappeared altogether. "You have more important things to focus on."

"So that's how you hid them on Earth." I squinted, searching for the wings.

"What are you doing?" His face softened. "Is something wrong? Did you get something in your eye?"

"No, I'm trying to see your wings." I didn't even question if I sounded crazy. "I could've sworn shadows were hanging around you in there with Nightbane, so maybe that's why I'm not seeing them now."

He scoffed. "I'm the king of darkness, nightmares and frost. I wield darkness when needed, but I'm not doing it now. Our wings fold into our backs, which you will remember shortly."

My head tilted back. "But everyone has theirs showing here."

"Because our wings are like our hands and feet." He shrugged. "We prefer to keep them loose, but I don't want you to worry about my wings right now. My two most trusted people are coming here soon, and I don't need them asking too many questions about you."

I ran my fingers through my hair, and they snagged in some knots. I felt gross from being in the holding cell, but I didn't have a change of clothes. Yet another problem for me.

"You must have the wrong person." If I had wings, I'd surely know it. "I don't have wings and definitely no magic."

"Sprite, there's no doubt you're the Seelie princess. I've tracked you nightly for years now." He moved toward me quickly, the distance between us gone before I even realized it. He tucked a piece of my hair behind my ear and whispered, "I watched your dreams before turning them into nightmares. I know more about you than you could ever suspect, and those dreams—they were your memories of your past life in Gleann Solas."

The small gesture felt so intimate, and my hormones tried to take over from my brain again.

A loud banging sounded on the door.

Tavish dropped his hand and wrinkled his nose while snapping, "Who is it?"

"It's me, Your Highness," Finnian's familiar voice answered. "I retrieved Caelan as requested."

Scowling, Tavish spun toward the door. He opened it, revealing Finnian and another man, who had to be Caelan.

"You're early." Tavish moved to the side, allowing the two men to enter.

"Actually, we're not." Caelan strolled past Tavish. He was an inch shorter than the king. He was almost as handsome as Tavish and appeared to be slightly older.

Where Tavish was coolly pale, Caelan's complexion was warmer, though still fair. He had dark-blond hair pulled into a bun on top of his head, which left his pointy ears visible.

He ran a hand over his scruff as his milk-chocolate-brown eyes focused on me. "We're a few minutes late because Finnian got distracted by the new servant."

"You blasted wildling." Tavish shook his head. "What have I told you about fornicating with women you can never be with?"

Finnian shut the door and smiled. "Oh, do you still believe in hierarchy and vengeance? Ever since this morning, I thought your stance might have changed."

Tavish scowled and crossed his arms. "Why in Ardanos would you think that? All of my actions have been to reinforce the need for rules and expectations. That will *never* change."

"Stop goading him," Caelan scolded and glared at Finnian. "We have much more important things to discuss now that Princess Lira has returned."

My body stiffened. Hearing him call me *Princess* didn't feel completely wrong, which didn't make sense. Maybe being here had made me more susceptible to manipulation?

"Things we probably should discuss with her," Caelan added while adjusting the white fur collar around his neck.

Biting the inside of my cheek, I focused on that pain instead of allowing my expression to change. Clearly, Tavish's plan to destroy me would begin soon. My heart ached.

"She's not going back to the holding cell, and that talk will have to wait." Tavish raised his head. "She's been attacked twice in the last couple of hours. Because of that, she'll be staying in my room with me, and my most trusted guards will keep watch outside my door. Our important message is to convey that Lira is not to be *harmed* by anyone. That her fate lies solely with me, and anyone who gets in the way of that will die by my hands."

Finnian somehow smiled bigger while Caelan blinked.

"You want her to stay in your room?" Caelan swallowed and paused like he needed to search for the right words. "Your prisoner, the *Seelie princess*, will stay here with you because guards want justice, and you'll kill anyone who threatens her. You must understand how this looks."

"It is *nothing* more than me protecting my prize until the time comes for me to avenge my parents' deaths and reclaim our rightful land." Tavish's face hardened, and darkness crept around his body. The temperature dropped several degrees. "We can't allow her to alert the Seelie before we're ready. I couldn't be sure that I'd locate her on Earth until I actually went there. Now, we must prepare, but her life cannot continually be in danger. Do you understand?"

This version of Tavish scared me. This was the man who had cut down one guard and almost slit another's throat, and he was staring at me with so much hatred that my chest constricted. He blamed the Seelie fae for his parents' deaths and the loss of their lands, and that put me in the crosshairs. At least his motives made sense, though he was clearly misguided.

"Right, and if the dragon prince shows up at our door asking for his betrothed, should I bring him to your room as well?" Finnian leaned back on his heels, smiling ever so sweetly. "Then you could have all the heirs of your enemies sleeping in the same room as you."

Tavish glared. "She still believes she's human, and she carries a child's toy as a weapon. I'm confident I'll be fine."

"And the dragon prince is not nearly as sexy," Finnian added, winking at me. "Which also helps with that decision, right?"

My face warmed, and I wanted to disappear. Hearing him call Tavish sexy felt wrong.

A muscle in Tavish's cheek spasmed, and he clenched his hands into fists.

"Finnian, stop." Caelan rubbed his temples. "Though I don't like the plan, Tavish is our king. Let's resolve the issue of her safety so we can then deal with the Seelie. I'll retrieve Torcall and Finola and bring them here to watch over her while we're gone."

"Excellent." Tavish nodded. "And take *him* with you. I can't swear that I won't slaughter him if he remains."

"I doubt slaughtering is what I'd witness if I were to remain." Finnian chuckled. "You would probably forget I was here if I stayed quiet."

Caelan's charcoal wings fluttered as he exhaled. "Come on." He marched to the door, dragging Finnian along with him.

When the door shut, leaving Tavish and me alone again, tension hung heavy over us. Once the guards were settled, Tavish would begin planning my future and the horrors that would go along with it. My mouth went dry.

Silence thickened, and finally, Tavish cleared his throat. "Why don't you take a bath while I attend to … business."

Yes, talking about my upcoming death outright would be in poor taste, though that was exactly what he was going to do.

"I'll retrieve a gown for you to wear, though you must remain in here." Tavish strolled to a door directly across from his bed and opened it. "I'll bring you food when I return. You must be starving."

I laughed bitterly. "So I can get clean and fat before you slaughter me like a pig?"

"A pig?" His brows furrowed. "I'm assuming that's something from Earth?"

"Yes, a delicious animal that I like to devour each morning." I tilted my head, letting my anger bubble out. That emotion I understood, whereas fear would lead me to do something more dangerous. "I'm assuming that won't happen here, just like, you know, me not dying."

Tavish flinched before his face turned colder. "I didn't choose this life for us." He took two large strides toward me. "You can thank your parents for this. I'm doing what I have to do for my people."

"Sure, because as long as it's for your people, that makes it okay." I needed to hang on to my anger and let it burn inside me. "You do realize that, even if my parents did have your parents killed and your people kicked out of ... wherever, I would've been only ten years old and not part of it, right?"

"It doesn't matter." Tavish shook his head. "Their blood and magic runs through your veins. It's as much your fault as theirs—that's the fae way. Never forget that."

Hell, I didn't even believe I was fae. But this was King Tavish's kingdom, and his word was law. I wouldn't have the privilege of having a jury hear me out.

"Just be thankful I'm protecting you now, sprite." Tavish strolled to the door without even looking over his shoulder at me. "Take a bath, and I'll get a servant to bring you clothes and ensure the guards are here before I leave. Do it now before I change my mind."

Though I didn't want to listen to him, after sleeping in the holding cell and being around all the blood this morning, I wanted to get clean. Besides, I needed distance from his stupid face.

I spun and marched into the bathroom then slammed the door. I leaned my head back against the wall as my eyes adjusted to the soft candlelight. The bathroom was dark, and a sense of Tavish's power ran throughout the castle.

Despite all that, I couldn't lie and say this place wasn't also hauntingly beautiful. A clear tub with a frosted bottom section sat on an elevated wooden floor. Paintings of lush trees decorated the walls, and a large wooden closet was set to the right of the tub. Directly across from me, shadows hazed the wall as if a dark forest lay behind it.

To the left of the tub was a dark toilet and a matching sink a few feet from it, with a basin like the tub.

I turned a lever in the tub, and aqua-blue water poured from the spout. I glanced around, searching for shampoo, conditioner, or soap, but found nothing.

As the tub filled, I hurried to the closet and opened it to find a robe hanging on the left and several gray, puffy towels folded to the right.

I laid a towel on the side of the tub and removed my clothing. When I was naked, I removed the dagger from around my ankle and placed it within easy reach under my jeans in case someone came in. For some reason, I didn't think they would, not while Tavish was determined to protect me.

When I stepped into the tub, my skin tingled. I sat in the warm water that was now as high as my breasts. I turned off the lever and leaned back. A huge, dark lantern hung above me, lit by candles.

Despite not having soap, I felt clean and fresh, so I leaned back and dunked my head under. I stayed under for as long as possible, enjoying the way the water rushed across my entire body and seemed to pulse in time with my heartbeat.

Back home, swimming was one of my favorite things to do, and in this small tub, I somehow enjoyed the water even more. It felt like the water ... knew me. Yeah, I had lost my mind.

With my lungs near bursting, needing air, I begrudgingly surfaced and took in a big breath. Not wanting to get out yet, I laid my head back and soaked with my eyes closed.

Even in this personal hell of mine, I'd found a slice of peace in the most unexpected place ... Tavish's bathroom.

The hair on the nape of my neck rose as if I were being watched, and my heart pounded.

Opening my eyes, I searched the room, hoping it was the servant Tavish had mentioned would be bringing me clothes. But, no matter where I looked, I didn't see anyone ... until my gaze landed on something faintly lighter than the rest of the room.

It seemed like a shadow, but there wasn't anything around to cast it.

Maybe Tavish had decided to begin my torture. He'd made me believe I was safe, and I had lowered my guard. Worse, I'd stupidly fallen for it like a dumb, naive girl.

"Tavish, this isn't funny." I lifted my chin, very aware that I was naked in a tub. I sat up a bit more, keeping my top half-submerged and trying to ignore my naked vulnerability. I reached for my dagger.

The shadows broke apart, revealing the person behind them. He had a coldness to his white eyes that not even Tavish could match.

His hand revealed itself out of the shadows.

No.

W hat the hell was Tavish's cousin doing in here with a dagger while I bathed? My foolishness would not result in me dying naked in a bathtub.

"Did Tavish send you?" I rasped, hating that my voice revealed how scared I was. I hadn't meant to ask that question, but I needed to hear the words so that my body would stop reacting to my terror.

Eldrin smirked. "Does it matter? The result will be the same." He held the dagger in front of him as he slowly moved toward me.

For some reason, it did matter, but if he knew that, he sure as hell wouldn't offer the answer. I had to handle this differently. I stood, letting the water pour from my body. This had to go perfectly for my plan to work without me tripping and falling. "Ah ... so the king doesn't want to do his own dirty work after all his talk about how he wants to handle my punishment accordingly. So he sent in the peon who must obey his command."

"Peon?" Eldrin paused, his brows furrowing, yet he still took the opportunity to ogle me. "You speak so strangely."

I wanted to slide back into the water because his leering made me feel dirty. Instead, I straightened my back, needing to come off like his creepy ass didn't bother me. "You know, a person who doesn't matter to the king. The people he orders around to do his bidding."

His head jerked back and his jaw clenched. "If Tavish had requested I do this, it would've been an honor."

My chest loosened marginally, though my situation hadn't changed. I didn't want to analyze why because Tavish was my kidnapper and enemy ... that was all. "You do realize that when he sees me hurt, he'll kill you. Don't you remember the guard who lost his wing earlier?"

"That's why you won't speak of this to anyone." He stalked closer.

A tingling warning shot through me, and I didn't want to learn his plans for me. His finding me naked and alone couldn't be a coincidence. Acid roiled in my stomach.

"If you do, I'll have no choice but to visit"—he smirked and tilted his head, pausing for dramatic effect—"Eiric. That's your sister's name, right?"

I tensed, understanding the threat. "You wouldn't."

"Oh, I would." He stood a few feet away, easily within striking distance if he wanted. "In fact, I hope you tell Tavish all about this so I can take someone you care for away from you, giving you the same courtesy you gave me." He *tsk*ed. "Now, what should I do with you?"

The time to act had come. It was now or never.

I used my injured leg to kick water from the tub, aiming for his face. He jerked back at the sudden splash. I spun and jumped out then squatted to retrieve my dagger from under my jeans.

The toes on my right foot panged, and my knee hit the wooden floor, forcing me to catch myself with the same arm as earlier and causing my attempted fluid motion to secure the dagger to fail. My kneecap throbbed, but I gritted my teeth and ignored the pain.

The sound of wings flapping echoed against the walls, and the gigantic bathroom suddenly felt very small. I slid my hands under the jeans just as Eldrin slammed into me.

He knocked me onto my injured side. I groaned, and he gripped my arm, forcing me to lie on my back as he straddled me, pinning me down.

A scream lodged in my throat, and I tried bucking him off, but he held me in place. His face turned a tad purple like he might be flushing, fae style.

"Stay still, or I will have your family on Earth slaughtered," he snapped, holding my wrists with one hand while he lowered the blade of his dagger to the top of my chest. The blade sliced my skin, the sharp sensation stealing my breath.

"I'm not going to sleep with you."

He laughed menacingly and lowered his face toward mine like he might kiss me. I prepared to bite his lips off so he could never try to kiss me again.

A few inches from my face, he stopped and spit, the liquid hitting my left cheek. He rasped, "I don't want anything of mine *in* a Seelie Cailleach-sgath. Don't flatter yourself. When I learned you were bathing in the *king's* chambers, I knew this would be the best place to get you alone. Nothing more than that."

My blood froze. "So you're acting against your *king*?" What could be so important that he would disobey his king and his own family?

"I'm doing what needs to be done." He sneered, and the lines in his face deepened. He dug the knife in more, and warm blood trickled down my body.

Placing the dagger into his mouth, he removed a bottle from his pants and scooped my blood into it.

That couldn't be good.

When he lowered his head a little more, concentrating on getting more of my blood into the bottle, I acted.

Bracing for the pain, I jerked upright and headbutted him. My ears rang on impact, and a deep throb pulsed in my head, but the agony was worth it when his grip slackened.

He snarled, but I yanked the dagger from his mouth and aimed to stab him in the shoulder.

He bolted, his gigantic wings flapping, and I sliced into his arm instead. Even though the wound wasn't that deep, his black blood dripped all over me. He held the container in one hand, his white eyes appearing to have more color.

"I should kill you," he spat, hovering over me. "Right here and now."

He screwed the cap onto the jar, and I noticed that my blood looked different. It wasn't red anymore but golden like honey.

I glanced down and saw that golden liquid had dripped underneath me. My mind ran in circles, but the threat remained. I couldn't lose focus. I lifted my head and met his gaze. "Do it. I dare you. Your death won't be far behind mine." I, once again, was using Tavish's obsession with breaking me himself against Eldrin.

"You'll regret that, sunscorched." He lowered himself to the floor several feet from me. "Your sister will pay the price for you."

Eiric.

My heart fractured into pieces, but I couldn't fall apart and become more of a target. These fae used fear to feel superior. "Do that, and I won't hesitate to tell Tavish what happened, including that you straddled me while I was naked." He probably wouldn't care about that last part, but if I said it with enough confidence, maybe Eldrin would believe it.

Eldrin glared, and the hatred in his eyes had my skin crawling.

"I got what I came for." He placed the jar in his pocket and smirked. "So don't speak a word, or your family will die. Do you understand?"

"I do." Even though I wanted to tell Tavish what had happened, I had no doubt that Eldrin would injure my family. "Now leave." I held his dagger tighter, ready for him to request it back.

Instead, shadows swirled around him, and he disappeared.

The door didn't open, but the moment he left, I knew. The chill in the air went with him as did my sense of safety. Not even in Tavish's chambers was I safe. Had the guards watching the entrance allowed Eldrin in, or could he hide from them too?

Unsure what to do with his dagger, I held it tight. There was no way in hell I was putting it down. I went back to the tub to wash Eldrin's spit from my face and clean the wound he'd made. I felt dirty again.

I drained the water before refilling the tub. This time, I washed myself quickly, trying to scrub the memory of Eldrin's touch from my body. My skin tingled more noticeably when the water flowed over the cut, reminding me of peroxide from back home.

No matter how many times I rinsed myself, I felt cold and violated. His strategy to attack me in here had been sound.

I climbed from the tub and wrapped the towel around myself. Glancing down at the wound, I noted that it was no longer bleeding. I sighed in relief. I wasn't sure how I could have kept it from Tavish.

Desperately wanting clothes, I hoped that the servant had brought them. Otherwise, I'd be forced to put my jeans back on, and they'd seen better days.

I grabbed my dagger as well and studied the weapons. I had to put them somewhere, or Tavish would see them as threats. I wondered if that was why Eldrin had left his with me, hoping I'd get caught with it. I refused to allow another one of his plans to come to fruition.

There was only one place I could hide them—in the toilet water tank. I doubted that Tavish went anywhere near that, and later, I could move them somewhere else.

I hurried over to the toilet and sighed when I realized that it didn't look like the ones back home. There was a small water chamber up top, so I opened it and put the daggers into the water. The fit was tight, but I pushed them down enough so the lid could close once more.

Satisfied, I exited the bathroom and glanced around. Even though I couldn't see the fae cloaked in shadows, maybe I could sense them. I would never again assume I was alone and safe.

I waited for something to indicate that I wasn't alone. Each second that passed allowed my breathing to get slightly easier until I could focus on getting dressed.

My attention landed on a flowy gray dress laid out at the bottom of the bed. My stomach tensed.

This had to be a joke. I despised dresses, especially with people waiting to attack me around every corner. I grumbled and considered putting on my jeans and shirt again. But the last thing I needed was for Tavish to get mad at me. If I wanted a chance to escape before he and his buddies determined the best way to torture me, I had to play the part of an obedient prisoner.

Pouting to myself, I dropped the towel and lifted the gown from the bed. I expected it to be scratchy, but the material was soft and smooth to the touch. I pulled it over my head just as the door to the bedroom opened.

I squealed, and my pulse pounded as I tugged the dress down, but with my body still slightly damp, it stuck to my stomach, not completely coming down, and I couldn't get my head out of the hole.

A deep laugh caused a lump to form in my throat.

"Oh, Lira." Finnian broke out into louder laughter. Footsteps headed toward me, making me desperate to yank the dress down. Somehow, I got my head out of the top of the dress so I could actually see what I was doing.

And boy, I wished I hadn't.

The dress was completely bunched at my waist, leaving everything from my ass down on full display. As if my night … day … whatever time it was, seeing as this place was always cloaked in darkness, could get any worse.

"I must say I never expected a water fae to have issues with moisture." A tear leaked from the corner of his eye, and his words were breathless. He didn't flinch when I glared at him but laughed even harder, holding his sides.

Water fae?

I wanted to ask more about that, but after my ass was covered. Tugging on the hem, I got the fabric down a little more, but not nearly enough. The material stuck to my skin, and I realized the dress was about a size too small.

Even better.

"Let me help." Finnian reached for me.

I took a step back and landed on my right foot. Pain flared up my ankle. I lifted a hand, blocking him from getting any closer to me. Cold air hit my ass, reminding me that another man had reached me while I was damn vulnerable. Now, I wished I'd kept the daggers with me.

Finnian's head tilted back. "Did something happen to you? You weren't this jumpy earlier."

I swallowed, hating that this man could read me so easily. I opened my mouth, but I couldn't get myself to say *no*—like, I physically couldn't. My throat worked, but my mouth wouldn't make the shape, nor could I make a fucking sound.

Something was horribly wrong.

My breathing quickened as fear strangled me.

"It'll be all right, Lira." Finnian took a slow step toward me. "Let me help you get your dress down before Tavish and Caelan see you like this. I promise I won't do anything more."

I nodded, my head woozy from the lack of oxygen.

Finnian gripped my waist, lifted me, and tossed me onto the bed.

I managed to keep my knees together to prevent myself from flashing him in a very intimate way. This wasn't how I wanted a guy seeing me completely naked for the first time to witness ... well—everything.

His hands gripped the hem of the dress, brushing against my skin. "Calm down. You're safe."

I waited for the buzz, but the sensation never came. Instead, his hands on me felt *wrong*.

What the hell?

I squirmed to get away, and the dress hiked up higher.

This was why my parents always told me to remain rational and not lose my head.

Finnian mashed his lips together, but his eyes twinkled.

"Let me help you. It'll go much faster, especially if you

stay still." He raised both hands like he wanted to prove they weren't weapons.

My face burned. I must look like a tomato ... or whatever was red in their world. "Fine, but don't look at my bare half."

His brows rose. "You think I've never seen a woman's vagina before?" He rubbed his fingers along his chest. "I've seen hundreds of vaginas and have loved each one."

Ew. Was he being serious? "No loving mine. Got it?" Of course he'd been with hundreds of women. And if he'd been with hundreds, I didn't want to consider how many Tavish had been with.

Not that I cared or anything.

He ran a hand down his face as if to prevent himself from laughing again. "I vow to you, Lira. Even though I find you extremely appealing, you are one with whom I will *never* succumb to my urges."

Ah, yes, here the insults came. "Because I'm *Seelie*?"

"No, that's not why." He winked. "I can make any type of woman scream. It's for reasons I won't get into with you. Either way, you're safe with me, unlike most others."

I believed him ... which bothered me.

Before I could force myself to tell him no, his hands grasped the hem of the dress and tugged it down.

The material gave, so I kept my mouth shut, wanting to reclaim my pride. He leaned over me, his arms working, and just as the dress covered my ass, the door to the bedroom opened.

My body heated despite the temperature of the room dropping a few degrees.

With those weird competing sensations, I knew who it was.

Tavish.

Our eyes connected, and Tavish's face tightened, and his nostrils flared. His wings opened, and he flapped over to us, grabbing Finnian's shoulders and yanking him away from me.

Finnian's grasp ripped a piece off the bottom of the dress as he was thrown against the wall.

"How many times do I have to say nobody touches her!" Tavish bellowed and charged at him.

No matter what I attempted, I couldn't get the image of Finnian standing between Lira's legs with his hands all over her from my mind. It was seared into my memory, and my chest ached like never before. She was my enemy, my captive, the answer to getting our rightful kingdom back for my people and seeking justice for my parents' deaths.

Yet, my heart pumped as anger warmed my blood, and I focused on that sensation. The anger comforted me because, ever since the day the Seelie royals killed my parents, fury had been my constant companion.

Rage had kept me alive, for my own people would've turned on me. The fury had turned me from a naive boy with hopes of uniting the fae kingdoms into a ruthless leader my people obeyed without question.

What made this situation worse was the fact that one of the two people I trusted most in all the realms had blatantly disobeyed me, and, of course, it had to be with *her*. I hated the thought of doing to him what I'd been forced to do to

Eldrin, but there could be no exceptions to the rules; otherwise, my people might attempt to revolt again.

"Tavish, be reasonable." Finnian raised his hands, but the tan lacy fabric he'd ripped from Lira's dress fluttered like a dragon breathing fire in the dark.

I wouldn't allow anyone to speak to me this way. "Be *reasonable*?" The words raked across my throat, making me more tense. My wings spread out, emphasizing my size and power. I could feel cool licks of darkness wisping around me, ready to cover me and take hold while I tore him limb from limb. "I made it clear that she's *mine*. No one else's." The words had left my mouth before I could take them back. That sounded an awful lot like claiming, but I didn't give a damn. She was mine to do with as I wished. Not *his*.

She snorted behind me and grumbled, "I don't belong to anyone but myself."

Something deep inside me *yank*ed, adding to my frustration, and I wanted to turn around and correct her. But first, I had to deal with Finnian.

The image of him between her legs popped into my head again without permission, and I punched him in the jaw.

His head jerked back from the impact, and he groaned. Still, bloodlust unfurled in my stomach, wanting more. He'd been all over her.

"Tavish!" Caelan exclaimed. "He wouldn't disobey you!"

I chuckled darkly, shaking my head. "Do you think I'm a moron? You saw the same thing I did."

"Her dress was stuck," Finnian started, but his voice had my vision turning red.

I removed my sword from the sheath at my side.

Finnian's eyes widened. "Listen to me."

"Oh, I saw everything I needed to see to feel comfortable with this decision." I readied to strike him, though I wasn't sure what my plan was.

"Wait," Lira gasped, grabbing the arm that held the sword.

That blasted jolt I experienced each time she touched me sprang to life. Her touch was like a warm twilight on a snowy day—something I used to enjoy as a boy when I'd thought the Unseelie and Seelie divide wasn't so large. Now, it was a reminder of the foolish dreams I'd had long ago.

"He was helping me." Her hands tightened. "Not—"

"*Helping* you?" I turned to her, and instead of an ache in my chest, she might as well have stuck me with a sword. Her attempt to defend him made the situation worse. "Sprite, if you wanted help like *that,* then—"

"The dress got stuck on me." Her cheeks turned a faint pink, which I'd never seen before. "I'd just gotten out of the tub, and in my haste, I didn't dry off well. The material got caught around my waist, and I couldn't get it down. When he walked in, he found—"

My blood boiled hotter than I'd ever experienced. "He walked in on you *naked*?"

Out of the corner of my eye, Finnian ducked, escaping my clutches. The wildling had used Lira's distraction to get away, but that wouldn't last for long.

"Blighted abyss." Caelan closed his eyes. "I feel like we're young winglings all over again."

I pivoted toward him, readying to use my sword on Finnian again. I wouldn't kill him ... merely make him wish he were dead. And maybe cut his hands off so he could never touch Lira again.

He ran to the table that held my chessboard.

"Don't make me do it." Finnian arched a brow and rested his hands on the edge of the board. "Just listen to me."

The imbecile knew that my games with Eldrin were important to me. I'd never won against him, and I studied my moves. This was the first game in which I was certain I would beat Eldrin, and Finnian knew it.

"Don't you dare," I seethed.

"Nothing happened between Lira and me." He moved his hand, waving the piece of her dress like a flag.

If that was supposed to be a sign of surrender, I viewed it as an active threat. I lunged at him.

Finnian grabbed the board and lifted it. The pieces fell onto the floor. I threw a punch, and he moved the board, blocking the blow. My hand pummeled through it, cracking it in half. Lira gasped, causing my head to become level once more.

I didn't want to bring her more distress. I yanked my hand back, but it was lodged in the wood. Finnian let the board go, allowing me to stumble several feet back.

"It might bode well for you to drop the piece of her clothing." Caelan sighed like he was bored.

In fairness, he probably was. I would be if I were in his shoes, and that thought alone froze me in place, but I still couldn't find it in me to care about how I was reacting.

"Good point." Finnian dropped the fabric and wiggled his fingers, showing he had nothing in his hand. "Tavish, I swear to the gods, there was *nothing* sexual going on. I didn't expect her to be naked, so I came into your room like usual. She was struggling to put on the dress, and I merely wanted to help her. She stumbled and almost fell, and that is the *only* reason she was on your bed like that. I would've helped anyone in that situation, even a *prince*. Would you rather I had watched her fall to the floor?"

The blasted wildling was too smooth of a talker, but I believed him. Even though I was still furious, my frustration ebbed enough for me to realize how irrationally I was acting. Another thing that had changed since Lira had come along in such a short amount of time.

"Then knock before entering next time," I rasped.

"Don't worry." Finnian scurried across the room toward the exit, standing on the other side of Caelan so he wasn't next to Lira. "I will. Lesson learned." He glanced at her and shrugged. "Next time, you'll have to let Tavish walk in on you like that and help you."

At that thought, my body hardened in *all* places. I was suddenly desperate to know what being between her legs felt like. I didn't understand what had changed between us now that we were older because I'd never felt anything this intense for her when we were younger.

Bringing her here might have been a huge mistake, but I had to find a way to navigate around it. The plan had been activated and couldn't change now.

"*That* won't happen again." Lira wrapped her arms around her upper chest. "Believe me. We *all* learned a lesson here."

I needed everyone to leave so I could process everything. Part of me still wanted to stab Finnian in the stomach. In fact, I kept my sword in my hand, ready to wield it at any moment. Unfortunately, the one person I needed space from was the person with whom I had decided to share my room. Another impulsive decision that might as well have been to skin my wings. I sheathed my sword and freed my other hand from the damaged chessboard. "You'll be retrieving a new chessboard for me within the next day."

Finnian rolled his eyes. "It might do you good not to spend so much time with your *beloved* cousin."

"You should stop while you're ahead." Caelan shook his head.

Eldrin was the one point of contention I had with Caelan and Finnian. They didn't trust him, and in fairness, when I was younger, I hadn't either. But he'd done so much for me and the kingdom since my father had passed.

Not wanting to expend any more energy, I pretended Finnian hadn't said anything. "The two of you should leave so we can prepare for dinner." I didn't want to attend dinner with everyone, but Eldrin had nearly danced with the sun when he'd learned that I'd moved Lira into my room. He'd demanded that we discuss it over dinner, and I wanted Finnian and Caelan there with me. They'd be on my side, putting Eldrin and me at odds, so I had to make the sacrifice to dress and attend dinner.

"Ah, yes." Finnian pursed his lips. "I can't wait to see how this particular conversation goes. It will be entertaining, seeing as I enjoy Eldrin's heat when he doesn't get his way."

"Unfortunately, he is right." Caelan frowned. "Having the Seelie princess remain in your room is reckless and something I never would have expected you to do."

I forced my hand away from drawing my sword. If I did, I might attack both of my friends. The idea of Lira being somewhere that any guard, servant, prisoner, or castle visitor could access and take out their frustrations with the Seelie upon her didn't sit well with me. It was *my* duty to decide how to execute her. "I want her protected until the right time comes, and I trust only the two guards outside and myself to ensure that happens."

"Hey." Finnian's brows furrowed. "What about me?"

I gritted my teeth, trying not to lash out. "You were part of that group until a few minutes ago."

"I can take care of myself, you know." Lira placed her hands on her waist, emphasizing how slender she was and how the dress clung to every curve.

The dress hadn't been as formfitting on my mother, but the way it looked on Lira had me believing it had been made for her. I fidgeted, trying to hide the growing bulge in my pants. Now would've been a good time to be wearing armor.

Frustrated by all the strange emotions she caused, I bit out, "Yes, sprite. I'm sure you could with the little toy you showed off earlier."

Instead of appearing hurt, she jutted her chin, which made me want to kiss her and make her quiver. I wanted to be the one to make her fall apart.

I needed to get away from her quickly. "I'm taking a bath." My gaze landed on Finnian. "And no helping me get dressed—or anyone else in this room, for that matter."

Finnian hung his head. "I'm never going to live that down."

I marched past the broken chessboard and toward my closet. But when I heard Lira giggle, anger coursed through my body. There was no doubt in my mind who'd made her laugh, and I wished I'd stabbed him earlier.

I dug through my clothes, looking for a tunic and slacks. We'd be eating in the formal dining hall, something Eldrin had insisted upon tonight, which meant we had to be dressed as royalty.

The doors to my bedchamber closed, and I selected a black outfit that would serve the occasion. I marched out the door to find Lira picking up the chess pieces that had fallen on the floor. The top of her gown gaped, revealing her ample cleavage and my gaze settled on something that appeared fresh ... a wound.

I dropped the clothes and took her arm, pulling her toward me. The cold magic of frost swirled within me as darkness clung to me. However, I couldn't remove my gaze from the cut on her chest. "Who did this to you?" I snarled then focused on her face.

Her bottom lip quivered. "I ... I can't tell you."

"Was it the guard?" Cutting off one wing hadn't been enough of a punishment for what he'd done.

She averted her gaze to the floor. "No."

"Then who?" I had to restrain myself from squeezing her more.

"Why does it matter?" She lifted her chin. "You keep saying you're going to do worse to me anyway."

The words were equivalent to her kneeing me in the testicles. "Just tell me who it was."

"I won't tell you." She glared. "Beat me, torture me, do whatever. You'll still never learn."

She doubted me. Good. That was what I needed. I leaned forward, allowing my lips to brush her earlobe as I said, "Don't worry, sprite. I'll figure it out on my own." A dark, dangerous sensation flooded me, telling me to harm everyone in the castle until I discovered the culprit, and the thought had merit. But that would have to begin after dinner. I had to get through that first.

She shivered, and that little action had me wanting more. My head screamed that I was being foolish, but I slid my lips from her earlobe to her lips. Her scent filled my nose as our lips touched, sending a jolt straight to a dark, cold place inside me that had been that way for so long ... ever since I'd lost everything. The strange sensation heated up something that needed to remain untouched and hardened so I could save my people and right the wrongs against us.

"I know whatever this is between us, you feel it too," she whispered, her eyes searching mine for something.

Her words brought me back to the present, and I pulled away. Whatever game we were playing wasn't safe. I had a mission. One she couldn't distract me from.

With every ounce of willpower I had, I forced myself to pick up the clothes I'd dropped and march into the bathroom.

With my hand on Lira's arm, I forced her to join me for dinner. Her only salvation for me not growing annoyed with her was that her foot was still bothering her, but she tested my patience with her inability to remain quiet.

"I'd rather die from eating poisoned food than sit down with you and your minions," she grumbled, trying to yank free of my grip.

Part of me admired her bravery, while an equal part wanted her to obey me like everyone else in this blasted place. I'd hoped that being raised in the human world would make her more pliable and moldable. Clearly, I'd been wrong.

We strolled into the dining hall where the long rectangular table sat sixteen. Four places had been set at the end near the windows overlooking the kingdom since no one had expected Lira.

Eldrin, Finnian, and Caelen were already there, and Eldrin frowned at Lira.

Two servants flanked the window, waiting to serve us. I glanced at the woman I'd grown up thinking of as almost a second mother. "Sine, please set another spot for the prisoner."

"What is she doing here?" Eldrin seethed.

I hated the way she tensed. When I reached my place at the head of the table, I gestured for Eldrin to move down a spot. "I brought her here to ensure no one attempts to poison her."

Beside Caelan, Finnian pressed his lips together.

Begrudgingly, Eldrin stood up and reached for his plate of fish and mushrooms to take with him.

"No, that's hers." I had purposely not told anyone she was coming with me because I didn't want them to know which plate would be hers. Too many people wanted to kill her.

I pulled out the chair for her to sit down.

"I'd rather have a fresh plate." Lira huffed and sat ungracefully in the chair. "I don't want his germs all over my food." Her gaze landed on the mushrooms, and she tilted her head. "I've never seen these before."

"They're unique to our realm," Caelan said solemnly.

He wasn't thrilled about Lira's presence here either.

"Interesting." Her cobalt irises sparkled as she lifted one. "I have so much to learn about the vegetation here."

Her interest shocked me.

"Tavish, have you lost your mind?" Eldrin remained, standing behind the chair I'd told him to take. "She's a prisoner, not a guest."

"If this is how a guest is treated, then y'all should learn some manners." Lira leaned back, crossing her arms.

I sat down, wishing she would be quiet. I needed her to be seen and not heard, but of course, that was impossible with her.

"Oh, forgive me, *Princess*, that you aren't wanted or

liked since your people are the reason we live here today." Eldrin's jaw twitched. He glared at Tavish. "What happened to you on Earth? Because my cousin isn't the same person sitting before me tonight. The person who returned is impulsive and rash, and that's something even your friends can't deny."

Both Caelan and Finnian picked up their forks and began playing with their food.

They agreed with him. I'd brought them here to be on my side.

"I'm not being impulsive and rash." I grabbed my goblet of water and took a sip. "All I've done is make sure our prisoner isn't mistreated until the time comes."

"Oh, she's not being mistreated." Eldrin crossed his arms as Sine brought out another plate and set it before him.

She hurried back to her spot beside the window.

Eldrin snagged his knife and pointed it at Lira. She flinched, which seemed out of character from what I'd witnessed of her.

"She's wearing your mother's gown, for the gods' sake." Eldrin grimaced.

I set the glass on the table. "It's not like any of us wear gowns. Where do you propose I find her clothes to wear?"

"What's wrong with the ones she arrived in?" Eldrin waved a hand at her. "She's supposed to be miserable."

"Oh, believe me, I am." Lira glowered. "I have to sit here with you, for one."

Finnian chuckled, and Caelan coughed to hide his laugh.

The two of them together would make this situation worse. I didn't need them to encourage one another.

"She's rude, including to members of your own family,

and you allow it." Eldrin placed a hand on the table. "This is unacceptable."

My back stiffened, and I waited for Caelan and Finnian to come to my aid. They normally would have jumped in and supported me by now.

"Tavish, Eldrin has a point." Caelan grimaced. "I understand that you don't want people punishing her, but you had her stay in the holding cell for only one night."

"And he carried her out of it after attacking a guard for wanting to scar her like he was," Eldrin added and sighed.

My stomach churned, but before I could say anything, Finnian interjected, "And you protected her against Night-bane. You even threatened the guard with death after he shoved Lira away from the beastly mutt."

"And you took her straight to your bedchamber, proclaiming she would sleep in there with you," Caelan added. "Let's not forget what happened when we came back after you threatened every guard in the palace about harming her."

All three of them were siding together, which *never* happened. But as they pointed out instance after instance of my odd actions since Lira's arrival, I hated to admit they were right.

"And now you've brought her to dinner with us, wearing the queen's gown. The very queen her parents killed!" Eldrin wrinkled his nose. "You're treating her like she's your betrothed, not your prisoner, and if you keep this up, your people will turn on you. Your irrational actions will get us all killed."

I sucked in a breath while forcing my expression to remain indifferent. I hated how right they were. Whatever was brewing between Lira and me was turning me into someone I wasn't. I needed to put some distance between us to clear my head. I had a plan, and I couldn't let anything interfere with it, including myself.

I wanted to stab myself in the gut. "Your opinions and advice are noted." I'd made one mistake after another, but I'd already declared she was staying with me. Every other nicety ended now. "Everything I've done has been to make her uncomfortable, but I hadn't considered it from my people's perspective, so thank you for bringing up your concerns."

"Yes, we wouldn't want the king to be seen as forgiving and graceful." Lira sneered and placed her fork on the table. She hadn't taken a single bite.

Good. Let her starve. I didn't care. I forced myself to harden toward her. "Forgiveness will never be given until your people have paid for their sins against us."

"Oh, and what exactly would constitute payment?" She turned toward me like it was a dare. "What is your plan to make my *people* pay? Clearly, it begins with me, so I'd like to know."

This was a test and one I had to meet head-on. I steeled myself, trying to cut off every damn emotion I felt toward her. The answer was simple ... four words that would make her hate me even more. So why were they nearly impossible to say?

"I will kill you."

My hands clenched in my lap as Tavish changed right in front of me. He'd been overbearing, controlling, and passionate, but his face had turned stony ... more calculating, like the night he'd thrown me in the holding cell.

"I will kill you." Tavish took a bite of his fish as if the words hadn't been hard to say.

Swallowing, I managed to hold my head in place and not allow it to snap back. He kept saying that he would hurt me, but since this morning, I hadn't fully believed him ... until now. Maybe that had been part of his plan, some psychological warfare, which I'd fallen for. "Then why haven't you done it yet?"

"Eager to die, sprite?" He chuckled, placing his fork back on the plate.

"If that's the only way I can be free of *you*." I'd rather die than lose all my dignity and break in front of him. He didn't deserve to break me, especially since I hadn't done a damn thing to him or his people. "*Nightmare.*" I added my own special nickname again, needing to remind myself that he was the enemy more than to actually hurt him.

He smirked like he approved of the name.

Bastard.

"It's a relief to hear that you do plan to kill her." Eldrin's shoulders relaxed marginally. "I'd begun to doubt your intentions. If that's the plan, why is she sitting here with us, and when is her execution?"

"Spilling the blood of the Seelie princess will restore the spirit of our people." Caelan lifted a black napkin to his face and wiped his mouth.

My stomach roiled, and I noticed how Finnian had bit his bottom lip instead of interjecting. I'd need to keep an eye on him—maybe he could become an ally.

"Precisely." Tavish placed his hands on the table. "The Seelie princess, which she isn't yet. We need her powers to awaken and her memories to return in order for the Seelie to feel her magic and know she's returned to Ardanos. They'll be desperate to find her, which will be when the four of us, with most of the army, will arrive at the Seelie veil they created to keep us from returning home and slit their princess's throat, allowing it to coat our bodies so we can finally enter the kingdom once again."

I was thankful I didn't have an appetite. Otherwise, I was certain my stomach would have emptied its contents. I wanted to believe I wasn't a fae, but between my blood color changing and every memory of my childhood gone, I couldn't discount it. Though, I still doubted I was the actual princess. Either way, I had to make an escape plan quickly.

Not having wings was extremely problematic.

Finnian leaned back and clapped his hands. "Very theatrical and vicious—your father would be so proud. No wonder you don't want her harmed until the time comes to reveal her soiled and broken right in front of her parents' eyes."

His eyes didn't sparkle the way they had when he'd teased me. I had to hope that meant something.

"Yes, he would." Eldrin nodded, a smirk firmly in place. "That is a plan every Unseelie can get behind."

My mouth went dry, and I took hold of my water. Even though I wasn't hungry, I couldn't risk dehydration.

The conversation turned to a prisoner dispute from earlier, and I got lost in my thoughts, trying to think of a good way out.

DINNER HAD BEEN AWFUL. I ate a few bites of some sort of barely edible sulfuric fish and two small mushrooms with a slightly sweet flavor. I had to keep my strength up to get out of here. From what I'd seen, there was only one set of large doors to the castle, which meant I'd have to climb out a window to escape.

The entire way back to Tavish's room, I took in every corner and crevice, trying to remember *everything*: where people tended to collect, the guards who flew along the hallways, and even which areas appeared darker than others, which I'd need to avoid since the fae here could blend in with the shadows.

In fact, light would be my best friend because a dark, shadowy blob flitting around would reveal that Tavish or his cousin was nearby.

Unlike on the way down, Tavish walked briskly, clutching my arm. My right toes throbbed as I walked quickly to keep up with him, and I began limping. His hand tightened on my arm, but he slowed slightly.

His touch still created that frustrating buzz, and despite the way he'd been walking, his fingers were firm but light, as though he couldn't make himself be more brutal. But I chose to focus on the pain and not on what his touch did to my body.

The two guards stood watch at the double doors to his room. I hadn't gotten a good look at them earlier, but now I took in every inch to determine what I'd be up against when I tried to leave.

One was female. I'd assumed that Tavish's most trusted would all be men, but once again, I'd been wrong. Her deep-set dark eyes focused on me, and she lifted a brow as she scanned me. A candle in a sconce burning over her head cast a warm glow on her light tan skin and reflected off her dark armor and long, thin, black hair.

"I'm assuming you haven't noticed anything, Torcall?" Tavish asked curtly, his fingers digging into my skin.

I flinched but swallowed the whimper. He wanted to prove a point to everyone, but that didn't mean I would help him. If his people revolted against him, even a few of them, that would give me a chance to break free.

"No, Your Highness," the other guard, a bulky guy, said from his spot in front of me. He had startlingly blue eyes that continually searched the area for threats. Between that and his dark skin and white hair, the man was very striking. "Finola and I haven't moved from our posts."

"Good." Tavish strolled by them, opening the door. "You two are dismissed for the night. Send your relief to take your station. I need you both back here in the morning."

He tugged me more gently, but my feet ached so much that I stumbled again on what I suspected to be broken toes.

Tears burned in my eyes, but I blinked to keep them at

bay. I wasn't sure if Tavish wanted to prove something to himself, to me, or both, but he was being awful.

I couldn't believe we'd basically kissed just an hour ago. My lips still tingled from the way his mouth had felt on mine.

"What's wrong, sprite?" Once the doors banged shut, Tavish eased his hold and slipped his arm around my waist. He took some of the weight off my foot even though he continued, "Are you not fond of mistreatment?"

Any butterflies I'd been feeling for him disappeared. I didn't need to get confused about my feelings for him, and his being a cold asshole helped.

Not wanting him to continue touching me and messing with my head, I limped away. "Nope. Crying because you smell so bad. Maybe you should put me back in the holding cell so I can actually get some sleep."

He laughed, and the sound was warm and genuine.

His hot-and-cold demeanor gave me whiplash. "Oh, are you back to being somewhat humane now that we're not around your besties and cousin?"

"Besties?" His forehead wrinkled. "What is that?"

"Your close friends—Caelan and Finnian." Even though we both spoke English, we had different vernaculars that hindered us from time to time.

He sighed and ran a hand through his hair, making it messy.

I hated how my heart skipped a beat.

"Everything they said is true." Tavish exhaled. "And I fear our past is clouding my judgment. I can't allow that. My people have suffered so much because of your family. My hands are tied, and whatever we're feeling can't happen. I have to kill you, sprite. Have no doubt about that."

His admission that he felt something for me made me want to close the distance between us. I couldn't do that. He'd made it clear where his loyalties lay, and it wasn't with me. I refused to bring up again that I'd had nothing to do with the attack. We'd already had that conversation. "You've made it clear."

He sighed and went to the bed, grabbing a pillow and the large comforter. He placed both on the floor. "This is where you'll sleep tonight."

"Why not just send me back to the holding cell?" I crossed my arms to prevent myself from shaking.

"Because I harmed a guard today on your behalf, threatened another, and informed the guards that you'll be sleeping in here since I can't trust them." Tavish's wings fluttered. "If I take you back, I'll look indecisive, which is unacceptable. And the truth is, I don't want you to be harmed until the time is forced upon us."

Not wanting to continue this conversation, I made my way to the makeshift bed on the floor. I wanted to close my eyes and go over everything I'd seen tonight before I forgot anything.

Preparing for another uncomfortable night, I wrapped myself in the comforter. It felt like silk on my skin, and as I nestled into the pillow, I could've believed it was a cloud. It was almost as comfortable as my bed back home ... and smelled like Tavish.

I wanted to stare out the window, but I turned to face the bed in case Tavish tried to kill me during the night.

He climbed into bed, and I couldn't see him anymore.

"Don't worry," he said softly, like he feared someone outside would hear him. "I won't hurt you until I'm forced to. Rest well."

A sob built in my chest, but I forced it away. I had to

focus on a plan ... a way to escape. Dad had told Eiric and me over and over again that if we ever got into a dangerous situation, we shouldn't waste energy on being upset but rather focus every last ounce of concentration we had on surviving until he could find us.

He was right. That was exactly what I had to do.

I had the two daggers, and I knew how to climb and how to fight. Now, I just needed to figure out how to use those three things to get out of here without flying fae catching me.

I faced the windows and examined them and every corner of the room I could see until I passed out.

TIME BLURRED TOGETHER due to the darkness surrounding me and the monotonous days. Tavish had left me alone today and had yet to return.

Being stuck in this room all the time with only my own company, I was certain I was losing my mind. My one solace was that Tavish still hadn't found the daggers in the bathroom. Granted, he hadn't been spending a lot of time in his room, coming back only after dinner with cold leftovers for me to eat before going to bed.

Now, I stood at the windows, trying to calculate how far away the edge of the rocky cliff was from here. It was at least twenty feet, which was too high for me to jump from, but maybe I could climb the way to the cliff instead.

Taking a deep breath, I pushed on the glass to lift it open and see what was directly beneath me. I hadn't been able to move around the castle again, so I had no escape plan from here.

As soon as the window rose an inch, the doorknob to the bedchamber turned.

Shit.

I lowered the window and took several large steps back just as Finola hurried in, her sword drawn. Her gaze locked on me and went to the window. She scowled. "Did you open the window?"

The other night, I'd realized why I couldn't lie. It was something I'd read in one of the folklore books my family favored. Fae couldn't lie, so I had to choose my words carefully. "Considering how fast you got in here, does it look open?" I rocked back on my feet, thankful that my toes didn't hurt anymore, though my middle one was crooked.

"Then what did I hear?" She tilted her head.

I hated the way she looked at me ... like she saw so much. It reminded me of Eiric, which meant I needed to redirect the conversation. I remembered how Finnian had been accused of trying to bed one of the servants, so that was a safe place to head. "There's a lot of noise around here. For all I know, it could have been Finnian trying to get you into bed." I didn't know why, but I'd expected Finnian to visit me. He'd been as missing as Tavish.

She laughed. "I do think, Seelie Princess, that if we'd met under different circumstances, the two of us could have been friends."

I tucked a piece of hair behind my ear, hating how it already felt a little greasy. Though I'd been brought new outfits that appeared to have belonged to servants, I refused to bathe again.

A faint scar still marked my chest from when Eldrin had caught me alone in the bath. I didn't want to re-create that moment ever again.

"Don't do something foolish and force Torcall's and my

hands to keep you in line." Finola sheathed her sword before heading back out to her post, leaving me alone.

I paced around the comforter on the floor, wanting to scream and throw a tantrum. Instead, I went back to thinking. One thing I had noticed was that there weren't many guards outside, and groups of people often lined up in front of the palace, chanting something, though I couldn't make out what. Most of the attention outside was focused on them.

Heavy footsteps echoed from the other side of the door, and Eldrin entered the bedroom.

His face was taut, and his lips pressed together as he hovered by the door. "Still no magic?"

"Nope." The guards came in every hour to see if they could sense my magic returning. Apparently, fae could feel the magic inside each other, though they might not be able to tell exactly what it was. So far, my scent and blood were the only things that labeled me fae. "Did you not believe the reports that are no doubt getting back to you?"

"Sometimes, I need to see things for myself." He wrinkled his nose and sneered. "But you should really bathe."

My stomach hardened. He knew why I wouldn't, and he loved it.

"Well, I have things I need to attend to with Tavish about our people." He blew out a breath. "But it would be really helpful for him if you could harness your magic and fast."

I laughed bitterly. "Oh, I'll get on that. I'd love to help him out so he can kill me." Even though Tavish returned each night, the distance between us had grown, and a stupid part of me missed him. I craved the buzz of his touch and wanted to taste his lips again, but that would *never* happen.

Besides, he seemed more than fine.

"Dragging out your fate is foolish. But what else should I expect from a sunscorched?" Eldrin rolled his eyes and left.

If I ever got out of here, I vowed to come back one day and kill the pompous asshole.

I bit the inside of my cheek, trying to channel my rage without causing a ruckus that would result in one of the guards checking on me again. The sweet taste of my blood filled my mouth, and my breathing turned rapid. I felt like a caged animal.

Suddenly, I heard a loud scream. It sounded like Eldrin calling for help.

I hurried to the door and pushed it open, planning to ask the guards what was happening, only to see them flying down the hallway toward the noise.

Leaving me unguarded.

My pulse pounded.

This was it.

The moment I'd been waiting for.

I was getting the hell out of here and never looking back.

Though I wanted to turn around and race for the daggers, I forced myself to remain in the doorway, searching the darkness for any hint of movement. I needed to take my chance to escape, but I didn't want to rush and fall into a trap.

Not sure what I was looking for; I squinted ... but I didn't see anything.

Another scream had me shuffling back and shutting the door. It was now or never, and if this was a test, so fucking be it. I needed to get the hell out of here instead of waiting for my death to arrive.

A faint *click* informed me that the door had shut, so I spun and raced into the bathroom to retrieve the daggers. Fortunately, I was able to fasten the one I'd brought from home to my ankle, and then I grabbed the dagger Eldrin had left after his attack.

As I reentered the bedroom, I heard more commotion outside, with someone yelling, "The attacker is toward the front of the castle!" followed by a group of guards flying by.

There was no way I could leave via the hallway, so I had only one option.

My breath caught as I turned to the windows, and the threat of tears burned my eyes. I would have to climb to safety and risk falling to my death.

But at least I'd die trying to survive and not at the hands of Tavish or any other fae.

Decision made, I ran to the window and lifted it, trying to open it as quietly as possible. I didn't want to be careless and have someone walking by notice what I was doing. I gritted my teeth, and when the window was open about two feet, I locked the top in place and stuck my head outside.

The ledge had a small platform, so I held the extra dagger in my teeth and crawled outside. The cold air hit my face and body, and my gray gown puffed underneath me.

I suppressed a shiver, turned so that my chest was facing the window, and glanced to my right. There were fairly deep grout lines from where the smooth stone material had been placed together. Each piece of stone was five feet wide and four feet long. Scaling the wall would be difficult, but there were indents where I could place my feet and hands.

Needing my toes for leverage, I kicked off my flat-bottomed slippers, letting them fall below onto the rocky embankment, and pressed my toes into a crack. A sharp ache shot up my legs, but I held my breath and climbed.

I tried to ignore the chill, but my body quivered. The stone felt like ice, probably from the snow that continuously flurried around me. I moved inch by inch carefully, but the longer I remained out here, the more numb I became, except for my hands and feet. They were on fire.

My teeth clacked against the dagger, and I stupidly looked down. The area below me was, at minimum, a fifty-foot drop with pointed, jagged pieces of rock sticking out of a thick layer of snow. A dark, wolflike creature was standing right underneath me, his lime-green eyes glowing up at mine.

Nightbane.

Shit. He was watching me, and he was alone, but that didn't mean his guard wasn't coming.

If I was the Seelie princess, I needed my wings to come out now. My heart thundered against my rib cage as I became light-headed.

I faced forward, my nose pressing against the smooth stone as I flexed my back muscles. If the blasted things were in there, now would be a good time for them to make their debut. I wasn't sure how much longer I could scale the side of the castle.

Of course, all I wound up with was a back spasm.

Great.

Focus, Lira, I chanted. *One task at a time.* I needed to get off this ledge. Then I could deal with Nightbane and whatever guards showed up. I'd either become free or die, but at least there would be finality to my dire circumstances.

With resolve, I moved again, though now I could barely feel my hands and feet. I thought about going back and seeing if I could find another way out, but when I glanced back, I realized I'd climbed halfway between the window and where the castle abutted the steep mountain.

I had to keep moving. Running down the hill would be easier in bare feet, even if I couldn't feel them.

My body shook as I continued, increasing my pace. My right foot lost its grip, and I scrabbled for purchase but couldn't offset the weight. My heart lunged into my throat as my body dropped. Flailing, I flipped frontward toward the ground.

I shrieked. The dagger dropped from my mouth, tumbling directly below where I'd be landing within seconds. I closed my eyes.

A faint whimper came from below me, and my body hit something soft and warm. I jarred as whatever had caught me dropped on impact, and I opened my eyes to find myself wrapped around an animal with dark, green-tipped fur.

Nightbane's body ran hot, warming me so that the frost eased from my body, and he quickly stood on all four legs again. He trotted, with me clinging to his back, his gigantic muscles working underneath me as he went to the dagger and used his teeth to lift it.

Raising my head, I expected to find guards hurrying toward us, but the area was clear. Still, Nightbane had caught me and knew I was a prisoner. I couldn't stay with him. I had to get away, though I didn't relish the idea of harming the animal.

Loosening my hold, I moved to roll off him, but he increased his pace and headed down the rocky spike of a hill.

I tightened my grip, not wanting to risk getting a spike lodged in my side. Once he tore off toward the front of the castle, I'd roll off and deal with the consequences then.

Enjoying the warmth while I could, I lifted my head to see dozens of fae standing outside the castle. Snow dusted their hair and clothes as they stood with their fists high above their heads. I expected Nightbane to veer toward the group, but he continued his trek downward through the spiky rocks to the stone road that ran through the village. He jumped over a small ledge, all four of his paws landing on the stone path, and darted through the town toward the sea.

My eyes burned as tears threatened to fill them, but I was confident that Nightbane planned on helping me get out of here.

I had so many questions, but I held them back. Now wasn't the time, nor could the animal answer them.

A young boy stood in the middle of the street, watching the people in front of the castle with four women beside him talking.

"It's the king's cù-sìth!" the boy exclaimed. He spread out slate-colored wings, knocking snowflakes off himself. He wore a light-gray tunic, making him stand out a little more than the people who lived in the castle. "Mother, look!"

My stomach dropped as the woman turned to me.

"It's her!" a woman screeched. "The Seelie princess! She's escaping on the king's prized animal."

Of course. I'd made it out of the castle, but one second in the village, and I might as well have been wearing a flashing neon light.

"Guards!" A woman with light-blue hair flung her hood from her face. "The sunscorched is out here!"

Nightbane continued pushing through as more doors opened, and a silver-haired man a few inches taller than I flew out, lifted me by my waist, and dropped me onto the stony path.

The chill covered me as I landed on my tailbone, throbbing pain stealing my breath. I jumped to my feet, removing the dagger at my ankle, preparing to fight anyone who might come at me.

Three other men joined the silver-haired man.

Nightbane growled, dropping the other dagger from his mouth and standing next to me. His eyes glowed vibrantly as he bared his teeth and circled me, staring down my potential attackers.

Behind me, the sound of a gigantic door opening warned that the guards had to be coming near. I had to get out of here, and now.

"The king should've known not to trust a Seelie wildling," a man more thick than tall snarled. Unlike most of the fae I'd seen, this one appeared older, with faint crow's-feet around his eyes and slightly thinner hair than the others. "You should be with the rest of the prisoners." He spat at my feet.

"Why? I haven't done a damn thing to anyone here." I hated how they treated me as if I was the person who'd attacked and banished them. It hadn't been my decision, yet they put as much blame on me as those actually responsible.

A boy flew from the window above me and landed right in front of my face. He couldn't have been older than ten, but he held a dagger larger than the one I had in my hand.

No wonder Tavish had called my pocketknife a mere toy.

"Their blood runs through you." He swallowed. "Because of them, I lost my mother. Your death will be celebrated by all of us." Then he attacked.

I ducked, the boy's dagger sweeping over my head. I leaned left and kicked him in the stomach. The impact sent him slamming into the house behind him, and his head hit the stone.

I wanted to run over and check on him. I couldn't imagine what losing a parent that young had done to him, and he wasn't old enough to know any better.

The four men moved toward me, and Nightbane leaped at the man with silver hair who'd removed me from his back.

Nightbane sank his teeth into the man's throat and ripped it out.

I stopped, nauseated, as the man gurgled, but the other three men came toward me. I raised my dagger. My feet were freezing, and so were my hands, but I'd go out like a warrior and not some helpless victim.

All three men removed short swords from sheaths at their sides and attacked me simultaneously.

Adrenaline pumped through my body, burning through the cold. My parents, Eiric, and I had sparred, but never like *this*. I inhaled, ignoring the way my lungs burned, and prepared to use the defensive moves I'd learned during the past twelve years.

Nightbane snarled and clawed a man with light-blue hair in the face then steamrolled into the man in the center, leaving me with one opponent.

I ignored the light-blue-haired man's screams as my attacker swung his sword at me. I jumped back several feet, and the edge grazed me, slicing through the center of my dress and nicking my skin. The pain stung, but I used his momentum against him and punched him in the jaw. His head snapped back as his wings expanded, keeping him from falling down.

His ink-black eyes widened, and his nostrils flared just as a far-too-familiar voice commanded, "Stop!"

Ink-black eyes glared at me, and I knew his intention. As he thrust his sword at me again, I spun to the side, allowing him to catch air, and Nightbane clamped his teeth down on my attacker's arm.

Black blood squirted over my face and chest as someone's arms circled my waist and lifted me. My buzzing skin informed me of my captor's identity, and I hated the relief his touch brought again. Yet, his warning from the first night we met rang in my ear. *I'm the very one you should fear.*

He hadn't been lying.

He flew me upward toward the castle, my backside against his chest, so I elbowed him in the gut as hard as I could.

It was like smashing into rock. Groaning, I used my other elbow to hit him in the face.

"Blighted abyss," he snarled as I jerked from his loosened grasp.

Then, I fell to the road but managed to land upright. My feet stung on impact. I pushed the discomfort away and spun around, readying for Tavish to come at me again. He'd needed me enough to hunt me down on Earth, so I had to hurt him to get free from here.

"Lira," he warned as dark blood trickled from his nose. "You need to stop. Don't make your situation worse." His eyes darkened to the ones from my nightmares, but this time, there was no hatred or malice in them. In a way, it looked like he was pleading with me.

I wanted to listen, but that was foolish. I gritted my teeth and struck with my knife, faster than ever before, aiming for his neck. Just before my blade would've sliced his throat, he kicked me in the stomach. I stumbled back, somehow not falling on my ass, but my tailbone nevertheless flared as if it were on fire.

Then Finola and Torcall were flanking me and restraining me, each grabbing an arm. I jerked to get free of their hold, but their grips were like vises. Torcall pried the dagger from my hands and dropped it. The blade clanked on the stone, the sound of my freedom being ripped from me once more.

This had been my one chance.

My one shot to not die by Tavish's hands was gone.

A low, threatening snarl had me glancing at Nightbane. Drool dripped from his mouth, and the hair on the nape of his neck rose. For some reason, he'd tried to help me tonight, and I feared what the repercussions would be for him.

"Nightbane, go to the prison and make your rounds," Tavish ordered, and the wolf turned his snarl on him.

"She's going to ruin us all!" a man yelled from the gathering crowd. "She's weakening the king, and the Seelie will overtake us, killing everyone!"

Eyes darkening, Tavish extended a hand, and Nightbane dropped to his stomach. He whimpered and whined as if something was killing him.

"Stop!" I shouted, trying to jerk free. "Don't hurt him. Hurt me instead!"

Tavish turned his steely gaze back on me and rasped, "Oh, your fate will be far worse than his."

"That's right!" A man smirked, his eerie, pale-yellow eyes shining. "A prisoner tried to escape and attacked the king. We all get to watch her die."

"No." Tavish shook his head and expanded his massive wings. "The plan is to kill her in front of the Seelie people. They need to feel her to know she's here before we take her there for all of them to see her death."

My stomach roiled. I hated how easily the words flowed from his lips as if my life didn't matter.

"What are you saying, *King* Tavish?" A guard beside Finola raised his chin. "You've killed your own people for her, and she sleeps in your bedchamber. The law is that if any prisoner tries to escape, then every prisoner must pay the price. Are you saying the *Seelie* princess is above the law? The very law you created?"

I glanced around and saw more people at their windows, watching the show.

Something significant was going on here, though I didn't know what. It appeared as if Tavish's people could be turning against him.

"Yes, King Tavish," the man directly behind me crooned. "If she dies in the gauntlet and we toss her body onto Seelie land, it will provide the same reaction. Why isn't she being held to the same standards as the rest of your people?"

The gauntlet? What the hell was that?

I didn't want to know.

The people closed in tighter behind us. I could feel their breaths on my back, and then a few shoved forward ... and chaos erupted around me.

I should've known that even a human version of Lira would be a pain in my ass. As a young girl, she'd loved to challenge her parents. She had been determined to find her own way and never molded to expectations. I'd always admired that about her, wishing I could be more like her ... until now.

The group of men behind her charged forward, coming way too blasted close to knocking her and my guards over. Seeing the way her dress hung open in the front, almost displaying her breasts, with golden blood trickling down and staining the material, I burned to unleash the damn protective streak inside me and kill everyone who'd harmed her.

Staying away hadn't lessened my emotions toward her; in fact, I feared my feelings for her might have intensified.

Alastor removed his sword from behind her, readying to lop off her head. The wildling enjoyed violence, and men like him had forced me to become the man I was now.

Unfortunately, I had no choice about what I had to do

next. If I didn't mitigate the desire for a revolt, civil war would break out.

I allowed frost magic to pulse from deep inside me. Unlike the darkness and the illusions I could manifest, this magic was light blue. I lifted my hand, allowing the frost to run down my arm and out of my palm, its rigidness turning my blood almost to ice, making me feel refreshed. However, I didn't have time to enjoy the sensation. I froze Alastor with his knife inches from meeting the back of Lira's neck.

My chest heaved as rage consumed me, and I clung to it. Not only was the sensation familiar, but it allowed me to amplify my magic. I needed my people to see what I could do if they chose to fight against me. The sky darkened as more magic hummed from me to the point that the moon disappeared and a haze hovered above our heads. Both my frost and darkness magic merged, which caused the snow to increase, allowing a coating to cling to our clothes.

With my magic on display, I bellowed, "None of you have the right or authority to make a decision that your *king* hasn't blessed!" With each word, dread pooled heavier in my stomach ... the sort of dread I hadn't felt since the day I regained consciousness at fourteen, only to find my parents, who lay dead, feet away from me.

Not only was I on the brink of losing control of my people, but the *one* way to protect Lira was to set her up to face the most vicious of them all.

"You're protecting a sunscorched at the cost of your people," Sablean shouted, hatred lacing his words and his dark-green eyes turning sinister. He marched toward the front to take the place of his best friend, not wanting him to have died in vain. "We will not—"

I flipped my wrist, allowing the illusions I cast in nightmares to filter into his mind as I flew over Lira's head and landed beside the man. The way my neck tingled with awareness, I knew Lira was watching over her shoulder, and the strange, pleasant sensation of having her attention soared through me even more. I placed the edge of my blade against his throat, and Sablean whimpered.

I had no intention of killing him—he hadn't posed any direct harm to Lira or myself—but that didn't mean I could tolerate his disobedience. I asked through gritted teeth, "Does anyone else want to challenge me?" I pressed deeper into Sablean's neck, needing his blood to spill. However, I didn't cut deep enough to end his life.

My stance had to be clear. Threatening or disobeying the king would result in death, but speaking one's mind out of turn would be forgiven once. I had to maintain control.

If a war broke out among the Unseelie, none of us would survive here. Our ground barely grew enough food to feed us, and only because the Seelie fae had allowed a handful of their people with earth magic to provide enough nutrients for us to skimp by.

A war would require resources we didn't have.

I made sure my gaze connected with each person who'd been protesting outside the castle, and I noted who had been at the doors, demanding I come out and explain myself to them.

Like I blasting needed to seek their approval when I'd been doing everything I could to take back what was rightfully ours ... by readying myself to kill the one person who had made me feel something more than the anger I'd breathed for the past twelve years of my life.

It was all for them.

And this was how they responded.

I wanted to punish each and every one of them. And I would, but not here. Not now.

The Unseelie who weren't outside were watching from their windows. If I injured anyone else, it would only fuel their hatred for Lira and encourage others to join the instigators opposing me.

Foolishly, I wished I could go back in time. I should never have brought her here.

Silence descended. The guards stood at my side, but they hesitated as if uncertain they wanted to protect me.

I'd allowed things with her to go too far. Eldrin had warned me, but not before the damage was done. I had to do right by my people ... do what my father would've done for them. My obligation was to them more than anyone.

I cleared my throat. "Good, because from this point on, anyone who speaks out against me will die at my hand." I paused, allowing my words to sink in. I'd already delivered on this promise once before, against one in my inner circle. "Now, I will say what needs to be said, and I won't tolerate any interruptions." I nodded to the frozen man I'd killed in front of them. "My plan was to take the princess alive and in good health to the Seelie kingdom's veil and spill her blood in front of witnesses. However, that plan has changed."

I had to be careful because I didn't need them to realize the truth. "I gave the sunscorched more privileges than she deserved to serve our greater good ... to have the most impact. But that wasn't enough for her. Not only did she try to escape, but she attacked me, which I won't tolerate." If I allowed her to do it, my people would turn on me. "As such, my guards are to prepare for the second-ever gauntlet. The sunscorched princess will take part, and you will get to enjoy watching her fight for her life."

The anger etched into every one of their faces turned to pure delight. I lowered my sword but continued to push my magic into Sablean and the world around us. Somehow, calling for the gauntlet made me feel more ill than the first time.

I clung to the lesson my father had beaten into me several times growing up. *The best way to control your people is to lead with fear. Ruthlessness is essential if you don't want someone to take the crown from you.* We hadn't been ruthless with the Seelie, trying to bridge peace at my mother's request, and because of that, my parents had died at the Seelies' hands.

"Take him to his home." I gestured to Sablean, refusing to relinquish control of his mind until later. This would be a punishment for him, and all would see what sort of state he'd be in after I released my hold on him.

Not bothering to wipe off his blood, I sheathed my sword and turned to Lira.

I didn't expect the way my heart skipped a beat when I saw her.

Her cheeks were golden from the cold, and her blonde hair was wild with snow in it. Her cobalt eyes looked hard as she stared at me with distrust and malice, and my heart stuttered. Her cleavage was on full display, her nipples taut, causing my dick to harden and my pants to get a little too tight at this very inopportune time. She was wild, feral ... and downright gorgeous.

"I'll take her back up," Torcall said, readying to carry her.

My hand inched back toward my sword at the thought of her being close to him. Clenching my jaw, I forced my hand to relax. I couldn't act irrationally.

I forced myself to nod at him, and as he took her away, I turned back to my people, knowing if I continued to watch him touch her, I'd lose my composure. Nothing had changed tonight between Lira and me. Her death had always been the goal. What I felt for her was irrelevant, and hopefully, when she died, the strange emotions would die with her.

Heart squeezing, I lifted my chin and slipped a neutral mask back into place. "Next time anything like this happens, you all will be placed in prison. I won't tolerate this behavior ever again. Do you understand?" I allowed the edges of darkness to swirl around me as the snow picked up.

As the Unseelie king, I had the most power over darkness, illusions, frost, and dreams. No one could do as much damage as I could, and they needed to remember that. Not even Eldrin could blend completely into darkness; he cast mere shadows.

"Anyone who threatens me also threatens the survival of our people." I spoke clearly, allowing the rocks to echo the message to the entire village. "And they shall be killed."

Two men flanked Sablean and took his arms while the oldest resident of the village flew high from his spot next to the door. "Yes, King Tavish." He bowed his head, his dark-blond hair gleaming faintly in the thick fog that hovered over us. "We won't doubt you again."

Some of the tension eased from my shoulders, though I kept my stance tight. "Good. Now hurry home and rest. It's late. Tomorrow, you'll need to double your workload since the gauntlet will start in two nights." I glanced at the guards by my side and at Nightbane, who lay miserably on the ground, tormented by dreams. "And take the dog to his cell and punish him. Do whatever it takes for him not to do something like this again."

The men who hadn't seemed appeased relaxed. They'd probably suspected I wouldn't set a date, which was exactly why I had. I had to give them every reason not to rise against me again.

Not wasting any more time, I expanded my massive wings and soared above them. I stared down at them until I blanketed myself in darkness and lifted into the fog. I wanted to hear what they had to say about their actions, but something yanked at me to go after Lira. I needed to reach her and check that she was all right, which was foolish. In two days, she'd likely be dead unless her memories came back, along with her wings and magic. There was no doubt the inmates would team up and work against her.

Acid inched upward in my throat, making me feel as if I would vomit.

I flew past my bedchamber and was heading to the holding cells when my attention landed on a window that had been lifted several feet high.

My mouth went dry. *That* was how Lira had escaped? Earth must have done a number on her, making her ignorant.

"Let me go," Lira snapped from inside my room. "I'm back in place. And where is Nightbane?"

"If you think we're going to leave you alone after *that—*" Finola started, only stopping when I flew through the window.

Lira stood in the middle of the room, her back to me, with her hands on her hips. I made sure to remain soundless, but I knew the moment she felt my presence.

Her body tensed, and she pivoted so she could see both me and the guards.

Excellent. She knew better than to keep her back turned to an enemy. Whether I wanted it to be that way or not, that's what we were. Her parents had made sure of that, and there was no way back.

"Your Majesty, we weren't sure where you wanted us to take her, so I brought her here." Torcall folded his wings behind his back and averted his gaze. "If you want us to take her to the cell to prepare, we can do that."

"Prepare for *what*?" Lira huffed and winced, touching her chest where she'd been cut. "And where is Nightbane?"

Two of her toenails were cracked and bleeding from being barefoot outside, and her hands were tinged blue from the cold.

"Leave her here," I rasped, a dangerous edge to my tone. "And go."

Her head snapped up toward me, and she clenched her jaw.

My stomach suddenly felt funny, and it wasn't from the bile anymore.

"Yes, Your Majesty." Torcall bowed his head. "We'll stand guard since you'll want to attend dinner."

"I won't be leaving tonight." I hated the way those words settled over me. I struggled to leave her every day and lay awake at night, watching her sleep from my bed. "I can't risk our little sprite sneaking out again. Between that and a brazen attacker in the castle, I need to ensure she remains well so everyone can see her in the gauntlet."

She huffed and stomped her foot, then cringed.

Good. It served her right for being so reckless. She had caused a ton of issues by escaping and attacking my people. I'd underestimated her, and that alone infuriated me. I'd accounted for seduction, trying to find a way to kill me, and escaping down the castle hall. I'd never dreamed she'd climb out the window.

"Go," I reiterated, my entire focus locked on her.

"Yes, Your Majesty," Finola replied, and the two guards left us alone.

When the door shut, I forced my feet to remain still. "What were you thinking, climbing out the window like that?"

She crossed her arms, blocking a portion of her chest. "Oh, I don't know, *nightmare*. Maybe I don't want to *die*. Maybe I want to get out of here so I can find a way back to my family and live out my life!" Her voice shook, but it wasn't from fear. Her nostrils flared, conveying every ounce of anger she'd harnessed. "And is Nightbane okay?"

I couldn't let her weaken me, but I still didn't understand her connection with the cù-sìth. "Nightbane is being taken back to his bed so he can be taught a lesson. He wanted to aid you in your escape and attacked other Unseelie. That is unacceptable."

"He was protecting me." She tugged at the ends of her hair. "Punish me instead of him."

"Oh, you'll be punished soon enough." I forced myself not to flinch, instead focusing on the goal I needed to accomplish. I pulled up the memory of my dead parents, blood soaking through their clothes and the Seelie guards hovering over them. My heart hardened, and some of the urge to comfort her slipped away. "And letting you go isn't possible." A lump formed in my throat, but I ignored it, making sure I enunciated every word. "You won't get to live out your life in Gleann Solas or back on Earth, sprite."

"And I don't have the option of living here either." Her bottom lip trembled faintly before she pressed her lips together firmly.

The one thing I wanted most in the realm could never happen—to close the distance and hold her in my arms. That would only further strain things between us. "No, you don't." There was no point in giving her false hope. "In fact, you'd better bathe and get some sleep so you can heal as much as possible for what lies ahead."

"Are you going to tell me what the fuck the gauntlet is?" The snow had melted in her hair, and the few flakes still speckled on her chest had mixed with her drying blood. "Are you lining me up for lashes? Hanging me in front of the crowd?"

"If only it were that quick and painless." That would be easier to witness than the hell she'd be experiencing. There was no doubt her death would be prolonged and painful. "Sprite, you have no idea what you got yourself into. You'll wish I'd slit your throat." I forced myself to smile, needing her to fear me and keep her distance.

Her jaw dropped, and her eyes narrowed.

I stepped toward her, though I hadn't meant to, and ran a finger along her cheek. That damn jolt sprang between us, but I bared my teeth, leaning down toward her. Her chest heaved, and I wasn't certain if it was from fear or attraction ... maybe both. Either way, it invigorated me.

I moved my lips to her ear, ready to tell her what she desperately wanted to know.

His musky amber scent filled my nose, making me dizzy. Those damn butterflies took flight in my stomach again, and I forced myself not to lean into him. After everything, I hated how attracted I still was to him and the way I longed for his touch.

Bastard.

"The gauntlet is three different games in which your only goal is to survive," he answered, his lips brushing my earlobe and his breath flitting across my skin.

I couldn't hide my shiver, but it clearly had to be from what he'd told me and not from his touch or proximity. Stepping back, I shook away my daze and focused on the words, *games* and *survival*. "What exactly does that mean?"

"You'll take part in three obstacle courses with dangerous challenges that include the other prisoners." Tavish leaned back and closed his eyes. "The prisoners will use the opportunity to kill each other without repercussions. Eldrin and Caelan will lay out the rules and the obstacles while I continue to handle the kingdom's issues."

I tried to swallow, but the lump in my throat was too

large. "They're all going to attack me, and I don't have wings or magic." My pulse quickened. I'd been determined to escape so I wouldn't die at their hands, and here I was, being handed over to them.

"Oh, I'm aware." Tavish opened his eyes, the color so dark it could have passed for onyx if I hadn't known better.

"All this time, you said you would kill me." I didn't know why, but out of all the options, Tavish would be my choice. I wasn't sure what that said about me. "Instead, you're going to stuff me and put me on a silver platter?"

His brows furrowed, and then he grinned cockily. "If you being stuffed by me is something you'd like to experience, I'm not opposed to making that happen. In regard to the silver platter, that's an odd request, but I'm sure we can come up with a solution to satisfy both your criteria."

My body warmed at his sexual innuendo, but I ignored it. There was no way in hell I would allow myself to lose my virginity to a cold, broody asshole who'd kidnapped me and put me in this mess to begin with. I lifted my chin and wrinkled my nose. "Not what I meant. I was comparing what you're doing to me to a turkey on Thanksgiving."

"Turkey?" He rocked back on his heels. "Thanksgiving. I'm unsure what you mean. Are we speaking the same language?"

Now *that* I understood all too well. It'd taken me a little bit to get used to the slurs here, but it was easy to catch on when insults were tossed only in my direction. "Never mind. I just meant you've been adamant that *you* would kill me, and now you're handing me over to be attacked by ..." I trailed off. I wasn't even sure how many prisoners they had here.

His jaw clenched. "I *didn't* do anything. You escaped, despite the nice things I've given you, and attacked several of my people. Not only that—but I was forced to kill yet another one of my people to protect you after you attacked me, trying to get away."

"You're still the one who made the decision." I wouldn't let him justify his actions like I'd caused this problem. "So don't blame me."

He closed the distance between us and moved me so that my back pressed against the wall. He lowered his face to mine and placed his thumb against my lower lip, pulling it down. The buzz shot through me, and I had to restrain myself from licking his finger to find out what he tasted like.

"If I hadn't announced the gauntlet, my people would've revolted against me, and you would've died tonight. At least this allows you a chance to prepare and survive."

I snorted, and before I could stop myself, I moved my head so that I had his finger between my teeth.

He smirked, stepping into me, and a velvety, earthy taste filled my mouth from his skin. I could feel him hard against me, and I had to fight my legs to keep them from wrapping around his waist, desperate to feel him between them.

"I should bite your finger off," I snarled, bearing down a little more on his skin.

"Now *that* is a sacrifice I'd be more than willing to make, sprite." He chuckled.

Goose bumps spread across my skin, and my breathing accelerated, but I couldn't tolerate him getting any more arrogant ... especially not due to me. I placed a hand against his chest and pushed him back.

He didn't fight me, and a part of me screamed in disappointment, but the sane part sighed with relief. When his finger left my mouth, I missed his taste as much as his touch.

This connection between us didn't make sense, but at least it affected us both.

"If you're expecting a thank-you, it won't happen." At the end of the day, he'd set my future. The only question now was who would kill me. "You still sealed my death."

"Yes. I did." His irises darkened. "The moment I located you and brought you back here. I've been honest about that since you foolishly separated from your sister."

The words knocked the breath out of me, forcing the walls to close in. My parents had always warned me that one wrong decision could alter my life and to never go off with strangers. I'd never been tempted until I had been by the person who'd brought me here. If I could go back in time and make some other decision, I would, though I understood he'd been determined to bring me here and that Eiric could've been caught in the cross fire. "It wouldn't have mattered."

His face morphed from arrogance to a deep scowl, and his frigid demeanor slid back into place. "You're right. Fate intervened and allowed me to find you. There isn't an alternative. The past is set, and the wrongs must be righted."

"Is that a mantra you repeat to yourself day after day, or only when you spend time with me?" I'd barely been around him, but I'd heard that line or something similar to it any time we remained in each other's presence. It was like he had to remind himself that this was the way things had to be. "Because if you're doing it for my benefit, message received."

He ran a hand through his hair, and the slight curls fell over his face. He opened his mouth to say something but paused. "The towels have been replenished, so you have what you need to bathe for now."

In other words, our conversation was over. That was for

the best. But I flinched and touched the faint scar from Eldrin's attack. The quick movement caused my tailbone and chest to ache from the injuries I'd sustained tonight. Yet the last thing I wanted was to soak in the bathtub. I didn't want Eldrin to ambush me again.

Tavish's attention homed in on the spot I was touching, and he huffed. "What's wrong?"

I opened my mouth to say *Nothing*, but no sound came out. Damn the rule of fae and no lying. I hadn't struggled on Earth, but *here,* when I needed to lie to save my ass, I became speechless. I settled on a partial truth instead and touched the area, which still felt hot from where the fae had stabbed me. "My chest hurts." I glanced down and realized my dress was hanging open and barely covering my chest.

The muscle in his jaw twitched, and his attention landed on the spot where Eldrin had stabbed me.

I had to do something before he asked more questions. We had enough tension and worry between us without adding more. I slipped from my spot and headed toward the bathroom door. I turned the knob and opened it, ready to get away from him and clear my head. "A bath would be good."

"I'll get a servant to bring a gown—"

"No need." They'd already put a new gown in the closet when they'd come to spot-check the room for things the king might need. "I have something already." Before he could say anything else, I shut the door and faced the tub.

I exhaled, wanting to make this quick. I didn't want to bathe, but it had been days, if not a week, since the last time I'd gotten clean, and I didn't want the new wounds to become infected.

I turned on the water and, as the tub filled, opened the closet door to snag a pale-blue towel. I scanned the room, focusing on the darkest corners but didn't see anything there.

With haste, I stripped off my clothes and stepped into the water, allowing it to cover me. As soon as I submerged myself, the water tingled all over my body, relaxing me and easing the pain from the wounds I'd received. Still, my brain ran wild, seeing flashes of shadows in the shadows. I blinked, and nothing was there. I was allowing Eldrin to mess with my mind, and I wasn't sure how to fix it.

I sank further into the water, allowing the dirt and grime of the night to wash away. My hands, feet, and chest tingled more than the rest of my body. They were cracked, scraped, cut, and bleeding.

After getting clean, I dried myself quickly and slipped the new dress over my head. I ran my fingers through my hair to untangle the knots to the best of my ability then hurried back into the bedroom, not wanting to be in the bathroom alone.

As soon as the door opened, I saw Tavish pick up the two pillows I'd been using and place them on the bed on top of the comforter.

He stilled, tilting his head. "That was quick. Was something the matter?"

That was a question I didn't want to answer, so I focused on what I wanted to know. "Am I moving back to the holding cell?"

"If you were going back to the cell, I would've put you there earlier." He exhaled and pulled down the edge of the comforter.

A wall of pillows divided the bed in the center, like a barrier.

He cleared his throat and rubbed the back of his neck.

"You need good rest so you can heal from your injuries, and you'll do better on an actual bed."

My breath caught. "You sound like you might not want me to die."

He took in a deep breath, and his frown deepened. "I don't want you to go into the gauntlet without being able to defend yourself. Your death will serve a greater purpose ... to save my people. However, the prisoners ... they'll want to kill you out of spite and for revenge, even if you aren't an actual threat. It's ... not what I intended. I don't want you to die this way."

Wow. Even if he was misguided, at least he wasn't taking pleasure in the thought of my death. Still, I remained quiet, unsure how to respond.

"If you're uncomfortable and would rather I sleep on the floor, I can do that." His wings folded tightly behind him.

I could only imagine one of the servants or guards coming in and seeing the king on the floor and me in his bed. I didn't need their hate for me to increase ... if that was possible. I didn't want to find out. "No, it's fine." The pillows were large and fluffy. They created a decent barrier.

"Good."

"Thank—" I started.

"Don't." He lifted a hand. "Don't thank a fae ... *ever*. That means you owe them, and the last thing I need is for you to be indebted to me."

For a quick second, an image of a boy popped into my mind, with eyes similar to the light-gray shade I'd seen only a handful of times and a genuine smile ... but then it vanished. My ears rang, and I wondered if that had been him.

He gestured to the bed. "Get some sleep. I'm going to get clean before climbing into bed."

I nodded, and we passed each other. I glanced down, taking in the charcoal gown that covered me. My latest wound was already healing, and the frost-bitten blue tinge had vanished from my hands and feet as well. The water tingling the way it had must have helped heal them. Maybe I should've soaked longer, but the thought of Eldrin watching me made me want to vomit. I couldn't stay in there.

Tavish shut the door, and I slipped into the bed. His scent overpowered me ... and made me feel like I was home. The mattress was soft like a cloud, and before I realized what was happening, I fell asleep.

My mind tried to wake me, but my body buzzed, lulling me back to sleep. I felt safer than I ever had since being brought to Ardanos.

Ardanos.

The realm's name popped into my head like it was meant to be there, but when I tried to tug at it and understand why, nothing more came. I had to know the name because Tavish had said it a few times. That was the only explanation that made any sense.

Still, shock opened my eyes, and I stared at the window I'd escaped through last night. My back was to Tavish, and something heavy and cool lay on my upper thigh, causing a pleasant sensation.

My head spun, and I lifted it to see Tavish's palm resting on my waist and his calf lay across my exposed thigh where the gown had risen during the night. His foot casually hung off the side.

I looked carefully over my shoulder to see his body pressed up against the pillow barrier and his right arm and leg over it, touching me.

My back was pressed against the pillow barrier. If it hadn't been there, we'd have been completely intertwined with one another. Thank goodness it was there, but how did I untangle myself without waking him? I didn't want him to stir and realize what he'd done during the night. After the little bit of progress we'd made, the last thing I wanted was for him to become distant again.

I shifted and wiggled out of his grasp while still pretending to be asleep, but Tavish groaned and tugged me back against the pillows.

Dammit. This wouldn't be easy.

I froze, listening to his breathing. Fortunately, it was slow and easy.

Good. I hadn't woken him up.

I bit my bottom lip, debating how to get the hell out of here gracefully.

Then the bedroom door burst open.

Tavish and I jumped awake and turned toward the door to discover the worst person in the world standing there, mouth gaping open.

Tavish gasped and lunged away from the pillows, back to his side. His wings spread out, and the edges brushed my arm due to their massive size.

"Aw." Finnian placed a hand on his chest while his other arm remained at his side with some sort of clothing. "I didn't mean to interrupt your cuddle time." He gestured to the closed door behind him. "Should I come back later so you two can finish up?" He waggled his brows.

My face heated, and Tavish froze like he might have turned into a statue.

Finnian smirked and turned toward the door. "I'll take that as a yes." He paused with his hand hovering over the doorknob. "Maybe there needs to be a sign for when you two don't want to be interrupted. Torcall or Finola could inform me that you're 'getting prepared for the day.' Then I'll know to come back in five minutes … since I'm sure, with Tavish's history, it shouldn't take him long to climax."

Heart skipping a beat, I clung to the last part of the sentence. I wasn't sure what that meant, but he made it sound like Tavish was either a virgin like me or didn't have much experience.

"Blasted abyss." Tavish shot upright. "Don't you *dare* leave. Nothing like that was happening."

"Oh ... so you're a cuddler." Finnian pivoted to face us again and leaned against the door. "You know, I never expected you to be that way, but now that I ponder your actions here lately, it makes sense."

Tavish's eyes widened, and his jaw clenched. "I'm not a *cuddler*. You know better than that."

"So you weren't trying to have sex with her, nor were you cuddling with her?" Finnian scratched his head. "What exactly were you *doing* with her?"

"*Sleeping,*" Tavish answered but closed his mouth like he should've known better than to say anything.

If I thought I'd seen Finnian smile before, I'd been so wrong. For Unseelie, his expression turned very bright ... almost on par with the sun. "Clearly. You didn't think that through, did you? I love seeing the noncalculating side of you. Still, anyone could've walked in here. You're lucky it was me and that I like the Seelie princess."

I snorted darkly. "Oh yeah. I'm sure you do. You threw me under the bus at dinner the other night when Eldrin didn't want me to be treated like a guest."

"Threw you under a *bus?*" His forehead wrinkled. "I most definitely did not throw you, and I'm not sure what a bus is."

Damn the cultural differences in our languages. I supposed I was fortunate enough that they spoke English, so I could understand and communicate with them ... *sort of.* "You told Tavish to treat me more like a prisoner, so I'm having a hard time believing that you *like* me."

"That's a bus?" He shook his head, but before I could

correct him, he continued, "And though I may like you, my loyalties lie with Tavish. I said all that for his benefit because he's my closest friend and king."

Unfortunately, that made me fonder of the charismatic Finnian. Still, he'd made one thing very clear. He would do what was best for Tavish and not me, and even though I wished he was more empathetic with my plight, I understood what to expect from him.

"Why are you here, and why can't you knock like everyone else before entering my room?" Tavish tossed the comforter off, threw his feet over the side of the bed, and stood.

Drool puddled in my mouth as his messy hair framed his face and the dark scruff on his jaw made him look more rugged. Through his thin shirt, his muscles were pronounced, and I wanted to trail my fingers over every curve.

I needed a very cold bath ... pronto.

"You were supposed to join us for breakfast ten minutes ago, and Eldrin is upset. I figured you'd rather I come get you instead of him." He arched a brow. "And I believed you would be walking out the door. I hadn't expected to come in and find you still in bed ... with *Lira*."

Tavish's face paled even more. "What time is it?"

"Nine fifteen." Finnian strolled to the end of the bed. "Which is unheard of for you. You're normally down there barking orders by eight on a late day."

"I don't know how I overslept." Tavish marched toward the bathroom. "I will change and come down."

Finnian's gaze landed firmly on me, and the corners of his mouth lifted. "You comfy in that bed?"

As a matter of fact, I was, but I refused to admit it to the pompous ass. I tried not to scowl as I climbed out, my feet touching the cool floor. I doubted Tavish would let me sleep with him again, especially after the cuddle mishap and Finnian walking in on us. Oh well, maybe I could sneak back in for a nap after the two of them left. They'd be none the wiser.

He snickered and strolled over to me, dropping a pair of pants and tunic on the bed. He then turned his palm over and opened his hand, revealing two mushrooms nestled there.

I glanced at them and back to his face, staying in place. My stomach grumbled, but I kept my face indifferent. "You didn't finish breakfast?"

"I saved some for you." He shrugged and closed his fingers over them. "But if you don't want them—"

My stomach growled even louder, answering for me. On Earth, I probably would've passed on food handled by someone else, but down here, food was scarce ... at least, for me.

His face softened, and he held out his hand again. "Here. Eat. I'll bring you more later."

I didn't hesitate this time and took the mushrooms from his hand. I hadn't eaten anything yesterday after my escape attempt. Maybe that was Tavish's way of punishing me, but I didn't think so. I'd been in so much pain that I hadn't been hungry.

As I took a bite, I noticed that Finnian had two swords on his belt. Normally, he carried one around like Tavish, but last night must have put everyone on edge. Fear had a way of making people irrational and causing more strife, but I knew better than to say anything.

Or did I?

"You think one sword isn't enough if you're attacked?" I arched my brow.

He rubbed his hands together like he was preparing to fight. "Oh, Lira. You have no idea what's in store for you."

My mouth went dry, and my bite of mushroom lodged in my throat. I coughed, choking, just as Tavish hurried back into the room, wearing his normal black tunic, leather pants, and boots. His unique, intricate sword was back on his hip, and I was relieved to see he had only one.

He glanced at me, then at Finnian, and asked, "Are you coming down again with me?"

Finnian mashed his lips together as if he wanted to hide his real expression. "I have some things to attend to, but you'd better hurry. When Eldrin learned Lira wasn't back in the holding cells, his shadows started to get the best of him. We don't want him to come here and see her in yet another one of your mother's gowns and me sneaking her mushrooms."

"Fine." Tavish exhaled and opened the door. "Just make sure you're there for dinner."

My head tilted back. After Tavish's last interaction with Finnian and me alone in his room, I'd never expected Tavish to leave us alone here willingly. Granted, my dress had been stuck around my waist with both my ass and vagina on display.

"Don't worry. I will be. Nothing will get in the way of food and me." Finnian rubbed his stomach.

"Okay." Tavish stepped through the door and faced us. "And if she gets stuck in any sort of compromising position, let her figure a way out of it herself. I don't want to walk in on anything like before ever again."

"Oh, believe me." Finnian laughed. "I learned my lesson. I had to special order the blasted chessboard to replace the one *you broke*. That's why I brought her clothing, so there's no chance of her dress moving to expose something you'd find inappropriate."

Now, the two of them were talking as if I wasn't in the room. I fisted my hands, allowing my nails to dig into my palms. "Excuse me, but if Finnian and I want to be in any sort of position, that is none of your concern." Not that I wanted to sleep with Finnian, but it was the damn principle of it! I made my own choices, not some arrogant Unseelie king who wanted darkness to cover the world.

Tavish blurred, flying toward me. He landed right in front of me, placed his hand around my neck, and pushed me against the wall. Darkness circled us, blocking us from Finnian.

This was the moment he'd kill me ... but he didn't choke me. Instead, he moved his hand and my chin up, forcing me to look into his eyes.

"You won't be with Finnian or anyone else," he growled. "I couldn't handle it, sprite. We have enough stacked against us—don't make things harder than they need to be." His face softened, and he released his hold, his hand running down my arm. "Please."

All my anger vanished because, for a moment, he looked broken. Instead of an arrogant king, a man stood before me, close to baring his heart. I wanted to prod and get him to open up to me, but we'd both regret it later. The last thing I needed was him acting cold and distant because I'd pushed. "I'm not, but don't talk about me as if I'm not in the same room."

"You should go to breakfast. You're taking way too long. Eldrin is probably on his way as we speak." Finnian cleared his throat, making his presence known. "Besides, what happened was innocent, and I understand what's going on, so I won't do anything to make either of you feel uncomfortable again."

Tavish took a step back, and the darkness that surrounded us eased. He took a deep breath. "I know. Just be careful with her. All right?" He looked at Finnian.

"Of course I will." Finnian bowed his head.

Tavish nodded and met my eyes before leaving Finnian and me behind.

The moment the door shut, a void filled my chest, and I wanted to go after him. The nicer he acted toward me, the harder it was to remember all the bad things he'd done.

None of that was my priority. I would be heading into the gauntlet, and I wasn't sure how to survive a battle with one flying fae, let alone a full-on war.

"All right, Lira. Go change." Finnian gestured to the clothes on the bed.

Not wanting to argue and curious about what he had up his sleeve, I quickly took the clothes into the bathroom and changed into a tunic and leather pants.

When I came back out to join him, he removed one of his swords and tossed it onto the bed. "Show me what you know."

My head tilted back, and I took in a shaky breath. This had to be a trick. "You expect me to fall for that? Are you trying to make Tavish look kinglier somehow?" I wasn't sure how getting caught with a sword would help. In fact, every scenario I considered would make him look weaker if I got my hands on his best friend's sword. But I understood where Finnian's loyalty lay. He'd been clear not even ten minutes ago.

"You're a smart woman." He crossed his arms. "You know that touching that sword would actually make people more upset with Tavish."

"Which means you must have a motive I haven't considered since you wouldn't want that to happen. In fact, you left no question that you would turn your back on me for him."

Finnian closed his eyes. When he opened them back up, he clasped his hands in front of him. "You dying in the gauntlet would impact Tavish a whole lot worse than someone catching you with a sword in your hand."

"Why? Because he needs my death to be by his hand?" He believed he needed to be the one to kill me. My chest ached at the memory, but I pushed the strange sensation aside. I didn't have time to dwell on something that wouldn't change. Either way, my days were limited.

"No, that's not why." Finnian shook his head. "I wish it were, but we must have done something to upset Fate. The only way you'll actually die is in the gauntlet. Tavish's wings are bound on that. Your connection with him won't allow him to actually kill you."

And here I thought Finnian was a smart flirt. Oh, how he was proving me wrong. "I hate to break it to you, but Tavish *will* kill me. Fae can't lie, and he's told everyone his plan."

"He wasn't lying when he said it, but the more time you spend together, the more I see what's brimming between you. Fate won't allow him to kill you, especially with his own hands." Finnian pointed at the sword. "But enough of this. We need to focus on preparing you as much as possible for the gauntlet."

I blinked and wrung my hands together. I needed to make sure this wasn't a trick. "You're going to spar with me?"

"Yes, but let's try not to actually wound one another." He gestured at his outfit. "I couldn't come in here in armor without getting questioned, and I couldn't bring you armor for the same reason. So we'll need to fight like this. You seem comfortable with a dagger, so that's a start. We just need to practice with a long sword so you can adjust before the battle."

With nothing to lose, I reached over and lifted the sword. It was over two times larger than my dagger and twice the weight, but other than that, it didn't feel foreign in my hand.

"If it hurts your chest, let me know." He removed his sword. "We'll take it easy at first."

I jerked my head down, having forgotten that my chest had been hurt last night. I moved the material of my shirt to see that the wound was just a scab. "How is that possible?" The water had made it much better, but this wasn't even a deep scab anymore.

"Fae heal fast, but I have to admit I'm surprised you forgot about it." He rolled his shoulders, preparing for our fight. "At least it won't hinder our training."

We moved into the center of the room, and he held his sword to the side. He gestured to me and said, "You attack first. Remember, the sword is longer, so account for the distance."

I swung the sword around to get used to the way it felt in my hand. The blade sliced the air, making a swishing noise, and my jabs were off balance as I compensated for the extra weight and dynamics. After a few more adjustments, I managed to balance it a little better.

I lifted the sword in front of me and swung at Finnian. Our blades clashed, and the impact vibrated painfully in my hand and arm. I gritted my teeth, trying not to make a noise, but I hadn't been prepared for that.

"Again." Finnian readied his sword.

For the next while, we sparred. I wasn't swinging hard but rather using the time to learn where to strike his sword and how to move more gracefully. My muscles burned from the exertion, especially since, for the last several days, I hadn't done much of anything but sit around.

My body was slick with sweat, and Finnian made suggestions and corrections. Soon, I was swinging harder, and we danced around one another more in tune, though I was not extremely skilled with the sword.

"Now, let me attack." Finnian straightened. "You need to know how to handle that the best you can."

I wanted to keep practicing my attack, but he was right. Our time was limited. I wouldn't perfect anything. I nodded, holding the sword in front of me.

Quicker than I expected, Finnian swung his sword down toward my right. I reacted, adjusting for the attack, but my sword didn't move as quickly as I was used to. I couldn't move it before he turned his blade at the last second to avoid stabbing my right arm.

Dammit, I would've been injured, and my dominant hand would've been taken out. I'd just gotten comfortable, and now he'd shown me how little I'd learned. I wasn't foolish—I knew I'd be more on the defense than the offense in battle. I hadn't seen the other prisoners, but they were likely hardened and knew how to use their magic and wings.

I had to learn and fast. "Again." I prepared for another attack.

A knock pounded on the door, and we froze, staring at one another.

Eldrin's voice called out, "I'm coming in."

Finnian rushed toward me, taking the sword from my

hand just as the door opened. Eldrin stepped inside the room.

"What's going on here?" Eldrin scowled, glancing at Finnian and me.

My heart thundered. Eldrin stared at me with such hatred.

"I figured Lira might want to know what a sword looks like before tomorrow." Finnian raised both. "Now she does. You know how she doesn't remember the fae and likes to play with toys."

Eldrin arched a brow, but instead of responding, he stalked over to me. He gripped my arm tightly and dragged me across the room toward the door.

"What are you doing?" Finnian called out, his voice strained.

Cold tendrils of fear tightened around my heart. I didn't want to go anywhere alone with him.

"Something you won't want to miss out on." Eldrin smirked as maliciousness danced in his eyes.

Worse than not knowing where he was taking me was Eldrin's cold hand clutching me, his fingers digging into my wrist. His skin was frigid, reflecting the essence of his soul.

My heartbeat quickened, and my stomach tightened, urging me to get the fuck away from him.

I dug my heels into the ground, though the smooth soles had me slipping along after him. He opened the door, and I noticed four additional guards standing in front of Torcall and Finola.

When the two guards turned toward us, they grabbed the hilts of their swords, readying to protect me.

Some of the tension ebbed from my body as I realized that they intended to obey Tavish about no one taking me anywhere.

"Where do you think you're going with her?" Finnian asked loudly.

"I don't answer to you." Eldrin's nose wrinkled.

Finola moved to block us from leaving the room.

For the last several days, I'd wanted to get the hell out of that room, and now, I'd do anything to remain in it. The irony clamped down on my shoulders.

"You may not have to answer to him, but you have to answer to us." Finola lifted her chin and glared. "She's under *our* protection."

Eldrin stopped, dragging me beside him in the doorway so that my body was crammed between him and the frame. My side ached, and when I attempted to take a step back, he yanked me against him even harder.

My skin crawled, but I clenched my teeth, not wanting to make him feel more powerful. He already had an inflated ego.

"This has been done at the request of King Tavish." His jaw worked, and I could feel a faint shake in his hand. "So, move aside before these four guards make you."

Torcall removed his sword. "King Tavish said that if the sunscorched is needed anywhere, he will personally tell us."

"And King Tavish informed me that Caelan and I are to handle the gauntlet, did he not?" Eldrin's fingers dug in deeper, though it didn't seem intentional.

In fact, I was certain he held a lot of rage, more than I'd realized.

"But that's not until tomorrow." Finola pursed her lips.

"That's what King Tavish said last night, but this morning, Caelan and I decided that to ease the tension among our people, the games should begin today."

I flinched, and Eldrin's smirk blossomed into a malicious smile.

Right now, that was the least of my concerns. Finnian and I had only begun defensive strategies, and I needed more time. Time Eldrin was determined not to give me.

"Caelan is notifying the people now that they're finished with their daily chores." Eldrin rolled back his shoulders. "And the prisoners are being prepped as we speak, which should include the *Seelie* princess."

The four guards he'd brought with him wrinkled their noses at the reminder of my supposed heritage.

Torcall and Finola glanced at each other while Finnian closed the distance between us, coming to stand at my back. The three of them remained silent, though I could see the strain on the guards' faces. They weren't sure what to do because Eldrin wasn't lying.

Another sound captured my attention—beating wings rushing toward us.

A *yank* in my chest grew stronger the closer the person came, and I had no doubt who it was.

Tavish.

"What is the meaning of this?" Tavish's voice boomed seconds before he appeared from a cloak of darkness. "The games start tomorrow." Lines of strain were etched into his face, and his hands clenched at his sides when he took in the way Eldrin was holding on to me.

Eldrin *tsk*ed and shook his head. "You know the people have been upset since last night. A few disagreements broke out between the fishermen today. It would have turned into a dire situation if we hadn't added more guards to keep an eye on our people. We need the games to start today so the people can see you're serious about punishments. This is to prevent more chaos, so why do you want to wait until tomorrow?"

The question hung heavy like a blanket. The insinuation was clear because everyone had seen that I'd gotten injured last night. Eldrin knew that Tavish would either be forced to admit he was giving me time to heal or allow him to take me.

Tavish's jaw ticced, the only indication that Eldrin had hit the mark.

I knew he'd relent. If he didn't, his people would learn that he'd held off the gauntlet despite two of his closest subjects wanting it to begin tonight. According to him, both his and my safety would be at risk if that happened.

"As long as you're confident that the trial will be challenging enough for our people, I won't stand in your way." Tavish folded his wings behind his back. "So I'll ask you—are you certain our people won't be disappointed?"

Eldrin chuckled darkly. "Oh, My King. I guarantee that everyone will be satisfied and entertained. I've been planning one of these for years in case something like this ever happened."

Somehow, I swallowed past the sizable lump in my throat. He sounded ecstatic.

Dark, stormy eyes met mine, and I swore I saw in them the regret that Tavish felt.

"Fine." Tavish crossed his arms. "Torcall and Finola, allow them to pass. But Eldrin, let me make it clear; if you and Caelan fail to make the games entertaining enough for the masses, you will be to blame."

"I shall bear the full burden if that's the case." He bowed ever so slightly then walked between Torcall and Finola, making sure his shoulders hit them while he dragged me along.

"Of course, you'd drag her to the games," Finnian scoffed.

Eldrin halted, and I ran into his wings. Even though his physique was nothing like Tavish's, his wings were strong, and the edges dug into my chest, right where I'd gotten injured the night before. The wound burned as if the scab had reopened slightly.

"Are you upset with how I'm treating the *Seelie* princess?" Eldrin turned and stepped to the side.

For once, I appreciated my height because he had to step around me to see Finnian and not have my face in his.

"I'm just noting that you're acting strong and overbearing with her when you've never acted remotely the same to other prisoners. You're grandstanding, like you're trying to make her believe you have larger testicles than you actually have." Finnian rocked back on his feet and shrugged.

"The other prisoners are Unseelie, and though they rose against Tavish, they deserve to be here," Eldrin rasped, twisting my arm so that a deep ache shot through it—like it could very well break. "Aside from the king's and queen's deaths and the Seelie forcing us from our lands onto this barren island, she is the reason that several of our people have died. It concerns me that both you and Tavish are struggling with her being mistreated."

"The situation is unique." Tavish lifted his hands, his wings folded tightly into his back. "You cannot compare her to the other prisoners." Even his words were short and harsh like he was furious.

"You have her staying in your room." Eldrin arched a brow in challenge.

I hated that I'd frozen and wasn't saying a word. I wouldn't go out like a coward, especially not around Eldrin. "He made it clear that my job was to keep him happy while I remained in there," I spat, regurgitating the words he'd said on my first night there. I'd been worried about what he'd meant, but he'd never pushed himself on me.

A guard snickered. "Did she follow through?"

Tavish blinked at me, surprised I'd spoken up to help him, but he recovered quickly, leveling a gaze on the silver-haired guard. "You have no idea." He smirked and winked at me. "She stayed for a reason."

"And here we thought he was getting soft on her." The pewter-haired guard chuckled. "That makes a whole lot more sense."

My stomach roiled at the innuendo and that these guards didn't have an issue with a man potentially forcing himself on a woman. I understood they viewed me as the enemy, but no one ... *no one* ... should ever be treated like that. No wonder Tavish had moved me to his room.

Tavish scowled. He didn't seem to like the jovial tone either.

"Since this is settled, we should hurry. The other prisoners will be ready, and the people are entering the coliseum." Eldrin tightened his grasp then turned and flew toward the cells.

My feet tangled underneath me, but I caught myself and remained upright to follow him. He hovered off the ground just enough to pull my arm slightly from my shoulder, and I had to run to keep up with him. Was he purposely trying to injure me and tire me out before the games began?

Mouth drying, I realized I didn't know much about what would happen. I understood it was prisoner against prisoner, but beyond that, I had no idea how the gauntlet worked. Between the drama of last night and training with Finnian, I hadn't thought to ask. Now, it was too late.

My side ached, but I couldn't slow down as Eldrin flew faster. My chest heaved, and my legs struggled to keep up. How the hell was I supposed to survive against Unseelie prisoners who had access to their magic and wings?

We passed the holding cell I'd stayed in the one night and headed deeper into the prison. The stench of feces and piss filled my nose, and I wanted to gag. Between the exertion, stench, and pain in my side, vomit inched up my throat.

I swallowed it down and ignored the way it lumped in my stomach. I would be enough of a target without throwing up in front of everyone.

The cells came into view. Each had a mattress that looked in better condition than the one I'd had in the holding cell, but that was the only thing that seemed nicer. Rodents ran across the floor, and some sort of odd, furry creature stuck its head from under one of the covers.

Ten feet ahead waited a group of people. Several wore standard guard armor while the rest wore tattered tunics and leather pants, their wings chained so they couldn't fly.

"Everyone is here!" Eldrin called out, slowing down and shoving me in front of him.

My chest heaved, and sweat dripped down from my brow as everyone focused on me. As if they wouldn't have figured out who I was on their own, but Eldrin offered me to them like they were dogs and I was their bone.

A familiar growl sounded from the front, and a few of the prisoners moved out of the way as dark fur headed my way.

Nightbane.

A woman with hair the color of dusk tilted her head at me. Her face, like the others here, was streaked with dirt, and her frame was very thin. "Ah, at least a Seelie has to live in our disgusting world for a time. Seems right, especially before she dies."

"If anyone gets to kill her, it's *me*," a man with pale-blue hair who was close to Finnian's size boomed. "She's the reason we all wound up here ... why we thought we had no choice but to rebel against King Tavish. We need to rough her up first and get her dirty. She shouldn't die resembling a princess. Let's return her looking like one of us."

The rest of the people cheered in agreement.

If I'd thought the guards held animosity toward me, it was nothing compared to the people I would be fighting against.

I lifted my chin high, refusing to cower. Maybe that was a mistake, but I suspected whichever way I reacted wouldn't change my fate. I had to survive against hardened prisoners who'd lived rough while I stood here in clean leathers and a shirt, courtesy of the king.

"Is everyone ready?" Eldrin asked.

The guard closest to the door on the left opened it a crack and shut it. "Yes. The stadium is full, and King Tavish and Finnian just took their seats in the front row with Caelan."

Eldrin chuckled. "Perfect." Eldrin flew overhead to the front. When he reached the door, he hovered and turned toward us. "The rules are simple. Because we don't want the spectacle to end quickly, we are keeping your wings and magic bound by your chains. You are not allowed to strike another prisoner until you have claimed a weapon." He stared at everyone in the group as if to make sure we all understood. "Enter the arena only enough so that you all fit inside. No one should move beyond the entry point until we blow the horn. You'll have one hour to survive."

An hour.

That wasn't as bad as I'd expected, but the length of time didn't matter. Every single one of them would work together to kill me.

Eldrin landed and opened the door. "Let them enter." As he walked out, the guards used the hilts of their swords and their wings to move the prisoners along. From what I could tell, I'd be up against fifty competitors.

Fifty people who wanted me dead more than anything else in their world.

The odds weren't stacked in my favor.

The group in front of me thinned, and strong arms shoved me forward. I fell, landing on my hands and knees as my body jerked from the impact. Pain exploded through me, and before I could stand back up, someone kicked me in the side.

Nightbane snarled and raced toward me.

"Get up, Seelie trash." A guard with dark, silver hair chuckled. "Though I do like you at this angle."

Not wanting him to get any additional ideas, I rolled to the side, ignoring the liquid on the stones. I feared I knew what it was.

As I pushed the awful thought aside, Nightbane rushed past me and leaped.

The guard yelped. "Get off me, mutt."

I quickly got to my feet, smelling worse than ever before. I needed Nightbane to calm down. I didn't want him harmed again because of me.

Nightbane lunged, taking the guard down on his back.

I rushed over and touched the wolf's back, whispering, "I'm okay." A faint, warm pulse came from inside me and filtered right through my hand toward the dog.

Nightbane whined, but he followed my hand as I moved him away from the guard.

"Get the cù-sìth off me!" the guard exclaimed.

Another guard moved to retrieve him, but Nightbane snarled and bared his teeth again.

I needed to step away before he got in more trouble.

"Listen to them. I'll be fine," I assured him then hurried out the door.

A loud, thunderous *boo* echoed like a storm rolling in, and I looked up. When they'd mentioned the Unseelie would be watching the gauntlet, I'd imagined a handful of people showing up. Nothing had prepared me for the massive space hidden behind the castle. Rows upon rows of spectators were there, from young children to adults.

It was an actual gladiator-style arena, the prisoners and me standing in the dirt at the bottom. The jagged mountaintop jutted behind us above the stands. Everywhere I looked, there were more and more people. Worse, Tavish was in the front row, sitting right in front of me.

Our eyes locked, and my chest squeezed uncomfortably. Darkness edged around him, and his expression twisted into what could either be anger or remorse. He faintly mouthed the words, "Stay alive," telling me everything.

Tears burned my eyes, and I took a shaky breath and tore my gaze away to look at the arena before I could fall apart.

Darkness cloaked everything except the small area where the prisoners stood. We couldn't strategize before the game began. No doubt, another thing Eldrin had planned.

Eldrin flew upward, his expression brighter than I'd ever seen it. "After twelve years, we're having our second gauntlet due to the *Seelie* princess attempting to escape and attacking our people, including our *king*." He spun slowly, ensuring each person got to see his face. "For this heinous crime, the gauntlet is the only acceptable restitution, per our king and the Unseelie people. That said, we've decided on an actual prize."

"Prize?" the man with pale-blue hair asked. "In the last

gauntlet, you had to kill a certain number of people to live. Is it not the same this time?"

A knot formed in my chest. Whatever this was, it couldn't be good.

"No." Eldrin's shadows curled around him. "In this gauntlet, whoever entertains us the most wins. The number of kills doesn't matter so much as who you kill and how each kill is performed. The more shocking, the more drawn out, the more gruesome, and the prisoner will have their sentence reduced, meaning some of you could be free by the end of the three games ... if you survive."

My heart skipped a beat. They wanted the deaths to be vicious, and I could feel each prisoner's gaze land on me.

My gaze went straight to Tavish, whose face had blanched.

The crowd went wild and began chanting, "Kill the sunscorched," over and over.

In other words, the person who killed me and survived would win.

Eldrin had added an even bigger target on my back as if I didn't have a neon sign as it was.

"For those who don't know, the prisoners' wings are chained so they can't fly, and the chain suppresses their magic. This first stage of the gauntlet is about punishing them and making them survive like mere *mortals*. Now, it's time. Set the clock for an hour," Eldrin called and turned with a sneer on his face. Then he lifted his hand, and a horn blew a mere few feet away.

Just like that, the darkness faded, revealing hell.

I hadn't realized how massive the space was until the full obstacle course came into sight. Though the area was still dark, the moon rose high in the first clear sky I'd seen in ages, illuminating the entire coliseum.

The ground was rock and dirt and shaped in a perfect oval.

I swallowed, taking in a massive fifty-foot-tall tower on our right. I wasn't sure how the darkness had obscured it, yet despite its height, it wasn't even half the size of the stadium.

Directly across from us sat an enormous axe gauntlet trial with double-sided axes swinging in different patterns. There was no way I would have tempted fate and tried to navigate that obstacle for any sort of protection, but then the moonlight glinted off the blade of a sword that was tied with other weapons right smack in the middle of the course. Weapons for protection. Something I needed.

I edged back to hide in the darkness as the people in front of me gave me dirty looks then took off, no doubt desperate to get a weapon to protect themselves and come back to kill me. I wasn't a threat to them.

I was thankful for that, but the reprieve wouldn't last long. They'd be eager to spill my blood, so I needed to get my bearings. I suspected there was more to this place than what I could see.

"Over here," the dark-blond man shouted, running left. "Let's get these. They're easy pickings."

I looked over just in time to see a cluster of weapons tied together on the ground.

The blond man and five other men ran toward the weapons while the rest rushed off toward the axe gauntlet. For the moment, I wasn't their main target, which gave me time to survey my surroundings for a chance to survive.

I scanned the rest of the area. A massive white rock took up thirty feet of space across from the tower. Numerous weapons had been laid strategically in the center on the top.

A *boom* pierced my ears, and a male prisoner screamed in agony. He dropped, and another explosion went off, but I couldn't make out what was happening. Ten people were between me and the person.

In a chain reaction, a platform sprang up on my left, hurtling the blond man and one other across the arena. Their bodies *smacked* against the tower, barely missing one of the eight people climbing to the top, and the sound of cracking bones reached me. Black blood sprayed from their bodies and dripped down the gray stone.

With the crowd in front of me now cleared, I could see across the entire arena. Four people in various spots in the center of the floor were sinking into the ground.

My throat clenched as I realized that the area around them was faintly darker than the dirt, and the way they sank faster as they fought told me everything I needed to know —quicksand.

The body of a man only ten feet away appeared to be missing a leg and half his side. He must have been in the explosion. Another *boom* sounded from the area between the axe gauntlet and the massive rock. A female with white hair that had frosted tips widened her eyes and stared down. Half of her foot was missing. She wobbled, trying not to fall, and searched the ground around her.

Then I noticed blackened rocks similar to what was under the man in front of me.

My chest heaved. This was worse than I'd expected. Not only did we have to fight each other, but there were booby traps all around us.

I could use that to my advantage if I thought quickly.

From the platform on my lower left, level to the ground, came groans from a man who'd jumped on the massive rock. Sharp edges stuck through his hands, and blood puddled from them and even out of his shoes.

A sour taste filled my mouth, and I tried not to let hysteria claim me.

Whimpers from the four fae trapped in the quicksand snapped my attention back to them. Blood pooled around them like the sand was ripping them apart. My heart quickened. It had to be porous quicksand, which was worse than the soupy kind. This kind would indeed rip them apart and push all the oxygen from their lungs, killing them before their heads went under.

Eldrin beamed from his spot beside Tavish. He was enjoying watching his own people die.

Tavish, Finnian, and Caelan all wore sober expressions like this was the last thing they wanted. The contrast between the four was striking and spoke volumes.

Tavish wasn't as coldhearted as I'd believed. He had baggage, but he hadn't gone down that evil of a road.

Knowing I couldn't help the trapped prisoners, I turned my attention to the axe gauntlet. There had to be more to it.

Another group of men was working together to figure out how to get the weapons from the platform, and I couldn't keep standing here. I needed to get a weapon or find a hiding place for the next hour.

People had reached the top of the tower and were climbing over the edge, which meant that it wasn't a place I could hide. My ears rang, and my blood turned cold when the truth settled over me. There was no place to go. I'd have to fight and hope like hell I survived.

My attention focused on the hidden platform. The weapons had been jostled during the launch, meaning the rope might have loosened. I just needed one of the men to loosen it further for me to grab one.

Two men squatted by a third man's legs and grabbed his ankles. Once their grip was secured, the third man inched across the platform, reaching for the weapons. The crawling man yanked on the rope, loosening one side just as the platform sprang.

The two guys tried to yank the third back, but they weren't quick enough. The man jolted upright, and the two of them rose a few feet off the ground. They released their hold on their friend, and he flew off the platform as the two of them crashed to the ground.

With the awkward momentum, Crawling Guy didn't smash into the tower but instead landed in the middle of the quicksand trap, which was still tugging down two who hadn't died yet. He landed facedown in the sand and died almost instantly.

The weapons he'd loosened landed a few feet from me

—one short sword, one dagger, two quivers of arrows, and a slingshot. The rest of the items scattered into the quicksand, including all three bows.

I took off running, needing to get there before the others. I had my eye on the short sword and the dagger, but ten others were rushing in the same direction.

I pumped my arms faster, but the others moved quicker. They reached the stash of weapons seconds before me and began fighting over the sword and dagger while I swooped in at the edge, grabbed a quiver of arrows, then snagged the sling. I pivoted to get out before anyone noticed me, but a gigantic, calloused hand caught my arm.

I got spun around to face a man with hair the color of coal. He sneered, "Not so fast, *sunscorched*. You don't get any of these." He reached for the arrows protectively tucked like a football against me, leaving himself open for me to kick him in the gut.

His breath *whooshed* out of him, and he stumbled back, taken off guard. Then, his feet began sinking.

I froze, realizing what I'd done.

I'd kicked him into the quicksand. I'd moved to help him when another man turned to look at us.

"Aron!" the sinking guy called out. "Help me."

"I'll help you all right." Aron chuckled, strode up, and sliced the man's throat with the dagger. "This death is better than one by that quicksand."

"Allies," the man gargled as he clasped his hands around his throat like that would stop him from bleeding out. Black blood trickled between his fingers and ran down his arms as death overtook him.

My body became heavy as I realized I'd caused the man to die. But if I continued to stand there, I'd die alongside him.

The nape of my neck buzzed like I could feel the prisoners' gazes around me. I didn't bother to glance at them, not wanting to acknowledge them or allow them to see my fear. Instead, I ducked, spun, and raced toward the side of the arena to keep my distance.

"The princess is *mine!*" Aron bellowed. "Her death will be at my hand."

I watched the ground in front of me for dark rocks and traps, listening to the pounding of the man's boots as he chased me. The other two men were still focused on the weapons on the platform, so I shifted direction and ran toward the outline now that it had sprung from the ground, and I edged around the men.

Aron was only a few steps behind, so I ran right like I was going to land on the platform. Just as my foot hit the edge of the line where I could see it would spring forward, I spun left. Aron ran onto the platform. I'd hoped that with his speed, he'd get off it before it launched since the others had needed to pull the rope first, but with my sudden disappearance, he stumbled over his feet. His right boot got stuck in the rope, and when he yanked to break free, the trap sprang.

The rope sent his body jolting up instead of toward the tower, but when the rope finally snapped, he soared forty feet into the center of the stadium in front of the spectators. He tried to flap his wings, but the chains still bound them, and he plunged to the ground. He clung to his dagger as the other weapons landed in front of the two men who'd been trying to reach them.

My heart lunged into my throat as Aron's body thudded to the ground, and the dagger sliced into his side. He didn't move, but his chest rose and fell.

This cache of weapons had three of each weapon—

swords, daggers, slingshots, bows and arrows, and short swords.

I moved toward the gigantic rock, hoping I could hide near it for a few minutes as I formed a plan. I'd seen a slingshot like this before, though I couldn't remember where and hoped I could figure out how to use it.

When I focused on my destination, a rancid, salty taste filled my mouth. A man was using two other bodies to climb the rock toward the weapons. He used one body to lean on while pulling the other body up to move toward the center of the rock. Blood coated the rock over the entire track he'd taken while two men and one woman below cheered at his progress.

I'd never seen anything so revolting in my life. He had no respect for the bodies of the people who had died. But I was guilty of helping to kill two people today, so I wasn't much better.

The walls closed in on me as the horror of what I'd done sank in, but I had to push it away. Falling apart would only get me killed sooner.

I moved around the rock, cold wafting from it into my skin. I paused and touched it lightly then realized what it was—ice with edges made into frozen spikes. I had no doubt someone had used their magic to create this.

More things exploded, and a person to my left screamed in torment.

I snapped my head around to see that a man had been sliced in two while walking on the wooden plank through the swinging axe blades. A sword had shot up from underneath him, stabbing him between the legs, and then an axe had sliced into him. The axe kept moving, slowing down only marginally as it chopped through the body. Blood and guts hit the wood and dripped onto the ground below, where someone was neck-deep in quicksand.

That had to be why the other person had tried to make it across the plank. It was either that or die trying to take a shortcut.

Everywhere I turned, I saw death, blood, torture, and chaos. The sounds were deafening. If we'd all just stayed in the entry area and refused to fight one another, things would've been different. There wouldn't be all this destruction and death, but that had been the point of the incentive for a reduced sentence and the directive to gain a weapon before attacking. Eldrin wanted us to fight each other and wanted this devastation.

The remaining prisoners had separated into small groups, leaving me to fend for myself.

I needed to do something to gain an advantage, so I scanned the area and noticed that the eight people who had climbed up the tower were watching the chaos from above.

For me to make it up there, they had to come down from their safe haven and fight for weapons.

I edged between the axe gauntlet and the frozen rock, noticing a couple of small pieces of black rock that had exploded just moments ago. I bent, gently picked a few up, and placed them in my slingshot.

Let's see if my plan works.

I swung my arm, spinning the sling over my head. At first, the motion felt strange, but then something natural kicked in. I homed in on the blue-haired man who'd spoken out in the hallway and flipped my wrist forward.

The rock soared from the sling to the tower, hitting it below the railing of the top platform. The rock exploded, and the tower shook, stone crumbling from the blast.

The eight men jerked their attention to me and realized I'd attacked them.

"It's the sunscorched!" the blue-haired man shouted as if no one else was aware.

Okay, I hadn't quite thought this through.

Two men climbed onto the platform with the swinging axes as I bent down and picked up two more exploding rocks to fling at them.

"Bran, we need to get down!" a dusky-haired woman said loudly. "She's going to knock the tower down."

The blue-haired man turned to her and scowled. "She can't possibly hit it again."

Wanting them to see I meant business, I slipped another rock into the slingshot. I aimed for Bran again. This time, I hit the tower platform right at his feet, causing the side closest to me to tremble.

"We got it!" someone exclaimed.

I turned toward the axes. The taller man was holding the feet of a dark-green-haired man and lowering him from the upper platform to grab a similar bundle of weapons as those on the spring platform. Once the dark-green-haired man had the weapons in his hands, he tossed them five feet away to a woman with the same color of hair as him. She caught the weapons and removed a bow and arrow then turned to shoot at three men barreling toward her. She fired in rapid succession, and the men thumped lifelessly to the ground.

Once the dark-green-haired man was back up on the platform, he patted the other man's back and laughed before giving the guy a huge shove. The bigger man tried offsetting the push but couldn't, and he fell into the quicksand below.

The woman with matching hair laughed so hard she hunched over.

These people were worse than I'd expected.

I had to get away from them now that they had weapons, so I turned to go back to the other side of the arena near the spring platform, but the man using the two bodies as his shields had gotten his own weapons.

My heart thundered so loudly that I couldn't hear the cries. Now that all the weapons had been claimed, they were all focused on me.

There was only one thing I could do, get to the platform and figure out a way to remain on it as it sprang up. Maybe I could use my slingshot to hold on to the edge or tie it to whatever it was that secured the rope that had bound the weapons.

I ran toward the rising platform, keeping close to the edge of the coliseum. As I rounded the spot where the spiked ice and platform were, a *hiss* came from beside me.

My feet dug into the dirt, and gray gas rose from a vent in the ground.

What the hell was *this*?

The gas funneled quickly, swirling around me, and my body did something that terrified me.

E ach breath burned my lungs, and my legs quivered like Jell-O. The same tightening sensation I had during my nightmares dominated my body.

I needed to get out of here. If the gas was causing this reaction, it would get worse the longer I stayed in it.

Gritting my teeth, I forced my legs to move, and I could've sworn I was treading in water with the air resisting like waves and holding me back. But this wasn't comforting like water. *This* was me struggling to control my own body.

When my right foot touched the ground and I put weight on it, I crumpled. I landed with a thud, dropping the quiver of arrows as pieces of rock and dirt flew into my eyes.

I sucked in a breath, trying to get my bearings, and my lungs caught fire. The pain intensified so that even shallow breaths hurt. Images of dark shadows crept into my mind.

My body tensed, and my heart rate skyrocketed. I searched for signs of Eldrin hiding in the shadows. I didn't doubt he'd use the gas to blend in and attack me, even in front of an audience. With the ruthlessness of the Unseelie fae, I suspected the others would urge him on.

The gas thickened, and I couldn't see my hands in front of me. My lungs stopped expanding, and everything inside felt as if it were on fire. This was worse than any nightmare I'd ever had. If Eldrin wanted to attack me, I'd never see him coming.

Remaining here wasn't an option. I could die if I didn't find a way out of the gas.

Not wanting to leave empty-handed, I clutched the slingshot and felt around for the quiver of arrows. My hand touched only rock and dirt until something pricked my finger.

The tip of an arrow.

My finger stung, but I followed the neck to the smooth quiver. Securing the shoulder strap, I slowly pulled it around my shoulder. I had to go.

My head pounded, and nausea added itself to my ever-growing list of problems. I was running out of time.

With darkness engulfing me, I closed my eyes. There was no point in keeping them open. Each time I blinked, they throbbed worse.

I concentrated on moving my hands and feet forward. The gas was coming from behind me and blowing toward the platform. I needed to head back past the icy rock and the axe gauntlet ... the very things I'd been trying to avoid.

Despite moving at a crawl, I felt like I'd run a fucking marathon. All I wanted was to wake up from this horrible nightmare and find myself back home.

The urge to lie down and never move again surged through me. Maybe that was the point of the gas—to see if we'd give up and die. But I'd never been a quitter, and I sure as hell wouldn't start now with all these people eager for me to do just that.

My irritated eyes watered, tears dripping down my face.

Any other time, I'd hate looking weak, but the tears would clear my eyes so if I did get out of the gas fog, I'd see the threats coming.

The fire ebbed slightly with each breath. I opened my eyes and saw the outlines of my hands.

My chest expanded with hope. The gas had thinned.

Keeping a steady pace so I didn't tire out, I moved inch by inch, focusing on small tasks while my chest heaved. It hurt to breathe, but it also hurt when I held my breath. The pain was the same, so I chose the lesser evil and kept breathing, hoping like hell I would find a way out of this mess.

After what felt like hours, the gas thinned further, and I could make out the frozen rock on my right. I raised my head to look forward and saw the blue-haired man and the dusky-haired woman standing several feet ahead of me, with five others, facing the axe gauntlet.

Behind the group, the dark-green-haired man raised a sword in one hand and a dagger in the other, readying for an attack, while the woman I suspected was his sister stood with her arrow nocked on her bow.

Two of the seven-member group were facing my direction, keeping an eye on the gas.

I'd be free of it soon if I kept moving, but I wasn't sure that would be better. I'd be facing nine fae, any of whom could attack me, but at least I'd go out fighting and not die because I'd given up or was too scared to face the real threat.

I crawled toward the frozen rock, hoping they wouldn't expect someone to willingly get close to the spikes protruding from it.

As the pain in my lungs lessened, I heard screams and the sounds of fighting. Blades clashed. More people had gotten weapons and weren't afraid to use them on each other.

Exhaustion crept into my bones. Confident I couldn't handle a physical fight, I had to come up with another plan.

When the edges of the spikes brushed my arm, I realized I'd made it to the ice rock. I paused, trying to take slow breaths. Though my lungs still burned, at least they weren't on fire.

Carefully, I gripped the tip of one spike and removed an arrow from the quiver. Using the sharp edge, I hit the spike, breaking it off in my hand. I continued to hammer more free, hoping to use them as weapons if needed. The ice froze my hand, but I ignored that pain and broke off ten more pieces. My wrist and hand cramped from the strain, but I focused on one spike at a time. I needed ammunition for the sling.

My lungs burned worse, causing me to blink and focus back on the world around me.

Shit. I gritted my teeth in frustration. I'd stayed too long in one spot, and the gas had thickened around me again. The handful of ice spikes would have to do; besides, I didn't want to keep them in my hand too long because they'd start melting. Not only that, but the arrow tip had been destroyed.

I tossed the dull arrow on the ground and moved slowly again. I crawled another ten feet before the gas thinned. Only one man was watching the gas; the rest had vanished. I kept the thicker part of the gas to my back, following the fuzzy line of where it receded so that no one would risk coming up behind me.

The last thing I wanted to do was come out of the gas crawling, so I stood up slowly. My muscles screamed, and my body ached, but I straightened my shoulders. If anyone saw that I was weak, they would be inclined to hit me hard and fast.

The man glanced at me, and his eyes locked with mine.

"The sunscorched—" he started. I placed one ice spike in the sling, but my hands moved slowly, and I dropped the rest as he finished, "—is still alive!"

He charged toward me, so I bent down to snatch up the ice spikes and stuffed them into my pants pockets. I didn't have enough time to get the sling working before he reached me.

Fortunately, he didn't have a weapon, which must have been why he'd alerted the others to my presence, and he ran full speed at me. I tried to pivot out of the way, but my legs moved too slowly, and he grabbed me and turned me so my back was pressed to his chest. His hands wrapped around my neck.

"The rumor is you enjoy inflicting pain on a man's tender region, and I won't make the mistake of giving you access," he whispered into my ear and squeezed my neck tighter.

The prick was choking me. My heart quickened, and I let all my self-defense training kick in. I shifted my hips to the left and elbowed him in the side. Pain shot down my arm into my hand as if I'd hit a wall, telling me how strong this prick was.

He grunted, his hold on my neck loosening, so I grabbed his arms and jerked forward. He sailed over my shoulder and landed hard on his back, deeper into the gas.

Before I could recover, someone slammed into my back.

I landed face forward with a thud as the man straddled me from behind. He forced my arms to my sides, and I used the opportunity to swing my head back. I hit something solid and heard a sickening crack. Warm liquid dripped onto me, and I tried not to think about what it was. I flipped over, knocking him off, and kicked him in the side, thrusting him farther away.

He whimpered and rolled to his feet then ran back to the spot where he'd been. "I need help killing her!" he cried nasally, turning toward me again. "Someone with a weapon!"

This time, I pulled an ice spike from my pocket and fit it into the sling. I swung the sling over my head. My wrist ached while my legs began to quiver again from the effects of the gas and physical exhaustion. I couldn't stand much longer.

Out of the corner of my eye, the gas resembled fog as it hovered over my shoulders. I snapped the sling forward, aiming for the guy's neck because the last two times, the stones had landed slightly lower than what I'd aimed for.

The guy jerked his head back, and the ice hit its actual target. It lodged into his neck, and blood squirted out. His eyes widened, his hand reaching for his throat.

My stomach dropped. I'd gone from not ever killing to being a murderer in the blink of an eye. My vision tunneled, but the sound of a scream kept me in the present. I watched the dusky-haired woman drop to her knees beside the man who'd fallen while I'd been freaking out.

I swallowed. It was time to face the consequences and hope like hell I figured out a way to survive. Though I had no clue how much longer we had to stay in this nightmare.

As I jogged away from the gas, I noted the sight before me. The dark-green-haired man and woman fought with their backs to one another. She readied to fire an arrow but held off, possibly because she had only two more in her quiver.

We were all running low.

Of the fifty who'd entered the arena, there were about fifteen survivors, and the gas filled everywhere but this corner, like they'd driven us here to fight one another.

"You!" the dusky-haired woman spat, her eyes shining like gunmetal. "Your kind always brings death to us." She barreled toward me, and I swung my sling, aiming for her shoulder, not wanting to risk killing yet another person. I'd caused enough death for one day, and unlike them, I didn't relish it.

Luckily, I hit my mark exactly as intended.

Her right shoulder jerked back, and she stumbled a few steps. "Someone help me kill the wildling!"

The pale-blue-haired man sneered, turning away from the green-haired duo and stalking toward me. "I get to kill her. No one else."

As he closed the distance between us and raised a sword, I put another sharp piece of ice into my sling and swung it. This time, my wrist moved much slower, and my legs wobbled.

Between the gas, emotional trauma, and the entire fucking nightmare, I was losing what little strength I'd gained. I released it, and the ice hit his right leg. He stumbled onto a dark-colored rock—the kind that exploded.

A *boom* echoed in my ears, and part of his boot and calf blew off. He blanched and hissed, but he hopped on one foot, still moving toward me. Blood gushed from his leg, and my chest heaved. This couldn't be happening again. My goal in life had been to become an environmentalist, but that dream seemed so far away now that I had blood on my hands. All I wanted to do was go back to when things were simple.

"It's receding!" the dark-green-haired woman shouted. "We can surround her. She can't make it to the next round."

I glanced over my shoulder to confirm what she'd said. Holy shit. This was the end for me. There was no other way around it.

I backed up to the edge of the gas so the others couldn't get behind me yet. All thirteen of them converged on me with one clear goal.

Kill the sunscorched bitch.

Well, they'd probably call me a bitch if they knew what the term meant.

My heart hammered, and I looked at Tavish. If this was going to be the end, I wanted to see the handsome jackass one last time.

He remained seated, but he was leaning forward with his elbows on his knees. I could see how tense his muscles were from here. His jaw was clenched, and he mouthed the word *won* for some reason.

Of course, the jackass was gloating that he had won. Why had I wanted to look at him? Still, something inside me didn't want to look away. My eyes took in every inch of his face, his full lips, his everything.

"Ahh, it seems she's taking a liking to the Unseelie king after all." The pale-blue-haired man cackled, but his malice fell flat under the strain of his injuries. Sweat dripped down his face, and more blood gushed from his leg.

The gas drew back farther, allowing the edge of the frozen rock to appear behind me, opening my entire right side to an attack. I noted every sword, dagger, and short sword they had.

The pale-blue-haired man charged, limping on his right foot as he lunged toward me, sword held overhead. His hands shook, and then he swung it at me.

I spun left, and the blade whooshed past me, coming closer than I ever wanted to know. I straightened, waiting for the next attack, and noticed black rocks slightly to my right. I didn't want to kill someone, but I also didn't want to die. I'd use those as a weapon only if forced.

"You're about to die, Lorne, so I'm going to kill her instead." The green-haired woman drew an arrow in her bow, the tip aimed at my chest. "I'm ending this."

I swallowed, watching as her hand twitched.

Then the horn blew, but she didn't stop. She loosed the arrow, and it hurtled toward me.

My heart pounded in my ears as I clutched the edge of my seat. Every muscle in my body wanted to charge toward the stadium and get Lira out of this mess. However, with nine fae staring her down and several more that would soon follow, I couldn't determine a way for her to make it out alive.

This was my doing. I needed her to die ... but something inside me couldn't stand for it to happen and kept demanding I help her.

The gas was receding, which would allow them to surround her. She needed to hold on for mere seconds longer, which I mouthed to her, though she looked at me with disgust.

The sentiment was fair. I was acting the fool, but I couldn't remain logical when it came to her.

Finnian leaned over to me and whispered, "Time is up. Why isn't the guard blowing the horn?"

I glanced at the moon, noting its place in the sky. Time *was* up.

My gaze turned to the guard with the horn, but instead

of it being in his mouth as it should have been, he was grinning maliciously.

Then I realized why, and my world halted.

The nine of them had ganged up on Lira. I jumped to my feet, wings ready to fly and save her, but Finnian grasped my arm.

"Get him to blow the horn," Finnian rasped. "Don't swoop down there and grab her. That will only make things harder on her in the long run."

Right. I could encourage the guard to blow the horn.

I allowed the nightmare magic to funnel from me, the thrill of the fear making my blood buzz in a way that used to scare me. I pushed the magic toward the guard, and his eyes widened. His asinine smirk fell. I made sure the illusion I created catered to his worst fears and told him to blow the damn horn. Fortunately, dreams occurred faster than reality.

The guard put the horn to his lips just as Rona strung her arrow and took aim at Lira.

No.

The horn blew, but Rona didn't falter. She was going to kill Lira despite the time being up.

I flew upward while pushing the cool darkness toward her. The darkness came on quickly, and her twin brother, Bran, shoved her in the side before they disappeared from sight.

The arrow shot from the darkness across the opening and lodged into Lorne's messed-up leg. Rona must have released it as her brother tackled her, causing it to miss Lira and hit Lorne.

Lorne groaned and crumpled to the ground, and I flapped my wings forward, finally able to move now that Lira was no longer in trouble. I knew I had to make the rules clear so it didn't seem like I was intervening only for Lira. Thankfully, everyone knew I was a stickler for rules. I had to be to make my people respect me.

"No!" Lira shouted from below, running to Lorne and dropping beside him. She touched right above his injury as she yanked the arrow out of his leg.

My heart hammered. What was she doing? Was she going to kill him?

Yanking back the darkness from the twins, I pushed it toward Lira. If she was breaking the rules, she'd have to experience the same thing as the others.

"Everyone, stop," I commanded, my voice echoing around the arena. "The horn has sounded, and this round of the game is over. If anyone disobeys that signal, there is only one punishment available ..." I paused for dramatic effect. "*Death*!"

I tugged the darkness back inside me, allowing all twelve remaining contestants to see once more. I was shocked to see Lira still touching Lorne, the bloody arrow at her side and both hands on his leg. The man watched her but didn't say a word.

What in the blasted snow was she doing?

I flew down and landed beside her then yanked her away from the man. She stumbled backward but tried to go to him again. Her hands were covered in blood.

"She's hurting him," the guard who hadn't blown the horn cried. "She must die."

Lira shook her head. "I'm not. He's hurt, and I'm trying to stop the bleeding. He took an arrow that was meant for me. I need to help him."

I grabbed her by the waist, yanking her against my chest. The jolt that I felt every time we touched warmed that dark place inside me and made me feel like the boy I used to be ... the one I couldn't be anymore, not after what the Seelie took from me and my people. "Sprite, you need to stop."

"Someone needs to help him," she said, trying to lunge from my arms.

I tightened my grip to contain her, and my people stood in silence. A Seelie was trying to save an Unseelie—something none of us had imagined we'd see—but here Lira was, doing just that after all these contestants had wanted to kill her.

How could she be so stupid? The people would use that weakness to exploit her.

None of this would've happened if the guard had blown the horn as required. My glare landed on the guard, and his Adam's apple bobbed.

He knew he'd made a grave mistake, and he'd pay for it.

The wildling would die. Tonight. Fortunately, I could hide the real reason for doing it.

He'd put Lira in harm's way and, worse, knowingly. He couldn't come back from that, not with me.

"Get someone to help Lorne and make sure that Rona sleeps in solitude tonight." I had to get Lira out of here before she made things worse for herself. There was only so much I could do to save her.

I should've never taken her from Earth.

I stiffened, the errant thought catching me off guard. Of course I should have. I had to save my people, or more would die. There hadn't been a choice!

Ten guards flew down, ready to take the contestants back. One of them came to me, waiting for me to release Lira. My arms tightened around her like there was no chance I'd let her go.

Her body shook, so I leaned in and whispered, "Don't

cry. You're safe for now." I forced myself to release her so she could follow the rest of the prisoners inside. "Don't harm any prisoners. They need time to rest and heal before the next game ... everyone but Rona, for not abiding by the rules of the game."

Rona tensed, but the guards shoved and pushed the prisoners out.

Lira's body shook as she gave the arena one final glance.

Death was everywhere, and some who had drowned in the gritty quicksand could be seen, their skin shredded and bloody. Even I had a hard time stomaching this amount of death, but this was the price of not abiding by the rules. Everyone here was guilty of treason. Well, everyone but Lira. She'd just abandoned me when her parents turned against the Unseelie.

As the prisoners were hurried off, I didn't hesitate. I looked at the guard with the horn, who moved back a few feet at my gaze. His cowardliness caused my blood to boil, making it warmer than I was comfortable feeling. I removed my sword, and a few spectators gasped.

I needed to make a point to each and every one of them.

I twisted my hand, allowing frost to trickle from it, and froze the guard's wings. His face turned purple as he strained to move them. Eventually, he dropped the twenty-ish feet to the arena floor, surrounded by five prisoners killed by the exploding lava rocks retrieved from the nearest volcano. He toppled onto his back, unable to stand.

When he didn't explode, I let out a relieved sigh. He needed to die by my hands for his crime against Lira. That hadn't been his decision to make, and everyone needed to know they weren't above the laws of their king.

I held out my sword and flew toward him.

"My king, the sunscorched was about to die." The

guard's lips trembled as he turned his head toward me. "We all deserve to see her blood spill for everything her people have done to us. I never dreamed—"

"What are the two things I hold sacred under my reign?" This wasn't a trick question. When I took over at the tender age of fourteen, needing to learn how to put grown men in their place to secure my crown, I had made two important rules to ensure we never became like *them*—the Seelie.

The guard swallowed. "We obey the king's command or suffer death, and we don't harm innocents."

"Two simple rules." With my left hand, I lifted two fingers. "If someone does you wrong, you're allowed to be as vicious as you want as long as it doesn't go against something I specifically commanded. I established the rules of the gauntlet, and you ignored them because you decided you'd rather see something that wasn't yours to allow."

I stood over him and lifted my sword so he and all the other Unseelie could see. When I was young and had to discipline or execute someone, I'd been composed, but afterward, I would hurry to my room to fall apart. Then, I'd hardened my heart and learned to soak in the fear of people who knew their time would come to an end at my hand. Now, under Lira's influence, I merely wanted to kill him so this lesson could end. He'd sealed his own fate.

"My King, I'm—" he started.

I stabbed him in the heart. My blade cut through his skin as easily as when I doused it in the sea to clean it.

His eyes widened, and I held his gaze, wanting my eyes to be the last thing he saw as he faded into the dark—the dark that even I couldn't access because his magic would leave and return to the land we couldn't access because of the Seelie.

With how silent the arena had become, a person could assume everyone had left.

But not me.

This was what happened when I made my point. When my people forgot I could be vicious, I had to remind them.

Once he stopped breathing, I placed my foot on the man's stomach, yanked out my sword, and sheathed it back in place. I wanted my people to see that blood didn't affect me, though I hated how it dripped onto my pants legs. That was a problem for later.

Standing upright, I took a moment to turn in a slow circle, taking in the entire arena. I wanted my people to feel that I was looking at them even though there wasn't any possible way for me to see everyone. "If anyone forgets these rules again, I won't be as kind as dealing a quick death. I hope everyone hears and remembers this."

Caelan and Finnian stood beside each other and nodded while Eldrin scowled. He wasn't pleased that I'd interfered and would have rather I'd shown leniency and allowed Lira to die. But we couldn't be like the Seelie and change our beliefs because it suddenly worked in our favor. The fact that we didn't change and stood firmly by our moral code would be the very thing that would cause the Seelie to lose against us because we were going to take back our land and theirs.

Without another word, I flew out of the arena, heading toward my bedroom. Even though the guards would learn what had happened, I didn't trust any of them with Lira. Too many wanted her dead, and I suspected they'd risk their own death to achieve it.

When I flew out the top, I realized I'd allowed the sky to darken to the point where the moon was no longer visible. The darkness coursed out of me and into the sky, reflecting my turmoil. My people could gauge my state of mind and say it'd been darker since Lira's arrival, a gross under-statement.

Two sets of wings flapped faster than the rest, informing me that Finnian and Caelan were catching up to me. They flanked me, and Caelan sighed. "Was that necessary?"

I jerked my head in his direction and arched a brow. "Yes. How dare you ask me that?"

"I fear the rules weren't the problem and more that a particular woman was almost harmed." Caelan inhaled deeply. "But please, don't answer that. I'd rather not know. You do need to realize she won't make it through the entire trial, and if she does, you'll be forced to kill her."

I wanted to flinch but gritted my teeth, fighting the reac-tion. I worried whether I'd be able to manage that, but I forced the thought away. I didn't have a choice, so my concerns didn't matter.

"At least she kept it entertaining." Finnian laughed loudly to lighten the mood. "She used that sling like she'd done it at least a few times."

My chest tightened uncomfortably. "She loved playing with the sling her father got her when she was a little girl. She enjoyed helping animals by knocking down their food from trees." I'd always liked to watch her because she'd always been kind to everything ... much like she had been kind to a man who wanted her dead.

"Shall we head to dinner and celebrate the end of the first trial?" Caelan asked.

I didn't want to. The one thing I desired was the worst thing I could do right at this moment—check on Lira. However, I knew that if I didn't eat with Eldrin, Finnian, and Caelan, especially after killing a guard, they'd wonder why and ask questions I didn't want them to entertain. "Of course. I'm starving."

As the three of us flew toward the dining hall, I tried to think about anything other than the woman who was becoming far more of a complication than I'd ever expected.

———

Dinner lasted forever, and it didn't help that Finnian demanded a second plate of food in the spirit of celebration and proceeded to take it to his room, leaving me with Caelan and Eldrin.

Fortunately, Eldrin didn't voice his discontent with my actions, and we all had a civil conversation about when the next game would happen. It would be in two days to give all the prisoners a chance to recover for a more entertaining match.

Half of me was sickened over that because Lira would be up against others who were back to almost full strength and, therefore, stronger than her. I suspected that was the point.

Finally, I excused myself because Caelan and Eldrin wanted to begin plotting the next game. It had to be more entertaining than the last.

However, I had a plan of my own. I would get clean and check on Lira.

I eagerly flew toward my room and found my personal guards already standing outside.

"What are you doing here?" They should've been keeping an eye on Lira in the holding cell. My voice lowered. "You're—"

"She's inside," Finola interjected and lifted a hand. "We

didn't realize you hadn't authorized her to come here. We can—"

My breath caught, and I shoved between the two, opening my door. "Under whose authority?" Who would dare make a decision of that magnitude for me?

"Mine." Finnian sat at the table, his second plate of food across from him. "I thought you'd be happy that I retrieved her. It helps that the guards don't notice me as much as they do you. So you're welcome."

Of course it'd be the wildling, but I couldn't find the anger or annoyance that should've been within my grasp. Instead, I relaxed more than I had since the gauntlet had started. He was right—I would've retrieved her myself. I didn't trust anyone else to watch her because no one cared like I did... or, unfortunately, like Finnian. "I didn't say thank you." I had to be clear so that he didn't believe that I owed him a favor.

I scanned the room, not seeing Lira anywhere, though I could smell her unique, alluring scent in the air. "Where is she?"

"In the bath." He gestured to the closed door. "She needed it. I'd planned on her eating first, but when I saw the state she was in ..." He trailed off. "She couldn't handle it."

"What do you mean?" I tensed again, ready to destroy whatever was bothering Lira. "What happened?"

"She's upset that she hurt people." Finnian shook his head. "She needed to relax."

For the first time since my childhood, I felt helpless. Violence was how I solved things, but if she was upset with herself, I wasn't sure what to do with that. "She's a water Seelie, so the bath should help her." She'd be able to connect with her element and hopefully regain a sense of calm even if she didn't understand why.

"I'm hoping so. She's been in there for a while." Finnian frowned. "I wanted to check on her, but I didn't want to—"

I snarled at the thought of him walking in on her naked.

"—upset you." He snickered. "Apparently, that was a good call."

I ignored him, stalking to the doorway, and heard a sound that shattered everything inside me.

She was crying.

"You need to go." I pointed to the door and glared at him.

Unlike usual, he stood and marched to the door, his forehead lined with worry. "Go take care of our girl."

I gritted my teeth at the word *our* but he left just as another sob came from the other side of the door.

I knocked on it gently and heard Lira suck in a breath like she was scared.

Something was wrong, so I didn't ask for permission. I opened the door, and my world fell apart.

I sat against the wall in the corner of the bathroom under two lamps that created the brightest area around me. There was nothing I wanted more than a bath to wash off the dirt, blood, and grime from the games, but I couldn't bring myself to undress and climb in.

What if Eldrin came again?

After the gauntlet, guards had taken me to a regular cell that smelled like feces with the green-haired woman who'd tried to kill me. If I'd thought she hated me before, it was nothing compared to now. She blamed me for her harming Lorne.

I suspected the only reason she hadn't attacked me was due to Finola and Torcall standing outside the cell, but that hadn't stopped her from promising to unleash all sorts of hell during the next part of the gauntlet.

Then Finnian had come for me. Instead of his usual easy grin and flirty demeanor, he'd stood cold and rigid and demanded he be allowed to take me someplace for his own form of torture.

The guards hadn't given him a hard time, and as soon as we'd turned a corner, Finnian's easygoing demeanor had slid back into place. He'd brought me to Tavish's room to bathe and eat.

All the chaos weighed on me: I'd killed a man, many people had died because I'd tried to escape, and there was the savageness of the Unseelie. Hysteria choked me, and every hair on my body stood upright, ready for yet another attack.

I might have had an easier time remaining with the green-haired girl, who I'd learned was named Rona. I deserved to be threatened and punished. Every time I closed my eyes, I saw blood spilling from the man I'd killed.

Now, in this bathroom, I swore something brushed my skin as if Eldrin were here to stab me again. I hadn't been this frightened ever ... not even when Tavish's eyes had haunted me in my nightmares. I'd surmised that the fear I'd felt hadn't come from Tavish but from the future that awaited me.

This hell.

A sob escaped, and I covered my mouth to hide the sound from Finnian. I didn't want anyone to find me like this, but when my hand stuck to my mouth from the drying blood, another whimper escaped. The taste of black licorice landed on my tongue.

The door opened, and I gagged, realizing what tasted that way—Unseelie blood.

"Lira." Tavish's voice broke as he hurried into the bathroom. He glanced at the full steaming tub, then at me, dressed in the bloody clothes from the gauntlet and pressed against the wall like a child. "What's wrong?"

I half laughed, and half choked, especially hearing my actual name roll off his tongue. "Is that a serious question?"

I hated that seeing him lifted a weight off me. Some part of me believed that he would do anything to keep me safe, which made me want to stomp and scream. He'd been very clear since the beginning that he planned to kill me. What sort of person was I to develop this false sense of security around him? I'd never considered myself stupid, but now I was questioning everything.

He flinched. "If I'd known—"

Anger warmed my blood, and I welcomed it. I needed something to fight off the cold that had sunk into my bones, especially since I couldn't get myself into the tub. "What? You would've killed me immediately instead of allowing your minions the chance to do it?"

"Blighted abyss!" He clenched his hands. "Do you not realize everything I've jeopardized by bringing you to Ardanos?"

I stood, allowing my anger to flow through me without regard. If I was going to die, I'd go out with dignity. "*I* didn't come here, remember? *You* kidnapped me, so don't you dare try to turn this around like I'm inconveniencing *you*. You've taken *everything* from me. My family, my future, and eventually my life." I needed to push him to kill me now. Not that I wanted to give up my future, but something inside me was changing. I didn't understand how I knew, but I'd felt a spark when I'd touched Lorne—something foreign and strong. Something I didn't understand had shifted within me. So I wanted to die as *me* before I became something the Unseelie made me.

"And I regret that I did it." He ran his hands through his hair, messing it up and making it fall into his stormy gray eyes.

My breath caught. I hadn't expected him to ever say

anything like that, but his expression had twisted into one of such conflict that my lungs struggled to work.

I remembered something my mom had said more times than I could remember. "Regrets won't make a difference. Only the decisions we act upon reveal the truth of a person's character."

"That sounds like a Seelie saying." He grimaced. "Always so pompous and righteous, especially when they feel they have the wind beneath their wings."

Here, it came back to the crux of our issue—Seelie versus Unseelie. So much anger and hate drove him, and the worst part was that I understood that and even felt sympathy toward him. Losing his parents so young had molded him into something I suspected he had never meant to become, and anger and fear ruled his decisions and emotions.

My anger vanished, and I leaned against the wall so I didn't topple over. "Why come in here just to argue?" Tears burned my eyes. I needed him to leave me alone.

His wings folded behind him, and he hung his head. "My intention was to check on you. I heard you were upset, so I feared something was wrong. I ... I don't want anything to happen to you."

I hated how my chest warmed at his concern. "I'm ..." I tried to say *fine*, but my mouth wouldn't allow me to form the word. Tears welled in my eyes, clouding my vision.

"Lira—" he said softly, again using my actual name. "Why aren't you in the tub? It will make you feel better."

I hated how it sounded better than any folk song I'd ever heard and how he knew that water calmed me. "Please, don't be nice to me." I already struggled to remember not to feel anything nice toward him, but his unguardedness risked shattering everything. "I need you to be mean and distant."

He nibbled on his bottom lip. "I've been struggling with remaining that way toward you, and there's no blasted way I could be that way toward you now. Why aren't you bathing? You need to get the dirt and blood off so you can eat and get some rest. The next trial isn't long from now."

The image of the man I'd killed flashed in my head as if he lay right in front of me. I closed my eyes and gritted my teeth, trying not to fall apart again.

Hands touched my face. My eyes popped open and connected with his. The buzz immediately started on my skin, and some of the horrors retreated. No matter what my mind screamed, I felt safe with him. I couldn't get myself to move away from him.

"Who did this to you, sprite?" he asked in a low rumble. His eyes focused on my chest where Eldrin had cut me not too long ago, and he winced like it pained him.

Even though my shirt hid the cut, a chill of warning shot through me as if he could see my scar. I swallowed, knowing that if I didn't force my lips closed, I could tell him what happened. But I *couldn't* take that risk. Eldrin had threatened to hurt my family if Tavish ever learned what happened.

"Your silence is louder than any words," he gritted out. "Were you in the tub when it happened?" He glanced over his shoulder as if the person responsible would materialize.

I had to say something. It was as if he could read me. Silence hadn't been the right answer. With words, I could at least deflect. He seemed to like to argue. "It doesn't matter. You've already determined my fate."

"Sprite, there are only a handful of people it can be if you were in here." His nostrils flared. "My wings are bound if it's one person in particular, but nonetheless, I still need to know."

"Why?" The question left my lips before I could stop it. With it already dangling, there was no point in not continuing. "It shouldn't matter to you."

"You're right, it shouldn't." He pressed his lips to my forehead and whispered, "But someone dared to hurt you. For the sake of my kingdom, I cannot show you any favor, yet something in me still responds to your scent and your voice. It reminds me of a future I used to envision. One long dead."

Butterflies fluttered in my stomach more intensely than ever before, and I desperately *wanted* to tell him who'd hurt me, though I didn't understand why. "I need you to promise me that you won't say or do anything to him because he's threatened my family. I don't care what happens here, but I need them to stay safe, and I don't want to cause more problems between you and your people." This was foolish, but this way, I could have some control over my life before it ended.

"I can't make that promise," he rasped, tilting my head up so our gazes remained locked.

"Then I won't tell you." I refused to give in. He had so much control over me, and I couldn't hand my family's safety over to him without his promise.

His jaw clenched as he examined my face. Then, his expression slipped into a mask of indifference. "Fine. I promise if that's what is required for you to confide in me."

"You promise? You won't act differently toward him?" With my understanding that a fae couldn't lie, I had to be precise with my words to bind him to our agreement.

"Yes, I promise. I won't change how I react to him or treat him differently while I count the days until I can provide justice for what he's done." He exhaled. "If it's who I suspect, I need to know." His irises darkened, reminding me of the night sky. Before I could say a word, he asked, "Was it Eldrin?" He flinched, prepared to hear the answer.

My stomach dropped. I hadn't expected him to suspect his own family. I opened my mouth to say no, forgetting it wouldn't work. He seemed to be bracing for betrayal, and I didn't want to do that to him. But then I couldn't make a sound, no matter how hard I tried, so I only had one choice, to tell him the truth. I nodded. "He hid in the shadows, and I didn't see him until he attacked me." My voice broke.

His chest heaved and his nostrils flared. He released me, stepping back as his face turned faintly purple. Then he pulled his hair at the roots like he was crazed. "He had to try to test me once again, and I can't do a blasted thing about it."

Heart hammering, I regretted telling him. The turmoil on his face had me wanting to close the distance between us, but the blood crusted all over me kept me in place. "Forget I said anything."

"I can't." Tavish's wings expanded behind him, their size massive and commanding. "The wildling doesn't deserve his affinity to darkness. He's not worthy of that power, not after what he's done to us." Darkness ebbed around his body, blending pieces of him into the surroundings. "But my hands are tied."

"What do you mean?" Despite not being around Eldrin and Tavish together often, even I could tell that Eldrin disagreed with most of Tavish's decisions. He scowled or frowned, and I couldn't remember him once ever offering praise.

He looked at me. "He saved my life, and I owe him." His head and wings hung like the weight of the world was bearing on him. "I owe him, and he reminds me of that often. If I didn't, he'd already be dead. Now he's taking advantage of the situation ... and my wings are clipped."

I stared at Tavish. Was he regretting the way he'd treated me? I wanted to ask him more but now wasn't the time. I was barely hanging on to my sanity.

"What can I do to give you a piece of your safety back?" Tavish placed a hand on his chest and leaned toward me. "Other than ensure you're never left alone like that again? Someone I trust will always be on the other side of the door when you bathe so you can call for assistance if you don't feel safe."

I blinked, unsure how to respond. Maybe I'd be safe here, yet I'd soon be heading into the second part of the gauntlet. I suspected I wouldn't make it out alive, though I had no intention of not fighting. "Nightbane."

"Nightbane?" He froze and raised his brows. "The cù-sìth?"

"He's tried to protect me several times, and I don't want another person in here while I bathe." Not only did I trust Nightbane, but I feared what trouble he might be in for protecting me.

"I'll make it happen." He headed out into the bedroom, and I heard the bedchamber door open. Tavish growled, "Bring Nightbane to me. I heard what happened earlier and need him brought here."

"Yes, Your Highness," Finola replied, and the door shut again.

With Tavish nearby and knowing that Nightbane was on his way, my entire body felt lighter. My pulse leveled out when Tavish carried in a dark-gray gown. He placed the dress in the closet, allowing it to hang down. "It appears you forgot something in the room where Finnian remained," he said tersely.

I mashed my lips, trying not to smile. I had no doubt he was thinking about when he'd walked in on Finnian attempting to help me get dressed when the skirt got stuck to me. "I was going to ask Finnian to hand it to me. I didn't want to touch it." I raised my hands, emphasizing the blood on them.

"You could wash them off." He leaned back and scowled.

Point taken. "True, but between Eldrin and today's events, my mind was elsewhere."

I hurried to the sink and turned on the water then scrubbed my hands. I'd rather not bathe in blood-soaked water.

I looked in the mirror, taking in my blonde hair, which seemed brighter and fuller despite not getting any sunlight. My emerald eyes seemed brighter too, and my complexion had turned a shade darker ... or was the dirt on my face providing that illusion? I'd go with that, especially with the honey-toned blood that had dried on my face.

Another reminder to them that I was Seelie and proof I couldn't claim to be human. Not anymore.

Someone knocked on the door before it opened. A familiar snarl sounded as Nightbane entered the room.

"He's here, Your Highness," Finola called out. "And angrier than usual."

"Don't worry," Tavish answered. "I'll handle him from here."

The door shut, and Nightbane sniffed. Before I realized what was happening, the enormous animal came rushing into the bathroom. His glowing lime eyes faded to a normal color as he ran to me.

I smiled and bent down, petting the animal. A warm *zing* shot from inside me, through my hand, and into Nightbane.

"I'll be right out here," Tavish said, and he shut the bathroom door behind himself.

After scratching Nightbane's ears, I stood and removed my clothing. As soon as I peeled the layers from my body, I eagerly stepped into the water, ready to wash off the day.

And if I spent part of the bath wondering about a certain aggravating fae king who became more contradictory and ornery the more time I spent here, well, that was my secret to keep.

I SPUN *the sling then jerked my wrist forward. The ice spike swirled around and hit my attacker in the neck. Blood squirted, and his eyes widened as he reached up to stop the bleeding.*

"Lira," a way-too-soothing voice called from far away.

I needed to save the guy I hadn't meant to kill. The ice spike was supposed to hit lower, in a spot that wouldn't kill him, just harm him. I wasn't sure what I needed to do, but this time, I couldn't allow him to die.

"Wake up," the same voice said, and I recognized who it belonged to.

Tavish.

Why was he interrupting me when I was trying to save one of his people? I pushed away and said, "I'm sorry. Let me help you. I didn't mean to."

The ground shook as if to keep me away, so I pressed harder. I just needed to close the distance between us to reach him, but every time I moved a step, the man I needed to save moved farther away.

A deep growl caught my attention, followed by a weight being flung off me. My eyes popped open, and I yelled, "Stop!"

I blinked, but each time my eyes opened, the scene remained unchanged.

Nightbane had lunged over me and pinned Tavish down beside me on the bed. The wolf snarled, drool dripping from his teeth and his mouth wide, aiming for Tavish's neck.

I'd normally fear for Tavish's life, but his jaw was clenched from anger, not fear.

"Get off me," he gritted, something dark brewing in his eyes, turning them onyx. "Or you will regret attacking me."

I remembered how Nightbane had cowered in fear when Tavish had punished him for protecting me during my feeble-ass escape attempt. I couldn't let either of them get hurt, and if I didn't intervene, one of them definitely would, and I feared it would be Nightbane.

"Hey, it's okay," I said, attempting to sound soothing. I sat up and petted the back of Nightbane's head. Tavish must have been trying to wake me from my hellish nightmare. "He wasn't hurting me. I had a bad dream, and he was helping me."

Nightbane stopped snarling, but he continued to stare Tavish down, his eyes glowing with clear mistrust.

I turned over, scooting my knees underneath me so I could lean more on the animal. His fruity smell comforted something deep within me. "I'm okay. I promise."

Turning his sizable head toward me, Nightbane scanned me for signs of injury. He huffed and moved off Tavish then sat right next to me.

I scratched behind his ear as Tavish opened his mouth and closed it, speechless.

That was a first. He should be silent like this way more often.

Between Tavish looking like a fish out of water and Nightbane's comforting presence, some of the horrors that had been plaguing me slowly faded away.

"What's going on between the two of you?" Tavish clicked his tongue. "He doesn't like being touched. The relationship between you doesn't make sense."

"Maybe if you didn't scare him, he wouldn't be that way with you." I cuddled into Nightbane's side, his body like a heater, warming me more than the blankets.

Tavish huffed, but instead of continuing the conversation, he touched my arm and asked gently, "Were you having a nightmare?"

His tenderness caught me off guard. These small moments when he showed me kindness didn't usually last long. After my bath, he'd sat at the table with me as I ate and then created the pile of pillows between us, offering me his bed again. Even though we hadn't talked much, I could feel the way he watched me, and it felt different ... more vulnerable, like now.

Even if I *wanted* to lie ... I couldn't. "No. It wasn't a

nightmare." A sob got stuck in the back of my throat, making me sound like I was gagging.

Lovely. That was worse than crying.

Nightbane narrowed his eyes at Tavish.

"If that beast doesn't learn respect again soon, I'll be forced to teach him again." Tavish frowned back at the cù-sìth.

I buried my side in Nightbane, the animal relaxing at my proximity.

"If you tried for respect, that might work better." That was the one thing I didn't understand about him. Why did he want to rule by fear?

"What do you mean?" His brows pulled together. "I demand respect all the time. The best way to ensure people don't act out is by having severe and absolute consequences."

"Like giving an animal nightmares or worse?" I already knew the answer, but I wanted to lead him down a path, so he realized it himself.

"Of course." He nodded curtly.

I rolled my eyes and patted Nightbane's head before settling back on my pillow. "That's ruling by fear. Your people don't respect you. They just don't want you to kill them."

He shrugged. "Either way, they obey and listen. I don't care how or why."

"But you'd have more loyalty from them if you tried to understand them and helped to find actual solutions that prevent the need to constantly scare and control them."

He scoffed and leaned back. "I'm trying to find a solution to our problem, but the current answer has backfired. That particular solution is lying next to me in bed, making me reconsider everything."

The corners of my mouth tipped upward, and I tried to hide my smirk as I settled into the pillow, getting comfortable, though I was wide awake. I didn't want to close my eyes and risk reliving the death and destruction from the gauntlet all over again. Whatever relationship was developing between Tavish and me was comforting, and at least I didn't have to fear him killing me anymore. After today, there was no doubt that everyone would team up against me in the second gauntlet. They hadn't been worried about me before, but by killing one of their own, I'd moved myself up on their priority list. "Don't worry. I suspect others will handle your problem in the next game." I tried to sound light, but my voice came out raspy. I didn't want to die, but there wasn't any way to escape either.

"That's not funny, Lira." His features turned stony, back to the man I was most familiar with. "Finnian is coming to train with you tomorrow. That's one reason you need to get more rest. You need to get more comfortable wielding weapons."

I swallowed. I did need more training, there was no doubt, but going back to sleep was the more imminent problem. The memory of the man's death was still so fresh that if I closed my eyes for a moment too long, the image reappeared. I stared up at the glass ceiling. The darkness was pulled back more than ever, and I could actually see twinkling dots of pink and purple that reminded me of stars and the moon shining high. It might have been peaceful if I could have found calm within me.

"Is the next game troubling you?" he asked, and his hand brushed against mine, my skin buzzing from the touch.

Some of my tension ebbed, but not the horror of what I'd done. "I wish that were the problem." The future might hover over me like a threat, but the past was anchoring me down, and I felt like I was drowning. Then, the next words tumbled out before I could take them back. "I killed a man tonight. How can someone get over that?"

As soon as the words left my mouth, I regretted them. Not only had Tavish killed probably tens, if not hundreds of people, but he'd killed multiple people just because I was here. Though I didn't relish it, I also didn't carry guilt; I didn't want to be here. Tavish had forced me to come, and I hadn't done anything to deserve their violence against me.

He turned toward me, propping his head up on his arm so I could only see half his face over the pile of pillows. "Blighted abyss," he groaned, removing his hand from mine and tossing the pillows beside him so that nothing remained between us.

My eyes burned, but I giggled at the ridiculousness of the situation.

He inhaled, and his irises lightened, causing my heart to pound in my chest.

"Are you okay?" The intensity with which he stared at me made my voice barely a whisper.

"I forgot what that sounded like." He reached over and tucked a piece of my hair behind my ear. "As a young boy, I always loved the sound of your laughter."

Loved.

The word had my chest expanding, which was absurd. It wasn't as if he'd proclaimed his love for me ... just my laugh. Still, my face warmed. "Uh ... then—" I cut myself off before I finished the word. *Never thank or apologize to a fae.*

He dropped his hand between us. If I moved my arm just an inch, we'd be touching again.

"The first kill is always the worst." Darkness edged around him as if to hide part of himself from me. "But you need to realize he was going to kill *you*. This isn't Earth, sprite. In this realm, it's kill or be killed. There's no in-between. You protected yourself so you could live another day. And I need you to do it again, even after the gauntlet ... even if it's *me*."

The air buzzed between us, and understanding weighed heavily on me. He hadn't just given me permission—he'd encouraged me to fight him if he attempted to take my life. "Are you—"

"Stop." He shook his head sternly. "Don't ask questions. I said what I meant, and I need you to remember that. Finnian is the second-best swordsman among all the Unseelie, beyond me ... even better than Finola and Torcall. If you stop fighting the training and open yourself up, your memories may come back, along with your magic."

I nodded as Nightbane settled at my feet. The bottoms of my feet pressed into his side, and his body warmed them until I realized they'd actually been cold. Huh, maybe I was getting used to the cold temperatures around here. "I'm not sure how regaining my memories will help in battle, but I wouldn't be opposed to having my magic and wings."

"You are the Seelie princess." Instead of bitterness, a faint smile tugged at his mouth, making him appear more like a breathtaking man instead of a godlike statue. "You were trained to fight, including with slings, swords, and daggers, by the best in your lands, beginning at the tender age of five. That's when you were able to access your magic and fly."

That had to be why I felt comfortable using the sling. He was right; maybe I was overthinking everything and holding myself back. "Still, that means I'll be expected to kill more people, and I'm not sure I can. They have people who love them."

"You want to believe there is good in these people, but there isn't," he said, and his fingertips touched my arm.

That was the second time he'd touched me, not including the way he'd tucked my hair behind my ear, which created two gigantic problems. I enjoyed each brush more than the last, and I didn't want him to stop. I was setting myself up for heartbreak and ruin, but I couldn't find it in myself enough to care. Who knew how many more stolen moments like this we'd share?

"Every single prisoner, aside from you, has either blatantly disobeyed me or tried to rise up against me. They are traitors who don't worry about harming innocents or finding the best way to get our people back to our rightful lands." He interlaced our fingers. "Sprite, these aren't just people who insulted me. They wanted to kill for nothing more than their own personal gain and cared nothing about the repercussions for our people. The people in all of Ardanos—not just Cuil Dorcha—are ruthless and won't think twice about stabbing you in the back. We're immortal, sprite. We don't value life the same as humans do."

I froze, and my jaw dropped. "Immortal?" That couldn't be possible. How could we all live forever? "How?" Could that be why my supposed Seelie parents had been okay with me growing up on Earth? But they'd still missed part of my childhood.

"Our magic keeps us young and healthy. The only time we face death is at the hands of someone else and the occasional strange accident." He yawned and lay back on his pillow. "We can talk more tomorrow. Tonight, we need rest."

A lump formed in my throat. Sleep was the last thing I wanted. Even though I believed him, I still struggled with what I'd done. I'd seen the way the man had fought me and the desire to kill me in his eyes. Tavish was right, but I didn't want to become hardened and cold.

"Look, I'll make sure I keep the nightmares away." He winked. "I have an affinity for that. I can sleep and watch your dreams. If I notice anything that might deter your sleep, I can redirect your thoughts for you."

"What do you mean? Isn't your magic nightmares?" I still remembered his eyes from my dreams on Earth, always watching and waiting, so much hatred shining through, but the man before me wasn't the same one who'd haunted me.

"Nightmare illusions come most naturally to me, but I can also deflect the fearsome thoughts," he reassured and squeezed my hand comfortingly. "I just don't do that very often, but I would have to access your mind. Are you okay with that?"

The thought both thrilled and petrified me, but I trusted him ... no matter how foolish that made me. A good night's rest would help me to survive. And it wasn't like he hadn't accessed my thoughts almost nightly for the past twelve years. "Okay."

His shoulders relaxed as if he hadn't expected that answer. "I'll make sure nothing but good images remain."

I expected him to release my hand, but he didn't. Instead, we turned to face one another as Nightbane gently snored down below. With my hand in his, I quickly drifted off to sleep, feeling safer than I ever had before.

THE NEXT DAY flew by with Finnian training me as promised. I tried not to overthink, hoping like hell that my magic, wings, and memories would return to me. But no matter what I did or tried, Finnian kicked my ass.

We trained hard all day, and when Tavish returned to his bedroom, Finnian left, and we spent the night together, similar to the last. We were still holding hands in the morning, and I foolishly lay awake, watching him sleep. His face was relaxed, and stubble coated his chin. He didn't look like a man burdened with ruling or wondering who might screw him over next. He looked like he could very well be happy.

Someone knocked urgently on the door, and Tavish's eyes flew open. Luckily, his attention shot directly to the door, so he didn't catch me watching him sleep.

"Yes?" he shouted groggily, then cleared his throat.

"The prisoners are being called to prepare for the next game," Torcall answered from the other side of the door. "The people are being alerted that the games will begin this morning before they start their duties."

My lungs stopped working. I'd expected to start in the evening again. "What? Why?"

"To catch the competitors off guard." His jaw clenched as he flung off the covers and climbed out of the bed. "I'll find you something to wear quickly—I need to be with Eldrin when the people arrive. I'll go see what else we have of Moth—"

"No." I followed his lead, standing. "I don't want to wear something of your mother's. I want the same clothes as the other prisoners."

He spun around and tilted his head. "Their clothing is worn and doesn't offer protection. You should at least wear leather to protect you and keep you warm."

That was part of the problem. They saw the Seelie princess wearing their former Unseelie queen's clothes. "Please. Just trust me. Besides, it'll help me blend in better."

"Sprite, you could never blend in anywhere you go," he rasped. "That's—"

"When I'm covered in dirt and blood and surrounded by gas, I'd have to disagree. I want to wear what they do. Eldrin is counting on me standing out."

His head jerked back, but he nodded. "You're right. Fine." He then shouted for Torcall or Finola to grab me something from the prison.

Wings fluttered, telling me one of the two had left, obeying his command, and he headed over to me. He kissed my cheek, his lips lingering there as he said, "Stay safe. Fight. Kill. Do whatever it takes for you to come back here tonight. I've got to go, but I'll be there, watching."

My mouth went dry as I watched him spin and leave me alone. I realized I hadn't responded.

The door shut, leaving me feeling more alone than I'd felt in my life, my heart cold and empty.

Minutes later, Finola returned and handed me dark-gray clothing that smelled faintly of urine and feces. I regretted asking for these clothes, but it'd been the right decision.

I held my breath and dressed, and then Finola and Torcall led me to the prison cells.

I missed a step when I realized what the guards were doing.

They were chaining people in pairs so they'd either have to move in harmony or fight one another. Of course, Rona and her brother had been split up, and there was only one person remaining who wasn't chained to someone. His partner would be ...

Me.

When my eyes met the prisoner's, I realized no amount of training could have prepared me to survive *this*.

O ut of every possibility, of course it would be *him*, the man who might want me dead more than anyone else here.

Lorne.

"What's wrong, *Princess*?" The tall guard chuckled, taking in my expression. "Too good to be chained to a man with a bad leg?"

Understanding dropped on my shoulders as I took in his mangled calf. I didn't know what I'd expected, but it wasn't the large scar, like his entire calf might heal despite the damage it had suffered.

The guard laughed, hitting Lorne on the back, almost friendly, and said, "Yeah, we're surprised he survived as well. However, you two won't make it far, based on what Eldrin has in store."

"And Caelan, right?" I lifted a brow, my gaze settling on him. I wanted to make it a point that it wasn't only Eldrin behind the planning. Eldrin already had too much power and control, and Tavish's wings were bound, just like the prisoners' wings, on what he could do. I hated that he owed Eldrin such a large debt, but in the next hour, that wouldn't matter. With all eleven of them teaming up on me, I'd be dead.

The blue-haired guard who'd been there the night I arrived shook his head as the tall guard scowled.

"Just like a Seelie to believe they can correct us in our own house," he spat and tugged on Lorne to move him forward to chain me to him. "You're the reason why the king has killed two of our own, and you deserve the slowest, most torturous death we can provide." He glanced at the other ten, ignoring Lorne. "Anyone who delivers your death for me will be heavily rewarded since I can't do it myself."

"Oh, don't worry." The dusky-haired woman rubbed her hands together. "She's our priority once the game begins. After what she's done to all of us and killing my boy, it'll be an honor and privilege to slice her neck."

My lungs seized, but I forced my face to remain relaxed. I didn't want to encourage them by showing fear. I'd already come to grips with what my future held. Instead, I focused on the guard and Lorne.

With each step Lorne took on his injured leg, he limped and winced.

He wasn't well enough to be part of the game, but pointing it out would be useless. No one cared. This was a form of punishment and a means of entertainment. Besides, most of the contestants here appeared to be his friends or allies, so that would gain him even more favor.

His injury gave me a slight advantage since it would impact his ability to lug me around. Despite his strength, the extra weight on his leg would cause him problems. He'd want to help me get to the end of the trial before he tried to kill me. I could only hope that meant he'd protect me in the meantime, but hatred did funny things to people. I'd realized that with Tavish. Underneath his hostility, he was kind and gentle, but his parents' deaths and his banishment from his home had changed him into something else entirely.

The taller guard reached me, and when he squatted, he slammed his armored shoulder into my side.

I stumbled back, but slender arms slid underneath my armpits, holding me up. "I got you," Finola grunted as Torcall appeared at my side.

Torcall wrinkled his nose, shoved the taller guard back into the dark-blue-haired guard and said, "Struan, you know better than to harm any of the prisoners before the gauntlet."

I managed to swallow, but my chest tightened more. I hadn't realized that Finola and Torcall hadn't left yet, and if we hadn't been in a roomful of other people, I very likely would've thanked them. Instead, I forced my feet back underneath me and stood tall. Finola released me.

"Of course the *king* would have his most trusted guards watch over his *pet*." Struan's wings spread out, fluttering to help him back on his feet. "I don't know how you can stand to protect her."

Torcall didn't flinch and instead leaned forward. "Because I'm loyal to the king of frost, darkness, and nightmares. His royal blood is the only reason we haven't been weakened more than we already are by these blasted lands we're forced to live on. Without *him*, we'd all be starving and near dying. You'd best remember that before your words and actions are seen as treasonous."

"I'm certain the people would be thrilled to have a new contender in the gauntlet," Finola added firmly.

"I didn't speak ill of the king, only of the Seelie sunscorched and why she's still breathing." Struan held the cuff and gestured to my leg. "I'm just putting this on her, so don't attack me."

"Then don't do anything foolish," Torcall countered.

Taking a moment, I scanned the area and noted the way the ten other contestants glared at me. They weren't even paying each other attention, making my blood run cold. Even if Lorne didn't plan on killing me right away, the others did. I needed to remember every damn attack and defense Finnian had taught me. They would come in handy.

The cold, dark metal slipped around my boot, and when the lock clicked, he dropped the chain, making me realize how heavy the metal was as it clanked against the cool, smooth floor.

"Is everyone prepared for the game?" the guard next to the door asked.

"Yes," Struan answered. "She's chained."

I forced myself to inhale and exhale slowly to calm my galloping pulse. We weren't even on the arena floor, and I could feel sweat gathering in my armpits. My only salvation was that Eldrin still hadn't arrived, which meant it wasn't time for the games to begin.

Then the guard opened the doors to the arena, and Eldrin stood a hundred feet away with the thick nightmare gas billowing behind him. The gas was more condensed, like when I'd had to crawl through it and could barely move in the last game. There wasn't a lighter patch anywhere, and I wondered if this was set up for the twelve of us to fight covered in gas the entire time.

I wasn't sure any of us would survive that.

"Move forward!" Struan shouted from his spot beside me in the back.

Lorne crossed his arms, his wings still bound, as were the others'. At least, that put me on more even ground with them, even though they'd trained with weapons for most of their lives and I had two days behind me ... that I could remember.

The other ten before us moved. They'd put Rona with the dusky-haired woman and Bran with the silver-haired man. I had no clue what most of them were capable of, but I'd learn all too soon.

The twelve of us filed into the arena in a line, with Lorne and me at the very back. He kept as far away from me as possible so our chain had no slack. This would only end with us in a disastrous situation, but if I tried to tell him that, he wouldn't listen.

"We'll be right here if you make it back," Finola whispered as I stepped into the lion's den.

Most of the Unseelie stood, cheering like the last time, but a handful remained seated without any bloodthirsty joy on their faces.

How odd.

My gaze inadvertently landed on the one person it shouldn't.

Tavish.

And I immediately wished I hadn't looked at him. His face was whiter than I'd ever expected was possible, and his hands were fisted at his sides. Finnian stood on one side, his hand on Tavish's shoulder, trying to look casual. But his grip was too firm, like he was holding Tavish back.

Eldrin extended his wings, making a show of them, though they weren't as large as Tavish's. I couldn't be sure if it was for the audience or a reminder to the contestants that they couldn't use their wings in these trials. Either way, it made me hate the bastard even more.

"For these gauntlet trials, Calean and I have ensured that the times and activities of each one are different." Eldrin rose a few feet off the ground, spinning slowly to take in the entire arena.

Despite it being morning, the sky remained dark, but a little sunlight shone through, casting twilight over the area.

"This trial will be different for many reasons." He gestured to our feet, pointing out the obvious. "Each person is chained to someone, which serves a greater purpose. This is not just a test of strength but of agility and grace, even when you're chained to a person who desires to end you."

The more Eldrin talked, the more I wanted to kill him. The urge was so damn overwhelming that it stole my breath, especially after reliving the death of the man I'd killed over and over again. *This* man was a problem, not only for me but for Tavish and his people as well.

"This trial will last two hours." He smirked, and there was a collective gasp from the competitors. Eldrin stared at us and said, "Some advice. Make sure you get on the platform, or the gas will consume you." He flew upward, heading toward his spot next to Tavish. "Without further ado, let the games begin!"

A guard blew the horn, and something hissed behind me. I glanced over my shoulder to see more gas rising from the ground, closing in around me.

"Blighted abyss," Lorne groaned as the other ten people hurried ahead, risking getting closer to the wall of gas directly in front of us, which began to dissipate. He moved forward, catching me off guard. My body jerked as his injured leg gave out, and he landed on that knee.

I managed not to fall into the dirt, and I hurried to his

side, wanting more slack in the chain so we each could move without fighting each other's weight. I reached his side and helped him to his feet.

He glared at me and took a few steps forward to gain distance. He rasped, "Don't touch me, wildling."

His reaction didn't surprise me. He saw me as beneath him and didn't want to risk even the illusion that I'd helped him.

I rolled my eyes and noticed that the wall of gas was closing in. "If you don't want my help, then move." I pointed over my shoulder. "Or we're both going to die."

The others were twenty feet away, watching us. The dusky-haired woman frowned, staring at Lorne, but the other contenders focused on me with giant smiles, anticipating my death.

Fuck that. I wouldn't let them win that easily.

"Come on, or do you want to die?" I bit out, moving forward without checking on him.

I almost expected the chain to snag from his refusal to move with me, but after ten steps, I realized he was keeping up.

When we were a few feet away from the others, Bran rushed forward. He threw a punch at my jaw, but I ducked at the last second, leaving his right side open. I punched him in the gut, and he doubled over in pain. I kneed him in the face, but the chain yanked me back, and I fell onto my back hard with a gust of dirt kicking up around me and getting in my eyes.

"You sunscorched Seelie," the dusky-haired woman croaked.

I opened my eyes despite the grit and saw the woman lunge at me. I tried to roll, but she landed on my side and clawed my face. I elbowed her in her side, making her groan, and changed my momentum so that I rolled on top of her.

My vision edged red as I straddled her stomach and punched her in the jaw. Her head jerked to the side, but before I could strike her again, someone reached around my shoulders, grabbed me by the neck, and lifted me off her.

I gagged, trying to gasp for air, and kicked my leg backward into my attacker with as much muscle as possible before my strength could vanish. The chain jerked, holding some of my strength back, but I'd caught the person by surprise, and they'd loosened their grasp on my neck.

Not wanting to lose my leverage, I reached behind my head, grasped a handful of hair, and yanked. A moan rumbled deep from a man's chest, but he didn't loosen his hold, so I dug my nails into his skin and ran my hand down his face.

Warm liquid trickled out as the dusky-haired woman recovered enough to stand before me. She bent down, grabbed the loose chain, and rasped, "Rona, get closer to me."

Rona moved, a smirk on her face, watching me struggle as the dusky-haired woman picked up more of the chain, readying to slip it over my head and choke me. There wouldn't be a way to get out of that, so my goal was not to get into it in the first place.

A noise clicked from below, and we all froze.

The sound was similar to the noise right before a bomb exploded ... from what I'd heard on TV.

Suddenly, a platform sprang from underneath us all, lifting us into the air, and then dropped back to the ground.

I landed hard on my feet before crashing on top of the dusky-haired woman. And just as soon as the motion stopped, it lunged us upward again.

Two loud screams echoed from below, and I lifted my head and counted. One of the six groups must have fallen off the ledge from the sudden stop.

Silence.

"Blighted abyss," Rona rasped, looking over the ledge. "I can't even see them below us now because of the gas."

I slowly climbed to my feet, all of us stunned and confused. Gas hovered thick below us, and we were suspended in the air, though I had no clue how far up we were because we couldn't see the ground.

Taking in our surroundings, I couldn't believe what I saw. If the last trial had been horrible, I wasn't sure how to describe this. It was some sort of obstacle course in the sky, but unlike the shows back home, I suspected these were deadly. There were five obstacles with a flat platform between each one, leading to one in the center. That had to be where we needed to go before the two hours were up.

I further understood why they'd paired me with Lorne. Even if the prisoners didn't kill me, it was unlikely we could get through all these obstacles with him injured. The platform closest to us, about two feet away, had the swinging axes from the last trial, and we had to crawl in the dirt to get through them. Next was a plank with swords below and around it. If that wasn't bad enough, the third course was a steep incline with a chain, a blazing fire underneath, and you had to climb up one side and down the other.

Something a man with an injured leg would struggle to achieve.

Then there was a collapsing walls course and monkey bars suspended over quicksand like last time.

Five obstacles that we had to survive, with an empty platform like the one we stood on between each one, and then the final one in the center after the monkey bars.

My heart stopped, and my mouth went dry.

The ten of us glanced around and stared at the course then at each other.

Then, there was another click, and my heart lunged into my throat.

I squatted on the platform to lessen the jarring of my body as I waited for the quick drop into the nightmare gas. My entire body clenched, remembering the misery of the gas from last time.

Would the Unseelie be okay with every single prisoner dying? Where was the fun in that, especially with the course from hell right in front of us? Why go to all that trouble to let us die here—but that could be the point, to make it more shocking and impactful.

Maybe that was why Eldrin had proclaimed that any survivors could have a reduced sentence—he knew no one would survive to claim it. That sounded like something manipulative he would do.

The platform didn't drop right away but, instead, creaked underneath our feet.

The other prisoners squatted as well. Lorne flinched, and his face twisted in agony as he tried to crouch like the rest of us. If he fell, he'd drag me down with him.

I'd bet Eldrin was enjoying himself thoroughly.

The anticipation of the drop had to be worse than actually experiencing it. I wished the damn thing would just go because, by how fast my heart was racing and how much sweat was pooling in my armpits, I was near cardiac arrest level ... or was that even a thing being a fae? I didn't fucking know anymore.

Something creaked into place underneath us, and the platform moved slowly.

This had to be a trick, so I remained in position, waiting. I didn't want to stand too quickly and be tossed off, but maybe if the drop was high enough, it would be a more pleasant death than inhaling poisonous gas.

After a few beats, Rona stood and glanced around. "Moira, we need to move. The other platforms aren't lowering. If we don't hurry, we'll be too low to reach the next one."

My hands fisted, my nails digging into my palms. They didn't plan on killing us all at once, but now I understood how they would force us to go through each obstacle course. We'd get to choose—die by gas or navigate the threat ahead, as long as we didn't run out of time.

"Then we should not delay." Moira straightened, pushing her dusky-colored hair out of her face and moving so the two of them stood side by side at the edge.

Rona jumped, but Moira froze, staring at the gas below. Rona landed on the other platform near the edge and gripped one of the metal pillars while holding on to one of the strings that ran to the end where all the axes swung.

The chain tightened, and Moira jerked slightly forward. Bran grabbed her arm, holding her back a second before she sailed over the edge.

There was no slack between them, and Rona gritted her teeth, holding on to the edge.

"What in the blasted fury are you doing?" Rona rasped. "I thought we were coming over *together*."

Now, the distance between each pair made sense. We had to move somewhat together or risk dying. I'd bet Lorne and I didn't make the first jump because I suspected he'd rather die than let the Unseelie watch him work with me. I could only hope I was wrong.

"I ... I might fall." She glanced down at the gas. "I don't think I can do it."

I blinked, and laughter bubbled out. A fae was scared of heights. I understood that her wings were chained and useless, but they all gave off such a tough and gruff persona that I hadn't expected *this*. It was such a *human* fear.

"You're going to die if you don't," Bran snapped. "So move, or I'll make you."

The other four pairs shuffled closer, all of them wary. The platform was about an inch lower than the other one, which wasn't a huge distance, but we were going to run out of time.

"If you won't jump, move out of the way so the rest of us can. I'll help you over, Moira," the darker-skinned man rasped as he took a few steps forward.

We were doing exactly what Eldrin had hoped—working against each other, which would lead to most, if not all, of us dying. Even though I knew they'd turn on me at the next opportunity, my hatred for Eldrin was stronger than anything else.

"Don't look down." My voice sounded raspy from dirt and trauma. I cleared it, the dirt like sandpaper against my throat. "Keep looking at Rona and pretend you aren't high up ... that you're on the ground."

Bran jerked his body toward me and sneered, "We don't need your help. We won't fall for your deception."

I wanted to roll my eyes, but I forced them to remain still. "I'm not deceiving you. The fear of heights is really tied to the fear of falling. Since she can't use her wings, she doesn't have that security. Looking down makes it look like we're higher up than we really are, so she needs to forget and pretend we're on level ground and stop overthinking it. This is a common human fear, so it's something I'm more familiar with than any of you."

"Oh, now you're comparing *us* to humans." Lorne spat, his nose wrinkling.

Lovely. He'd remembered how to speak.

I much preferred his silence.

"In this instance, yes." If they wanted me to coddle them, they'd be sorely disappointed. "But if everyone wants to die and turn on each other, then please continue." I waved a hand, indicating I would stand back and watch. I hoped my condescending tone would motivate them to prove me wrong.

Moira lifted her chin. "I'm not fearful like humans." She turned around and jumped over the ledge. The chain between her and Rona went slack, and Rona released her death grip on the metal.

Some of the tension eased from my shoulders, and I looked at Lorne. "Are you ready to go?" With only a two-foot distance, I hoped he wouldn't struggle to reach the other platform. The lower we got, the harder it would be for him to get across.

"You aren't crossing before us," Bran said and patted the darker-skinned man's shoulder. "Dougal, take a step now."

The two of them moved in tandem and made it easily over the barrier as Moira and Rona crawled underneath the axes.

Another pair tried to get in front of us, but Lorne

stepped up to them and shoved one of them off the platform. The man dropped from sight with a yell and the man
he was chained to reached for my arm to help him not fall
over. On instinct, I almost took his hand, but Lorne
knocked my arm away, and the second man fell after the
first.

"Don't you *dare* get us both killed." Lorne's jaw
clenched. "I don't plan on dying today, not even while stuck
with you. Do you understand?"

Two sickening thuds came from below just as I nodded.
My stomach churned as I realized how close I'd come to
dying ... *again.*

"Ready?" He arched a brow.

I nodded. We were about four inches below the platform, and Dougal and Bran were crawling under the axes.

"Now!" he barked, and we stepped over in tandem.

When my foot hit the other platform, the weight on my
shoulders lightened. Even though we hadn't gotten far, I'd
learned that Lorne was willing to work with me enough to
survive. That counted for more than I'd expected.

Lorne had stepped forward with his hurt leg, leaving his
healthy one to anchor him from behind. When his injured
foot hit the second platform, the area around his eyes tightened in pain, and he dropped to his knee.

I moved to help him but stopped short. I didn't want to
embarrass him in front of his people and ruin the marginal
goodwill brewing between us.

Though I doubted we'd survive with his mangled leg,
especially given the third obstacle we'd have to get over,
which would push his leg to the max, I wanted to take it one
trial at a time and not get ahead of myself.

"Move, or we'll trample you," the white-haired man
called from behind us. "We're not going to wait here to die."

Lorne moved in front of me, not bothering to get back up from where he'd fallen.

I understood why. He wanted to pretend he'd meant to drop since we needed to crawl anyway, and I wouldn't bruise his pride.

He hunkered close to the ground and moved forward as an axe swung right above his back. As I dropped to my knees, I watched Moira and Rona hop to the next empty platform. From this vantage point, I noticed there were thirty axes we had to move under. Some swung lower than others. Great. I'd belly-crawl if that's what it took to get through this thing. I could only hope it was enough for the super-low areas.

The chain yanked on me, and Lorne turned to glare and rasped, "Get moving, sunscorched."

I dropped to my stomach, ready to move, but the next axe sliced into his shoulder as he faced forward again. He groaned, and guilt swirled through me. He'd gotten injured because I'd been too slow to follow. I couldn't do that again, especially since we were hindered enough as it was.

I lay back down and moved my legs and arms forward. They were stiff from when I'd fought at the very beginning, but at least I wasn't injured. As I moved through the dirt, the axes *whooshed* over me. At times, I could feel the air against the back of my neck, causing fear to choke me, but I pushed it away and continued my trek forward.

I wasn't sure how long we had left, but it felt like I'd been crawling forever when the platform underneath us began to creak like the last one had before it lowered.

My ears rang, and I inhaled, taking in a deep breath of dirt. This whole course was timed, which meant that, even though we had two hours, we didn't have time to dawdle.

The dirt irritated my throat and lungs, and my entire

body convulsed into a coughing fit as I forced myself to move. I turned my head to the side to keep from getting more dirt in my face, and a sharp pain sliced across the tip of my ear.

I hissed, wanting to see what damage had been done, but I couldn't risk moving and getting injured.

"Come on, wildling," Lorne said coldly. "You're at the end. You're almost out."

Those words were enough to get my panic under control and move out, but something grabbed my ankle and dragged me back.

I yelped, unable to swallow the noise, and tried to free my foot.

"I want it noted that I am the one who killed the Seelie princess," the white-haired guy chuckled. "Make sure you scream loud and give them a good show." He lifted my leg, making his intention known.

He wanted an axe to chop it off. The axe directly over me swung past, so I turned to my right. He had both hands on my right ankle, with his face looking up to watch me. Using the few seconds between axe swings, I kicked the dick in the nose, resulting in a sickening crunch.

He groaned, and his hold loosened on my ankle. I kicked both feet as hard as I could, and when he released me, I crawled forward as quickly as possible.

The sound of flesh tearing came from behind me.

Out of the corner of my eye, I saw the metal poles marking the end, so I crawled until Lorne's feet appeared beside me ... nothing else. He had to be standing, so I pulled my legs underneath me and stood.

I spun around, wondering if the white-haired guy was right on me, but bile inched up my throat. The man's head was cut up and bloody, and he lay limp on the ground. His partner was behind him, trying to shove him forward to get through.

The world shrank around me at the realization that I'd killed yet another person.

"We need to keep moving," Lorne rasped, turning my attention to him. "Or we die. Though I'd love to see you fade into oblivion, I'd rather it not be while you're chained to me."

At least we were on the same side ... for now.

Pushing away the horror, I focused on the task ahead. "Let's go."

We moved easily to the next platform, but the second obstacle course—a thin beam with swords sticking out from all around—had already begun descending.

We were taking too much time.

The other two groups had already made it to the caged steeple with the fire underneath. A sour taste filled my mouth. That one would be hard for Lorne, so we needed to reach it as soon as possible to give ourselves as much time as we could get.

Lorne must have realized the same thing because he moved up the stone steps and waved for me to follow.

He balanced on the thin piece of wood and waited. Growing up, I'd never been one for gymnastics, desiring to be out in the woods, swimming and kayaking. At this point, I wished I'd gotten familiar with the balance beam.

I tightened my core and stepped on, hoping like hell I could balance.

I held out my arms, helping to keep me centered, and took a step. My foot wobbled, and I swayed from side to side.

"Don't overthink it!" Lorne barked. "Just focus on the end. Use your own advice."

A laugh lodged in my throat, but I swallowed it, not wanting to add more instability to my balance. I inched forward.

The two of us moved with caution, and each time he had to use his bad leg, he wobbled as well. I didn't call him out on it—that wouldn't help him since it wasn't something he could fix.

When we got to the midway point, the platform jerked, and something clicked behind me. I started, and my foot wobbled on the beam, so I placed the other one down, forcing myself to center.

I turned and saw that a sword had shot a few inches upward.

Lorne continued, so I cleared my mind, needing to catch up before the chain strained between us. Keeping my eyes on the piece of wood in front of me, I tried to tune out the rest of the world.

At the end, I stepped onto the level platform and noticed we were six inches lower than the other platform.

That wasn't a good sign. We were getting farther and farther behind.

Lorne and I glanced at each other, and no words were needed as we stepped onto the next empty platform. But when we looked at the towering wall of metal chains we had to climb up and down, icy tendrils of fear curled around my chest.

The two groups in front of us were moving at a much faster pace, but Rona and Moira were still making their way to the top, and Bran and Dougal were on their way down. The second group had taken the lead, but even they were moving slower than I'd expected.

Not wanting to insult Lorne, I tried to keep my tone light. "Are you ready?" Of all the challenges, this was the one likeliest to kill us. The climb would take both arm and leg strength to complete.

"I'm fine," he muttered, telling me more with his curt reply than if he'd used more words.

We made our way onto the third platform and stood at the bottom, looking up. The incline was forty feet high, with a blazing fire underneath to make us sweat and overheat while we strained every muscle.

I decided to take the lead. He might need me to support some of his weight as he climbed, and we'd already wasted too much time. At least the platform hadn't begun descending yet.

Taking a deep breath, I gripped the first chain to pull myself up, but the skin on my palm burned. I gasped and jerked away, stumbling back, and the heel of my foot missed the back of the platform.

My body tipped backward.

My toes dug into the front of my boot, and I threw my weight forward. My knees crashed into the platform, and pain exploded while my hands felt like they were on fire.

Lorne had almost gotten to his knees, reaching for the chain as if to prevent me from falling, but with his injury, we would have both dropped had I not overcorrected.

Chest heaving, I gritted my teeth and regulated my breathing, though it was hard. My eyes burned, and I blinked back tears. I didn't want to cry in front of the Unseelie, despite the fact that my reaction was just because of the suffering.

"What was that?" Lorne rasped, but with how his voice broke, his question was almost inaudible. "You almost killed *us*."

Us.

Of course he'd only save my ass to keep himself from dying. Any other time, he would've gladly pushed me off. I had to remember how these people operated. They were nothing like my family back home. "If you'd touched the chain, you'd understand why."

I glanced at the two pairs left with us. They were moving as quickly as possible, but the soles of their boots had already melted off, and they weren't even on the other side yet. What had looked so easy wasn't, and their movements were jerky and uneasy.

I looked at my palms and winced at their toasty-pink color from where I'd gripped the chain.

He turned back to the chain. Since we'd arrived, the fire had gotten larger, the flame tips heating the metal. "Blighted abyss. The longer we stay down here, the higher the flames will go, making the climb over harder. They're punishing us for already struggling."

"We'd better get moving." Even as I said the words, every cell within me wanted to never touch that chain again. I spun and noted that the first two platforms were no longer visible, already encased in the foggy gas, with the third one about two feet above it and the one we'd just jumped off two feet below us.

There were no choices other than to continue forward or die.

Death wasn't an option. I wasn't ready to give up and accept that fate. I believed there was more to my life than *this* ... or I hoped so with every cell of my body.

My hands burned at the thought of touching the chain again, and I wanted to chastise them. If they hurt now, I didn't want to know how they'd feel when we started the climb.

"Rip off the bottom of your shirt and tie it around your hands for protection. If it begins smoking, we need to suck it up and keep moving forward." Even though we'd still feel the heat through the fabric, it should prevent massive burns.

"Why would it smoke?" His brows furrowed. "Do human clothes catch fire?"

For the first time since, well, *ever*, I wanted to thank the fae for their differences. I ripped the bottom of my shirt, turning it into a crop top. "Yes. If the fire's hot enough to burn the bottom of boots, it will burn clothes."

Even as we talked, the chains lowered a little, putting them deeper into the flames. I ripped the material in two and tied a piece around each hand. Lorne followed my lead, and soon, we were as ready to climb as we'd ever be.

Lorne straightened his shoulders and glanced at me.

I nodded, and dread pooled in my stomach with each step closer to the chain we took. At the edge, I watched as Bran and Dougal jumped over the top of the incline, black blood dripping from their hands and feet. I didn't need to know why; we'd be bearing similar wounds soon, if not worse.

We reached for the chains, and the heat seared through the material. Thankfully, it wasn't my skin like the first time, but the heat made the burn that marred my palms worse. As we climbed, the heat from the flames caused sweat to bead on my brow and chest.

This was worse than summer in Georgia, which spoke volumes. We moved at a slow pace, pausing each time Lorne had to use his injured leg to move up to the next level. In the moment that we waited, I shifted back and forth between my left and right side, hoping that would prevent the soles of my boots from melting as quickly.

The women finally reached the top, Moira's bottom lip quivering. Hers and Rona's skin looked black on the bottoms of their feet, where the chains had melted away the soles of their boots.

They climbed over the top, their faces purple with

exhaustion and pain. They faced us but began descending, moving quicker.

Lorne grunted. "My blasted boots have already melted through," he gritted out, bringing my attention back to him.

Holy shit. This wasn't good.

The last thing I wanted to do was lose progress, but I went down a little past Lorne's ass, put my right hand underneath it, and pushed up. Lorne took the step he'd been struggling with, and I smelled the putrid stench of whatever the bottom of our boots was made out of burning.

We moved up a few chains, and when we got back to where his injured foot needed to bear his weight, I shoved his ass again.

Tears clouded my vision as my hands felt like they were on fire and my feet became hotter. Between that and the way the flames charred my skin, I had to look like a burned chicken nugget. My skin tightened, making me feel like I was getting close to being well done.

My right arm ached from shoving Lorne upward, but after what felt like years, we reached the top of the incline.

At least now, we'd be going down, which would help our momentum. As we threw our legs over the edge, something dripped into my eyes, giving everything a golden hue.

When I glanced at Lorne, I saw black blood oozing from cracks in his face, confirming I had to be bleeding as well.

The flames were only a foot from our faces.

I took a moment to look behind me and realized the platform we were on was already a foot below the next one.

We were running out of time.

"We need to hurry," I rasped, my face throbbing from barely moving my lips to speak. My mouth was so dry, and I desperately wanted to drink water and soak in a tub—two things I would be able to do only once we were finished with this stupid game. "The platform is already descending."

Lorne clenched his teeth, and we tried moving faster. My arms were tired, especially the right one, since I'd used it to help push Lorne. That arm shook, then gave out, causing my bare stomach to press on a link. An intense burning sensation engulfed me, and I jerked my feet up, causing the bottom of one shoe to rake off so that my bare skin was on the chains.

I hissed, trying to move so that no part of my skin burned, but no matter what I did, my foot touched the chain. A sharp, throbbing burn engulfed me. I positioned all my weight on the other foot, but the bottom of my sole heated, warning me that I was about to have no protection there either.

For a moment, falling to my death sounded appealing. The impact would be hard and solid, ending my suffering ... unless the wildlings hadn't actually placed us high, which meant the nightmare gas would provide a slow, painful death on top of the burns.

I wouldn't give Eldrin the satisfaction.

Peeking over my shoulder, I realized we couldn't jump down yet. We needed to get halfway down this massive, slanted wall before we could land on our feet without risking worse injuries than we had now.

Lorne groaned, but he quickened his descent. I noticed the way his legs shook, which I hated. I needed him to hold on, but he'd been dealing with the burning of his feet longer than I had since he struggled to move his body as easily.

"We just need to get halfway down, and then we can jump." I cringed, thinking of him jumping with his blistered feet and injured leg, but it would be better than letting the skin melt from our bodies—if we could wait until then.

As we climbed down, dark spots edged into my vision. The torture was so severe that my stomach churned, and bile inched up my throat. If I thought I'd experienced injuries before, they'd been nothing like now.

My tears thickened so much that all I saw was a blur, and vomit lurched into my mouth and spilled from me. It hit the flames, and the fire roared higher, the tips of the flames reaching my hands.

I yelped, and unable to hold on any longer, I let go. With my last bit of strength, I pushed with my legs, hoping like hell that we cleared the rest of the chains below us.

As my body tumbled, the chain yanked on Lorne. He hissed as he couldn't hold on, and we both fell backward. The air blew my blonde hair forward into my face so that I couldn't see anything.

Within seconds, I landed on something solid and hard, knocking the breath out of me. Lorne landed beside me, and he didn't move either. For a moment, I lay there, trying to clear my vision, but even though we weren't touching the chains anymore, the burning continued to blaze throughout my body.

Move, Lira. Eiric's voice popped into my head, even though that wasn't possible. On Earth, she was my voice of reason whenever I wanted to give up, and the sound had my heart aching in a completely different way.

Dammit, I missed her so much it hurt to breathe.

Don't make me find a way to you just so I can bring you back to life and kill you myself. Get on your feet and move. I need you to come back home to us.

A sob built in my chest, making my body ache worse. *I can't come back to you. I don't have a way.*

If anyone can figure it out, it's you, Lira. Her voice

turned sterner than I'd ever heard it. *Now get up and find a way to survive. We need you back with us.*

My gaze immediately found the spot where Tavish sat, and somehow, I could see him clearly through the chaos like he was the only one who mattered. Our gazes connected, and realization tingled through me, along with the chill of what felt like magic retreating from me.

He mouthed the words, *Get up and survive. I need you to win.*

A pleasant warmth spread through my chest. That wasn't my mind pushing me on—it was him. A little bit of adrenaline pumped through me, taking the edge off the pain.

I will, I mouthed back, not wanting to disappoint him. I forced myself to sit up as the need to be with him again surged through me. My skin felt as if it might rip off, but I forced myself to push through the pain. I turned my head and swore I'd been turned into beef jerky—all dried out and wrinkled. "Lorne, can you keep going, or would you rather keep lying there and die?" I asked, knowing there was one thing that drove him—pride.

He bared his teeth. "No, we're going to prove to them that an injured Unseelie and a sunscorched can make it through this."

I stood and reached for his hand to help him.

He paused like he was considering not taking it, but then he let out a breath and took my hand. I helped him to his feet, ignoring the way my body shook from the torture and how one foot felt melted into the platform.

When he got to his feet, his face twisted in agony, but we pivoted to see that the platform was now two feet above us.

This would be much trickier since we were both

injured, and we wouldn't have any slack to give. We had to work together perfectly, or we'd fall over the ledge.

"Go on the count of three," I croaked. "Got it?"

"Yes, let's proceed," he snapped, but his voice was hoarser than mine.

"One, two," I inhaled, bracing for what came next. "Three."

Lorne used his good leg, and we stepped upward. I moved quicker than him, but not so fast that our chain tightened, and we stumbled to our knees onto the next platform.

My attention homed in on the one after it, where two walls were closing in toward each other, and not very slowly. Right now, there was enough room for about three of Lorne to go through abreast, but the gap closed with Moira and Rona limping around the corner at the end, almost a quarter of a mile down.

Crap. We weren't out of the woods yet, especially with Lorne's fresh injuries.

He'd already climbed to his feet when I straightened. I waited until he'd rolled his shoulders back, which he did whenever he was ready to move forward, like he was psyching himself up for the next threat.

This platform was only six inches lower than the next one, but that didn't matter. We were still behind.

We moved in tandem, not even needing to discuss what we were doing, though it helped that I was limping almost as bad as him. We made it to the next obstacle course with the wall as wide as maybe two and a half of him.

"Run," Lorne commanded.

My heart hammered, and I took off first, knowing I might have to tug him the rest of the way. Each time I landed on my left foot, fire exploded through me. I tried to run at a steady pace, but Lorne continued to move slower and slower.

The space between the walls was now about two of him, and we'd made it only a quarter of the way there.

"You need to run faster." I glanced over my shoulder, and my eyes widened as I took in his state. A thick trail of blood followed him, and I could only imagine what his feet looked like underneath the boot ... not that I wanted to know.

"We're almost there." I reached down and snagged the chain, yanking it. I *needed* him to go faster. I'd been so focused on the slanted wall that I hadn't considered *this*.

"I'm trying," Lorne grumbled.

I yanked on the chain harder.

The walls continued to close in around us.

He grunted, picking up his pace, but it wasn't enough.

I was almost at the end, but Lorne was a full two feet behind me and moving slowly.

If I didn't do something, he'd die.

I had to save him, especially since we'd been helping each other this time around. I wouldn't leave someone behind when things got hard.

In a last-ditch effort, I rushed back to him and grabbed his hands. I ignored the warm liquid I felt on my hands from his.

The wall was almost on him, moving faster like we were out of time.

Not wanting to lose traction, I moved my hands to his wrists so they didn't slip off, and I yanked harder than I ever had before.

The muscles in my back strained, and something felt like it ripped. A warm pulse shot through my body into my hands. Slicing pain throbbed through me, and the sound of something tearing tickled my mind.

My body shifted as I flexed, and our bodies sailed the last few feet, breaking us free of the closing walls. We fell onto our asses. Something strange shifted behind me, and I turned to see sparkly sea-green wings that reminded me of the water in the bathtub.

I blinked, trying to understand what was going on, but when my back tensed, the wings folded in toward my back ... like they were mine.

Blighted abyss! I had *wings*.

Even though my blood was gold, seeing the wings made all this more real. My vision grew fuzzy, and I tried to understand what the hell was happening to me.

"Bless the gods," Lorne whimpered. "I don't understand how this is possible."

He wasn't telling me anything I didn't already know. Even though I was coming to terms with being fae, I hadn't expected *this*. "I guess Seelie have wings too." Now I was worried this would prevent him from working with me, the wings a big reminder that I was his *enemy*.

"Of course Seelie have wings. But that's not what I'm referring to." He pointed to his feet and rasped. "Look at this."

I tore my gaze from my wings to see what he was talking about. He had his foot propped up on his leg, staring at the bottom.

The bottom of his foot wasn't blistered anymore. It had a few faint scabs, but the severe injury was gone.

Holy shit.

"How did that happen?"

Then the platform we sat on creaked, the sound more rushed and frantic than the others.

He lunged to his feet. "Let's get to the next platform."

We hurried to the edge, and he readied to leap onto the next platform. I tried to move my wings, but they jerked, so we jumped together.

When we landed on the next platform, it made a popping noise and dropped with Lorne and me on it.

As we dropped toward the gas, my hair flew into my face. I reached out and grabbed Lorne's waist. When our bodies were almost submerged, my back muscles moved like a reflex, and my wings flapped, holding us steady despite the way my arms shook from his weight.

I glanced down to see that I was shoulder-deep in the fog. If I didn't move us upward, the gas would engulf us, and we'd die.

My muscles tensed and ached, and I tried not to over-think it like Tavish and Finnian had coached me.

I was fae, and part of me knew what to do, even if I couldn't consciously remember. I needed to focus on keeping hold of Lorne. If he fell, the momentum would take me with him.

"Hold on to me," I gritted out, wanting my whole body to take the distribution of his weight and not only my arms.

He didn't argue, wrapping his arms around my neck and his legs around my waist, putting me in the most inti-mate position I'd ever been in with a man. All it took was a life-or-death situation to get a man to cover my body with his.

Loud boos came from the audience, who were clearly not happy that we'd survived. I hadn't heard any of their noises before, but I hadn't been this high up in the coliseum. That had to be why.

But wow. The Unseelie were such lovely people.

"You're going to have to do more than this to get us out of danger," Lorne whispered.

He had to weigh twice as much as me, and my entire body was straining just to keep us at this level. My back muscles burned in ways I'd never dreamed of. "I ... don't ..." With the amount of pressure from carrying him yanking on me, I struggled to say each word. "... know ... how ... to fly."

"Focus on where you want to take us," he huffed. "Your wings will do the rest."

Yeah, I seriously doubted that, but I didn't have the energy to spare to argue with him. So instead, I locked on the beginning of the monkey bars obstacle, and my wings moved faster, though the burn intensified and my back screamed. Lorne's weight resembled an anchor trying to drag us to our deaths.

I clenched my jaw so hard that it cracked, and I tried to push through the searing pain. Between my feet and stomach burns and now this, I'd never been in misery like this before, and that was saying something.

With each flap of my wings, my back muscles became more tired, but our bodies lifted. After a while, the sensation didn't feel quite as strange, and something inside me filled with faint joy.

Even though I didn't remember it, a freedom that felt slightly familiar confirmed that I loved flying ... without the extra weight.

Lorne clung to me, his body rubbing my raw skin, but I swallowed any complaint. Tears filled my eyes, and I refused to look down to see what little progress we'd made. I focused on the platform, desperate not to lose sight of it, fearful that my wings would stop moving. Sweat beaded my body, causing my skin to burn even more, and Lorne struggled to hold on.

"That's it. We're almost there," he encouraged as we neared the bars.

I wanted to snap back at him, but I didn't have the energy, every ounce of strength needed to push us higher. Then, my back muscles cramped and spasmed.

"Get on the bars," I gritted out, fighting through the pain.

Looking over his shoulder, Lorne released one of his arms from around my neck and reached for the monkey bars. Tears fell from my eyes and down my face, hitting the cracks from the fire. Every single part of my body throbbed or burned.

His hand missed the bar by a few inches. My body screamed in protest.

I'd clearly pissed off fate or something else out there that was determined for me to die in this trial, but I'd gone through too much to give up.

Not caring how weak I sounded, I screamed, letting out the torment I'd been in while giving myself one last little bit of strength. I managed to fly up one more inch, but no more.

"Got it!" Lorne shouted with relief, and his legs tightened around me. He then said, "Now it's your turn to hold on because my leg isn't healed all the way." He released his other arm, and as soon as he held his own weight, my wings gave out and flopped limply behind me.

Even though I didn't remember having wings, I didn't

have to be a brain surgeon to know that having them hanging flat like that wasn't a good sign. My back had a deep ache from the strain I'd put on my body.

Lorne didn't move as he adjusted to carrying our weight, and when I glanced up, I saw the strain on his face. I needed to get up on the monkey bars too, though my arms felt like mashed potatoes.

Taking a deep breath, I reached out and took the bar in front of him.

"I can carry you across," he insisted behind me.

I untangled my body from his, and the hair on the nape of my neck rose like a warning. If he helped me, he would believe I owed him, and I didn't want to get in the same situation as Tavish was with Eldrin. My arms strained, but luckily, my wings had taken the brunt of his weight. My dad had always made sure that Eiric and I pushed our bodies to the limit, so I should be able to push through the shaky sensation as long as Lorne moved quickly enough. "I'm fine. Let's get going. This platform could collapse at any moment." I didn't have to add that I couldn't fly again because my wings were convulsing faintly at my sides.

He moved forward, joining me on the same bar, wide enough for us to work together. We locked eyes and nodded then moved to the next one. With each bar, my arms weakened more, and we had at least thirty more to go.

On the platform in front of us, Dougal, Bran, Rona, and Moira fought the person they had been chained to. It was clear that Bran and Rona weren't part of Lorne's group, and everyone wanted to reduce their sentence the best way they knew possible—by killing each other.

My stomach dropped. There was no telling what awaited us. How could Tavish have created this sort of cruelty for his people to enjoy in the name of justice? No wonder his subjects had no problem turning on him when things got rough—that was the attitude he'd allowed Eldrin to encourage.

Anger roared through me, and adrenaline burned off the edge of pain and soreness and drove me on.

But Lorne slowed beside me.

Now, it was my turn to annoy him and tell him something he already knew. "Only ten more bars." The end was in sight, and this was the last bit we had to push through. "If we die now, I swear I'll find a way to bring you back just so I can kill you with my bare hands, night fiend." The insult rolled off my tongue, though I didn't remember hearing it before.

Lorne laughed, startling me. The material of my shirt was still wrapped around my hands, which was the only reason I didn't slip off the bar.

"I never would've thought I'd be so happy to see your wings and memories coming back, but I won't lie. I'm relieved." He continued forward like a little bit of energy had infused him.

Dougal stepped away from his fight and glanced at us. His jaw dropped as Bran rounded on him, but Dougal pointed at us. "Blighted abyss, Lorne and the sunscorched made it."

"That's blasting impossible." Bran pulled his punch and blinked like we had to be a mirage. He then spat, "And the wildling got her wings."

All four of them forgot about fighting each other as they stared me down with hatred etched in every line of their faces.

My heart dropped to my stomach. I already knew how

this would go down. They'd team up on me, including Lorne, and why not? As long as they killed me without me falling off the platform, Lorne would be fine. We'd made it through the obstacle course to the end of the second gauntlet.

It'll be fine, I lied to myself. *I made it this far. I can finish the last bit without dying.* Even as I tried to motivate myself, my blood ran cold. The truth told a different story. I was wounded, exhausted, and dehydrated. The last thing I needed was a fight, but by the same token, they should all be as bad off as me. We'd survived the same obstacles, though none of them had been paired with an injured person.

We reached the end of the bars, and the four of them stayed back, no doubt waiting until Lorne was safe before attacking. Even the siblings seemed to hesitate when it came to Lorne, which made me wonder whether he held some sort of power over them.

Needing my strength, I dropped to the platform. Pure agony raged from the bottom of my feet, raw from the fire, and my knees went weak and wanted to crumple. I forced them to lock and my feet to stay firm on the ground. I refused to show my weakness.

Lorne landed next to me, and we faced the other four, but I knew that wouldn't last long.

Rona moved forward. Her eyes darkened as she readied to fight me again.

They'd have to blow the horn soon, surely.

Not wanting to be near the edge of the platform, I moved toward her, and her eyes widened with surprise.

She threw a punch and nailed me right in the chin. My head jerked to the side, and a sharp ache shot through my face, but I punched her in the stomach.

Stumbling back, she let out an *oomph,* but my victory

was short-lived. Moira grabbed one of my wings and yanked, pulling the muscle away from the others. My body moved toward her to overcompensate for the strain, and she stomped on my foot.

A strangled cry escaped me, revealing how much pain I was in. I tried to move away, but the chain linking me to Lorne tightened, keeping me right in their grips.

Of course he'd turn on me now that he was safe. Our little bit of teamwork didn't mean anything long term.

"I'm getting in on that." Bran chuckled darkly. "They can't have all the fun."

I swallowed. There was no escape, but I wouldn't die without a blazing fight.

I leaned toward Moira and slammed my forehead against hers. Her body wobbled, allowing me to free my foot—though it felt like I left a slab of skin behind on the platform—and yank my wing from her grasp.

Rona slammed into my side, forcing me toward the edge of the platform. I kept waiting for the men to attack as well, but then I heard the punches and groans of fighting.

As long as it prevented them from reaching me, they could rip each other in half.

I spun toward Lorne, having no option with our chain, catching Rona off guard. Clearly, she hadn't expected me to head toward the men.

Elbowing her in the back, I focused on Lorne, who was fighting Bran and forcing Dougal to stay back. I wouldn't complain about that.

Rona landed on her knees, and I kicked her in the side, moving her to the platform's edge. Her hands gripped the side to prevent herself from going over, but something came over me. If I didn't end her, they'd tag-team me in the next round. Pushing her off the ledge would eliminate two enemies.

I'd taken two hurried steps, ignoring the pain and readying to kill Rona, when my heart caught up with my brain.

What the hell was I thinking? How could I end someone's life just because they'd been raised to believe this was how they needed to be? This wasn't her fault; this broken kingdom and, unfortunately, Tavish were to blame.

Arms wrapped around my waist, jerking me hard so that the side of my body hit the floor and throbbed with debilitating pain. I could've sworn I'd been skinned and filleted.

Moira sneered as she stood over me and rasped, "You could've ended us, but you froze. Ignorant sunscorched." She straddled me and reached out to strangle me despite the blackened blisters on her palms.

She gripped my neck, and I inhaled deeply, readying to make the last move I could with the remaining strength I had.

When her hands touched my neck, warm blood from her seared hands coated my skin. Her face twisted in misery, and she couldn't squeeze hard enough to constrict my air.

Not wasting any time, I lifted my head like I was going to headbutt her again. She jerked back enough so that I rolled, throwing her off balance. She landed on her side, and I struggled to my feet just as the horn blew.

Relief soared through me, and I dropped back to the ground, unable to stay upright. My body burned like flames engulfed me, and I was certain this was how death felt. *Please tell me I didn't survive the game just to die as soon as it's over.*

The platform began to lower, and I opened my eyes. All six of us lay there.

This trial had been so much worse than the first one, which made me fear for the last one. How could any of us survive something worse?

With every inch we lowered, I waited for the nightmare gas to engulf us, but the arena walls came into view, indicating we were close to the ground. The fog had dispersed.

Once the platform was lowered, Eldrin flew to us and scowled at me. "Congratulations to the six of you. The fighting and obstacle course of the game is over, and you'll officially be through when you exit the arena and the guards unchain you." He steepled his hands and smiled. "After this round, we'll select the team of two who won and give them access to their powers for the final challenge."

My heart sank. He wanted all of us to get up and walk across the dirt to complete the trial. At that moment, Eldrin became the one person I could kill with zero guilt.

He was a monster … and something tugged at my brain like it wanted to be known.

I tried to sit up, but my body refused. What would happen if I couldn't make it to the door?

Lorne got up slowly beside me and stared down at me. He flinched, and a sour taste filled my mouth.

He was going to drag my ass out the door.

Instead, he squatted beside me, and cold tendrils of fear squeezed my heart. I lifted my hands, ready to keep him from strangling me. I doubted anyone would stop him.

"Blighted abyss, Lira." He shook his head and frowned. "Don't make this any harder than it has to be. If you don't fight, it'll go much faster and easier."

After all this, he thought I'd lie here and allow him to kill me?

I glanced at Eldrin to see if he would intervene, but he only smiled.

Lorne leaned forward, extending his hands toward me, and I clutched a handful of dirt, ready to throw it in his face.

Then, he did something I never expected him to do.

I n my entire existence, I'd never struggled with self-control until I brought Lira back into our realm. Watching her in this blasted game was excruciating. I'd almost interfered with the trial multiple times, and had it not been for Finnian holding me back and her sprouting wings to save herself, I would have rescued her.

Of course, the man who'd risen against me was the one she was chained to and whom she'd saved time and time again. Another dig toward me by Eldrin, no doubt. Eldrin hadn't expected them to succeed.

Eldrin finished his speech, indicating that if the prisoners couldn't make it through the doors back to the prison, they didn't officially survive the game, which had my frozen blood thawing. Caelan's head minutely tipped back with surprise. That hadn't been the plan. Eldrin must have made the change because Lira was completely exhausted.

I hated the debt I owed to Eldrin. Being around him now made me want to cloak him in darkness and strangle him slowly for what he continued to do to Lira. But my hands were tied, and I couldn't help her to the doors since he hadn't officially ended the game, just the fighting.

Lira's face was strained, and her head lifted as she tried to get up.

Something in my chest ached.

My breath caught, the sensation overwhelming, reminding me of the moment I'd stirred back to consciousness to find my parents dead at the feet of five Seelie soldiers after they'd taken Dunscaith Castle by surprise.

The Seelie had frozen my heart solid by killing my parents. Of course, their princess would warm it back up to ache once more. The bitter irony filled my mouth with the taste of copper.

I stood, ready to push another vision into her head. I wasn't sure what she'd seen, but whatever image I'd prompted had inspired her to continue. And ... she knew it had been me.

Lorne closed the distance between them, causing all three types of my magic to pulse. Somehow, the wildling was moving better than he had when the trial started, and I wondered if his injuries had been an act to wear Lira down so he could ultimately be the one to kill her.

I couldn't do a damn thing unless he tried something that went against the gauntlet rules, but my hands tensed, ready for the moment my sword could slice through his neck. Every one of them would die after the games concluded because each person had tried to harm her. I just had to wait until the end and dream of all the ways I would destroy them and make them suffer twice as much as Lira.

My wings spread as Lorne reached down. I made sure to watch every movement he made, knowing how smart the wildling could be. He'd had me fooled for a few months while he and Eldrin had tried to turn my people against me.

Lorne got to be a prisoner for life, and I made Eldrin pay as much as I could with the debt still hanging over my head. Thankfully, he'd fallen in line these past eleven years and had helped me take back control because losing him at my side would further fracture our people's trust.

Lorne touched Lira, and primal rage ripped through my body. I flew upward, ready to attack, when he stood, lifting her in his arms.

I froze, waiting for the first sign of her distress, but he cradled her to him and headed toward the prison door.

My heart pounded, and my hands clenched as my vision tunneled. The rest of the world faded from view except for the way he held her against his chest, cradling her the way only I was allowed to do. The fact that I couldn't kill him turned my vision red, and I readied to swoop down there and rip her from his arms as soon as they reached the door.

"What is he doing?" Eldrin grumbled below. "He should be dragging her, *not* helping her."

My focus on Lorne touching Lira was the only thing that kept me from killing Eldrin. He purposely set her up to die, and I wasn't certain how she hadn't. Worse, her heart beating comforted me more than it should.

She deserved a happy life. I should never have brought her here.

My breathing seized as the magnitude of what I'd thought crashed over me. *No.* I couldn't think that way. Bringing her here had been my only option. If we didn't strike the Seelie hard and fast like they'd done to us, my people would die, and *that* was unacceptable. It was one life for thousands, and we needed her blood to take down the veil protecting the Seelie from us.

Finnian chuckled, pulling my attention from the

dangerous thought I'd had moments ago. He said, "I think you underestimate the Seelie princess, Eldrin. The fact that she doesn't act like the monster we've painted her kind as may be impacting the Unseelie more than you anticipated. She is strong, only defends herself, and keeps rising above the occasion despite not having her memories."

The admiration coming from the mouth of one of my best friends had me snapping my head in his direction. Finnian was used to getting any woman he wanted, but Lira wasn't one he could take to bed. The thought alone had me wanting to stab his eyes out so he could never look her way again.

Something was horribly wrong with me.

"King Tavish, is something bothering you?" Caelan asked, his brows furrowing as he scanned my face.

"Oh, that's putting it mildly." Finnian grinned and placed his hands behind his head as he leaned back. "I believe irritation would be an understatement as well."

Normally, his goading didn't bother me, but he provided an easy target for my frustration.

His eyes widened as he realized he'd pushed me too far, but the sound of the door creaking open came from below.

Lorne walked through the doorway with Lira in his arms. Finola and Torcall stood at the door, and when Finola took her from Lorne, some of the strange sensations in my chest eased, though I now had a new hatred for Lorne I suspected I'd never shake.

Wings flapped as Finnian hovered next to me. He patted my shoulder and whispered, "She's out of danger."

Even though that was true, her safety was temporary. She'd be involved in the next gauntlet, the gruesome game I had created. If she survived, it would fall on me to kill her.

That agonizing pain burst through my chest, reminding

me that, no matter what, her death had always been the fate I'd given her.

I hadn't considered the possibility that I'd carry the guilt of my decision for eternity.

I rubbed the spot on my chest directly above my heart to ease the discomfort. "But for how long, really?" The future weighed on me, and the need to rush to her and mend her wounds overtook me.

I had to be smart about it and not let Eldrin know. He already focused on her too much, and if he did more, I risked killing him.

Moira and Rona were the next pair through and I couldn't wait any longer, especially with Dougal and Bran just a few feet behind them.

Tearing my gaze from the door, I scanned the stadium. More than half of my people were grinning, enjoying every moment of the pain inflicted upon the traitors. That didn't startle me. What did was the quarter of the watchers who were frowning like they weren't happy with everything that had happened.

As soon as the last pair made it through the door, I turned to my group and said, "I have something I need to attend to now that the game is over."

"We all do, King Tavish." Eldrin rolled his eyes and flew toward the open sky above the arena. He called over his shoulder, "Our real day is just beginning."

All that prevented me from following him and punishing him was my intense desire to check on Lira. Torcall and Finola knew to bring her to my room, and if I argued with Eldrin, especially in front of my people, he'd want to discuss the state of things between us, thus keeping me from Lira.

"Caelan and I will find volunteers to do the work the

prisoners normally do," Finnian offered. "Meet us for dinner, and we'll catch you up on everything."

Maybe not killing Finnian had been the right decision after all. Instead of responding, I flew upward. I'd need to take the long way back to my room.

I heard Caelan mutter, "Where is he going?"

I knew better than to fly to Lira, but I couldn't stop myself. The way her golden blood had trickled down her face and her wings had hung limply sprang back into my mind, pushing me to reach her faster.

After taking the longer way around the castle, I flew into the window closest to my bedchamber, noting Torcall standing guard outside the door alone.

My wings suddenly felt as if someone were pulling me to the ground. I landed right before him, searching for Finola and Lira. Had they run into issues while coming here? Surely, the other guards knew better than to cause problems. "Where are they?"

The corner of Torcall's eyes tightened, and something strange formed in the back of my throat.

As I readied to head to the prison, Torcall cleared his throat and said, "They're both in the bedroom. The Seelie is struggling."

I hurried past him and shoved the door open. I found Lira crawling to the wall and propping herself against it. She reached for Nightbane, who crouched between Finola and her. Drool dripped from his teeth as he snarled at Finola, making it clear he viewed her as a threat.

"Nightbane, calm down." Lira reached forward, her face twisting in worry. "She helped me, so don't be mean." Her fingers reached his tail, and she ran a hand along it. "It's okay."

Seeing her broken gutted me. I was quite sure I'd rather

be stabbed repeatedly than see her this way. I couldn't keep my distance from her anymore, and my feet began moving before I gave them permission.

"You can leave, Finola," I rasped while squatting next to Lira, not bothering to look at anyone but her. Even bloodied, beaten, and injured, she was still the most gorgeous woman I'd ever seen.

"Yes, sire," Finola said with relief and darted out the door.

Heart clenched so tight I feared it might burst, I touched her shoulder, hoping it was a safe place.

She flinched and whimpered.

I jerked my hand back, and the words *I'm sorry* sat on the tip of my tongue, but I forced myself to swallow them. Instead, I settled on something else. "Where does it not hurt?"

She licked her lips and the center of her bottom one split. "Everywhere hurts, but I need water," she replied hoarsely.

Water. That was something I could do for her. I hurried to the bathroom and turned on the tub faucet. She'd meant to drink some water, but soaking in the tub, especially with her affinity for water, would rejuvenate her faster than anything. I could get her settled in with Nightbane and then get Torcall or Finola to get her a large glass to drink.

As the tub filled, I snagged a towel from the closet and placed it on the edge so it would be easy for her to reach it. With that settled, I headed back into the bedroom. The door to the room opened, and Finola stuck her head in while holding a gown.

"I thought she might need this," she said and held it out for me to take.

Right. She needed something to wear. I still wasn't used

to taking care of anyone but myself, especially a woman. "Excellent." I took the gown and added, "Can you get someone to bring her water too? She needs to drink."

She nodded and glanced at Nightbane before shutting the door again.

Maybe having the beast in my room wasn't a bad thing after all. People didn't loiter.

Nightbane lay flat on the floor beside her. He looked as worried as I was, and I realized the impact Lira was having on both of us. Another thing I had to refuse to allow myself to analyze.

"Let's get you in the bath." I tossed the gown over my shoulder, readying to carry her. The image of her in Lorne's arms took over, causing that damn rage to surge back. I needed to scrub that memory from her brain, preferably with me.

She winced but nodded. "I should get my wounds clean before an infection sets in."

"Infection?" I lifted a brow. I had no idea what that was.

"Yeah, the dirt and germs that make you sick." She placed a hand on the floor and groaned as she tried to sit upright. When she placed her foot on the ground to stand, she hissed and fell back down.

I slid my arms under her wings and knees, and the jolt sprang up between us, stronger than ever. Her breath caught like the strength of the sensation had taken her by surprise as well, making me realize that my touch impacted her just as much as hers affected me.

Why did that sound familiar? I couldn't recall, though the importance seemed significant.

I needed to tend to her and get her rested and in bed. Eldrin might call for the last game to begin tomorrow, though with how severely the contestants were injured, I doubted he would. He'd want to make sure they were healthy enough to kill her.

"I'm going to carry you to the tub, and Finola is bringing you water." I scanned her face, wishing I could take all the pain away from her. She didn't have much longer to live, and she deserved to spend that time pain-free. "You ready?"

She nodded but bit her lip, causing blood to ooze from the wound once more. I stood, and the way her body fitted to mine made the gesture feel so natural.

With each step I took, she moaned softly, making my dick harden in my pants. Even though the sounds were from pain, I imagined they were similar to how she sounded during sex.

Once again, she was testing my limits, but there was no way in Ardanos I would ever take advantage of her, especially in this shape. I moved slowly, Nightbane at my side, not letting her out of his sight like he thought I would harm her.

The water had filled the tub, and I gently set her on the edge. She winced, rolling her feet onto the heels. I bent down to remove what was left of her boots and took in the bottoms of her feet. That red haze clouded my vision again. Her skin was burned black from the fire-heated chains she'd been forced to climb.

No wonder she'd struggled so hard, yet she'd helped Lorne even when the closing walls could've broken the chain that bound them together. "Why didn't you let him get crushed so you wouldn't have to struggle like you did?" I hadn't meant to sound so gruff, but the idea of her risking her life to save *him* had me wanting to knock sense into her.

"He wasn't trying to harm me," she answered simply and factually, like it made perfect sense. "What sort of person would I be if I could help someone but decided it wasn't worth it? Besides, you made it clear I'm dying soon anyway. This way, it will be somewhat on my own terms."

"He wouldn't have thought twice about killing you if the roles had been reversed." I needed her to see that her decision was flawed so she wouldn't take a foolish risk like that again. "He leveraged your weakness so you'd save him."

Her laughter sounded raw. "Valuing a life doesn't make me weak. It makes me not a monster. I won't let the gauntlet change me. I want to die knowing who I am." Her voice gave out at the end, revealing how weak she was.

I chose to drop the conversation for now because she needed to get into the bath to heal, but I didn't want to. She had to see she wasn't thinking like a fae ... what she really was.

After untying her laces, I helped slide off the boots. Each one caused her to whimper. Luckily, that noise helped the issue I had with my pants because those sounds tugged at my heart.

I tossed the boots to the corner of the bathroom and readied to leave so she could strip down and get into the water. "Nightbane will stay with you, and I'll be right outside the door if you need me."

She nodded, and I left, wanting her to get in the tub as quickly as possible.

I stopped just outside the door, waiting to hear her get into the water, but for several minutes, nothing happened. A heavy knot formed in my stomach.

I knocked gently. "Are you okay?"

"No." She whimpered. "I need your help, but—"

Before she even finished the sentence, I opened the door ... and froze.

E ven if my skin hadn't felt like burned leather, I had no doubt my face would still be feeling hot now. I wanted to cover my body with my hands, but that was part of the problem. I couldn't move without feeling as if my skin might crack and fall off. This must be how snakes felt when they molted.

When he opened the door and stepped in, he stopped in his tracks.

I almost wished I had the power of darkness or even shadows to hide myself. I'd tried to take off my leather pants, but sweat had stuck them to me, and I couldn't get them off without nearly passing out from the agony. I could barely even stand, let alone undress myself. "I ..." The words died on my lips, and it had nothing to do with how parched my throat was. "... need help." I shouldn't have asked him, but my wings were limp. I had no choice, and who cared if I owed him? I'd be dead soon, either from the next trial or at Tavish's hand.

He swallowed, his Adam's apple bobbing as he remained frozen in place.

I wanted the floor to open up and engulf me. He didn't want to help me. I couldn't blame him. I could only imagine how awful I looked. "Never mind." I tried to force a smile, but my skin didn't want to stretch. "I'll figure it out."

"I don't mind assisting," he said loudly and entered the bathroom. "I merely don't want to make you uncomfortable."

"We both know we're way beyond that," I whispered. The words held many meanings, and even I wasn't sure which one I meant. He'd kidnapped me, brought me to a realm I didn't remember, made me feel things I hated and didn't understand, and took care of me. Every one of those things made me uncomfortable, but in very opposing ways.

He winced, and I could've sworn his face tightened with remorse for a second before he continued toward me.

The air between us turned electric. Something tugged in my chest hard, and if I hadn't been in such a horrible condition, I would've helped close the distance between us. As it was, it took him an eternity to reach me.

When he stood before me, he bit his bottom lip. "What do you need me to do?" he asked in a growly voice.

Heat flooded my body. The kind that didn't resemble pain in the least, other than feeling like I might combust if he didn't touch me.

"Help me undress." Three words I'd never said together, and of course, they'd be to him. This man had the ability to take everything from me, but this time, I'd give it to him willingly. Thank fuck my body was in complete misery, or I very likely would've done something stupid. "I ... I can't get my pants off, and just thinking about getting the shirt over my head—" I cut off with a shudder.

He nodded and reached out a hand before pausing. "Uh ... what do you want help with first?"

Good question, and surprisingly, the answer was easy. "My shirt." I would be a lot less uncomfortable standing around without my top while we removed my pants instead of being commando and him touching my top half.

Hands shaking, his fingers slipped into the collar of the tunic. "The shirt's ruined. I'll just rip it so you don't have to strain your back and wings to get it over your head."

"Good idea."

His fingers brushed my skin, and the buzz thrummed, taking the edge off my pain. I didn't understand how or why, but his touch felt better than ever before, and that was saying something.

Gripping the material, he ripped the shirt open in the front.

Cool air hit my breasts, and he glanced down then closed his eyes. He breathed through clenched teeth as he lifted his head before opening his eyes again. His breathing quickened, and he slowly eased the tunic off one arm at a time.

Even though he was gentle, the material gliding off my skin might as well have been raking me raw. I groaned.

"Blighted abyss, sprite," Tavish gritted out. "We're both going to be in misery if you keep making those noises." He dropped the tunic on the floor and straightened.

I started, my wings fluttering and my back muscles spasming again. I jerked forward, and my body pressed against Tavish's chest. My nipples hardened from the buzzing and cold as my feet hit the floor.

Excruciating agony crumpled me. Tavish wrapped his arms under my wings, my body buzzing everywhere we touched. He slid his hands back under my knees the way he'd carried me before. Unlike last time, my top half was bare for him to see.

He gritted his teeth, and his eyes focused on my breasts again before he averted his gaze back up to my face. "Let's get you undressed and into the tub before you get hurt worse."

As he placed my butt against the side of the tub, Tavish's magic of darkness crept around me. The cold sensation blanketed me, and when I glanced down, he'd covered me from the waist up. I relaxed my shoulders, thankful for the privacy, though my chest tightened in disappointment. He clearly didn't enjoy looking at me.

But why should he? Not only was I bloody and hurt, but he planned to kill me.

As I enjoyed the coolness against my raw skin, Tavish gripped the waistband of my leather pants and pulled them down gently. My legs weren't as bad off as my upper body and feet.

When he got to my ankles, his face was right in front of my crotch, and I wanted to die inside. In less than an hour, I'd had two firsts—a man who hated my guts had held me tightly because he'd feared death, and a king had put his face right in front of my vagina. When I imagined revealing my naked body to a man, I always thought it would be with him pleasuring my body instead of mere circumstance, which was definitely not sexy.

Tavish hissed, scrunching the pants hard together and removing them carefully from my legs. With the darkness now hiding me from the cooch up, I didn't feel nearly as uncomfortable.

As soon as he was finished, he turned his back to me.

My chest ached. This whole experience had to be miserable for him. I hated that I'd asked him to undress me, but he'd been right about needing to clean my wounds.

"Do you need any additional help?" he rasped.

There was no way in hell I'd ask him for anything else. "I'm good. Th—" My lips slammed shut, stopping me from thanking him. I couldn't forget he was the reason I was in this situation. "Therefore, you should go." My words were terse, but I was more upset with myself than with him. How could I have allowed myself to almost be that careless?

He cleared his throat. "If you need anything, I'll be outside the door." He went to the door, but I couldn't help but notice he was walking ... not quite as easily.

Had I hurt him? If so, how?

When he shut the door behind him, the darkness around me faded, and I ached for the coolness once more. Instead, I slowly turned my body around and winced as I prepared to dip my feet into the water.

I had no doubt it would sting.

Inhaling deeply, I touched my soles to the liquid, bracing for torment. But something cool and refreshing inside my chest trickled down to my feet like it was reaching for the water. As soon as it came, it vanished as if it had found what it'd been searching for.

The throbbing eased, and I lowered myself, shifting so that my wings slid inside as well—a little awkwardly, but I managed. My skin tingled, and my muscles relaxed, so I submerged myself, needing the relief on my face. I held my breath for as long as possible, enjoying the way my body felt underneath the liquid. I opened my eyes and turned my head to the right, where Nightbane lay, watching me. I could see him through the glass bottom of the tub.

Soon, my lungs ached, so I surfaced, laid my head back against the edge, and closed my eyes.

Something warm sparked next to where the cold, refreshing sensation had been, lulling me to sleep.

"Lira, are you okay?" Tavish slurred from the other side of the door. "I'm not trying to rush you, but you've been in there a blasted long time."

My eyes popped open, and I sat up. My back ached, but nowhere near as much as it had after the trial. How long had I been in here?

"Sprite?" He knocked louder. "Are you still in there?" He chuckled loudly. "Of course she's in there. Where else would she be?"

His unguarded laughter tugged at a memory I couldn't quite grasp. I shook my head, my hair dry except for the ends that dipped into the water. "I fell asleep. I'll be out in a moment."

"Well, I'll be here waiting." Something thumped against the door, almost like he'd placed his head against it. "I'm not going anywhere. Not unless I take you with me."

I slowly reached for the towel and noticed that my skin wasn't burned anymore. The water had healed me, and I wouldn't complain. Though I was moving slower, I no longer wanted to cry from the pain.

"Do you need assistance getting dressed?" he asked a little too loudly. "Because, believe me, I wouldn't mind."

My breath caught as I snatched up the emerald gown—my favorite color—and slid it over my body. Thankfully, my wings instinctively knew how to move and slide into the slits in the cloth, though my back ached gently. "Thanks, but I'm okay." I didn't want to live through another embarrassing moment.

He huffed and muttered, "That's a disappointment."

My wings folded behind me as I straightened. Surely I hadn't heard him right.

Not wanting to make the situation between us more awkward, I gently placed my feet on the floor, waiting for the debilitating pain, but all the arches of my feet did was ache. I sat on the edge of the tub and examined the bottoms to find the charred skin gone with fresh golden skin in its place.

I looked over my shoulder at the water. What sort of magic did it hold? I'd never take it for granted again.

Nightbane climbed to all fours, and we padded to the door. Though I still limped, I was thankful I could actually stand on both feet.

When I opened the door, Tavish stumbled into me. One hand caught the doorframe while the other wrapped around me. He buried his face in my neck and took a deep breath. He murmured, "You smell so nice." Then he swayed on his feet.

I placed my hands on his shoulders to steady him. "Are you all right? You're acting strange."

"I'm better than perfect," he answered, his lips brushing my earlobe.

A *zing* shot down my spine, and warmth flared between my legs. Definitely a reaction I didn't need to have with him. My heart hammered, and I took a step back. His actions were not in line with his usual behavior, so something wasn't adding up.

I scanned the room and saw one clear container that held water and a second that was half-empty, holding red liquid that reminded me of wine. "What is that?"

"Spirits." He smacked his lips and leaned back. "Sweet, but I bet you taste even better."

My face burned from embarrassment. "Maybe we should sit down."

"Or we could lie down." He waggled his brows, reminding me of Finnian.

I snorted and quickly covered it with a cough. "Why don't you go do that, and I'll grab myself some water?" Even though the bath had made me feel substantially better, my throat remained dry.

"No, I should take care of you," he insisted, taking my hand and leading me to his bed. "Sit and allow me to do this for you."

Before I could argue with him, he soared to the table where his chessboard had sat before *the incident*. Knowing there was no point in arguing, I sat on the edge of the bed.

He filled a glass to the brim with water for me then filled a second one with spirits.

Something he'd clearly had enough of already.

He hurried back to me, liquid somehow not sloshing over the rims. His pain-in-the-ass self would still be careful, even when plastered. That sounded about right.

"Here you go, sprite." He held out the water glass.

I gladly took it and drained the liquid in four large gulps. Just like in the bath, my throat immediately tingled and felt better. "The water here has to be full of magic." That was the only explanation.

"Your magic must be returning." He took a large sip and plopped beside me. "Your wings coming out is a big deal. It makes things more complicated."

I bit the inside of my cheek. "What do you mean?"

"This was the point, the reason I'd intended to take you back to Gleann Solas, so I could drain you of your blood in front of your people to take down the veil." He lifted his glass and watched the liquid swirl around it. "But I can't do that now that you're part of the gauntlet, and I'm relieved."

I arched a brow as anger heated my blood. "You're

relieved I'm stuck playing a game where all the competitors want to kill me, and you want to drain my blood."

"Yeah, I need your blood to take down the veil. It's the only way to save my people. And Lorne didn't want to kill you tonight." He wrinkled his nose. "That wildling will die for touching you like that. You'll see."

I stood, ignoring the way my feet twinged. "Are you fucking serious? You want to kill him for saving me? If that's how you feel, why keep me in your room and help me bathe to feel better?"

"Don't be foolish, Lira." He lowered his glass to the bed. "I'm not upset with him for *saving* you. Nobody touches you but *me*."

"You mean gets to kill me." I crossed my arms, hating the way so many emotions were surging within me, making me feel off balance.

He sighed and hung his head. "No, for touching you. I blasting don't want to kill you. Not anymore." He looked up at me through his lashes and messy hair, which had fallen over his eyes. "I wish I'd never brought you here. You don't deserve any of this. But I'm also glad I did because I got to spend time with you again."

I swallowed, my pulse pounding hard. That damn *yank* in my chest fired, trying to pull me toward him. "Tavish, you're drunk. You don't mean any of this." I reached over and took the glass from him. "It's best for us both if you stop drinking."

He surprised me when he yielded the glass without a fight. As I walked to the table, he said, "Don't pretend you don't feel the same attraction. Do you know how hard it was to walk away when you were naked in front of me?" He laughed. "When I say hard, I mean it was in *all* ways."

The image of how he'd moved strangely while leaving

the bathroom suddenly took on a whole different meaning, and desire pooled in my stomach.

Smirking, he stalked toward me, reminding me of the night we'd met on Earth. I felt like the prey, but the thrill had my pulse beating quicker.

Wrapping an arm around my waist, he pulled me flush against his body. His eyes homed in on my lips, and he lowered his mouth to mine.

Everything in me wanted this to happen, but I found the strength to lean back and place a hand on his chest. "No. Not like this."

His irises darkened, and he frowned. "Why? Is there someone else?" His arms tightened around my waist. "Is it Lorne?"

I blinked. "*Lorne?*" I must have misunderstood him. He thought I wanted a kiss from the prisoner I'd been chained to and who hated my guts? "Have you lost your damn mind?"

"Knock, knock, wildlings!" Finnian's voice boomed from the other side of the bedchamber's door. He flung the door open as he continued, "See, I knocked this time instead of—" He cut off as he and Caelan froze in the doorway.

Tavish didn't move, his face locked on mine as he commanded, "Leave before I make you."

Caelan's face tensed. "What is going on here?"

My patience snapped. I glared at Caelan and said with heavy sarcasm, "Tavish just informed me that you chained me to Lorne because I have the hots for him."

"Hots for him?" Caelan scratched the back of his neck. "You're a water Seelie, not fire."

Of course, they wouldn't know what that meant. Fine. I'd make it clear for him. "Apparently, I want to fuck him."

"I knew it," Tavish hissed and released me. "I can't wait

until the gauntlet is over to kill him. He will die *tonight*."
Then he soared across the room to the door.

"Tavish, she didn't mean—" Caelan started, ready to block him, but Finnian stepped out of the way, waving his friend on.

"Remember, he's got the hurt leg!" Finnian called out as Tavish vanished from sight.

What the *hell* was going on? My stomach clenched, and I prepared to go after Tavish to stop him.

My wings expanded behind me as I readied to push through both men and the guards. I wasn't sure how I'd accomplish that, especially injured, but I'd flutter across that ocean when the time came.

Caelan shoved Finnian in the chest and growled, "Are you trying to get our people to turn against him?"

"Of course not." Finnian gasped and placed a hand on his chest. "Why would you even suggest such a thing?"

"Because you allowed him to leave the room," Caelan gritted through clenched teeth. His normally calm demeanor had vanished, and his face twisted into anger or annoyance ... I wasn't sure which. Not that it mattered.

"I did?" Finnian dropped his hands to his sides in shock, but the corners of his mouth tipped upward like he was struggling to hide a smile. "Why would I do that? Him attacking Lorne before the gauntlet is officially over would set things back for all of us horrendously." He pointed in the direction Tavish had left. "You better hurry and get him before he reaches the prison. He's drunk, and you know he doesn't fly well that way. I'll stay here and determine what happened with Lira."

Caelan huffed. I waited for him to beat the hell out of Finnian, which he sort of deserved, but Caelan shook his head and said, "I'm not sure I should leave you with her, but I know you won't stop him. You're forcing my hand, and I don't like it. The three of us will discuss this once I retrieve him." He turned and flapped his wings then quickly disappeared from sight.

Some of my tension eased, and my wings responded by lowering into a more comfortable position. I waited for Finnian to turn around and comfort me, but he moved methodically like Tavish wasn't in danger of doing something stupid.

"Make sure if anyone arrives, they knock on the door before entering. I need to have a private conversation with Lira." Finnian took the time to glance at Torcall and Finola, making it clear he expected them to obey.

I tried to keep my hands steady as I took my glass and refilled it with water. I hadn't processed what had happened between Tavish and me because so much had been said, and he'd acted like a different person ... until he didn't. I wished I'd allowed him to kiss me because I wanted to know what it'd feel like to have his lips on mine and how he'd devour me, but not like this. Besides, what sort of person was I for wanting the man who'd kidnapped me and planned to kill me? Yet I could see how he struggled with the decision and wished he could change his mind. Worse, I believed him.

The door shut, and Finnian's face became uncharacteristically solemn.

He rubbed the bridge of his nose. "What happened, Lira?"

"I ... I don't *know*." Needing a moment to collect my thoughts, I chugged another glass of water, enjoying the refreshing sensation as it slid down my throat. Still, I worried that Tavish would get to Lorne and do something before Caelan could intervene. "Will he be okay?"

"Caelan?" Finnian's brow arched. "I'm sure he'll be fine."

I glowered, wanting to smack him. "Him and Tavish."

"Tonight isn't what I'm worried about." Finnian strolled to the table and plucked the glass from my hand. Before I could retaliate, he poured some spirits into my glass and took a sip.

"Please tell me *you* aren't going to get drunk." I was exhausted, and all I wanted to do was curl up in bed and rest. The gauntlet had taken everything out of me. "I don't think I could handle it."

"Intoxication isn't my goal, but I suspect it wasn't Tavish's either." He took another sip and sat down in one of the wooden chairs that had been painted like shadows to blend in with the room's ambience. "Mind informing me what happened so I understand how I need to support Tavish?" He scanned me from head to toe. "I can see it's not irreversible yet, which is surprising."

He kept talking in riddles, but I didn't have the energy to ask any more questions. With Tavish leaving like that and my body relaxed from the bath and water, fatigue settled into my bones. "I don't know what you mean, but he was drunk when I finished my bath. I came out to find him acting strange and talkative." The words Tavish had thrown out repeated in my mind. "But he mentioned he plans to drain me of my blood. Care to elaborate on that?"

"Blast." Finnian took another sip. "He's struggling. I'd

hoped he'd come talk to me instead of *this*." He put the glass on the table and hung his head.

Like Tavish, he pretended my question about draining me of blood wasn't a big blazing deal, but it was. I crossed my arms, and my feet ached a little deeper, informing me I'd been on them too long. I sat on the bed, my muscles jarring and the soreness clenching more. "*He's* struggling? I'm the one fighting in a gauntlet, sprouting wings, and in pain. And no one will answer my question about draining my blood!"

"Lira, he won't harm you." Finnian lifted both hands. "I've told you not to worry. His getting intoxicated, especially during the day, informs me he's coming to the realization on his own."

"He still plans to kill me." Even when he'd spoken about his regrets, he hadn't said he wouldn't do it, even if I survived the last game. "Nothing has changed. But the draining of my blood part was a surprise, and I'd love to hear more about *that*." It sounded like my death would be excruciatingly slow and unkind. Panic expanded in my chest, and I couldn't breathe.

Shoulders hunching, he sat beside me on the bed. "You're of Seelie royal blood. In order for all of our people to get through the veil and back to Cuil Dorcha, we need all your blood to take down the barrier. Otherwise, more of our people will starve."

"Starve?" Though they didn't eat three meals a day here like on Earth, I'd thought that was cultural. "Why are your people starving?"

"This land was never ours. When the Seelie and the dragons attacked our kingdom, they killed our king and queen and kidnapped Tavish. Eldrin saved Tavish and hid him from the Seelie. The dragons and Seelie ran us from our home and forced us onto this island that the dragons had ruined." He gestured out the window toward the desolate, jagged mountains. "Dragons slowly ruin the lands they live on, which is what they'd done here. The Seelie healed the ground enough so we could grow mushrooms. But most of our people remain hungry. We've lost over five thousand of our people in the past twelve years since we were exiled here."

Dragons. For a moment, the image of a blond-haired man with eyes the color of embers flashed through my brain before disappearing, but the feeling of dread and obligation lingered. Yet another memory that seemed within my grasp, but I couldn't fully hold on to it.

"So that's why he keeps insisting he needs to kill me to save his people." Even though I didn't agree with it, at least he didn't just want to kill me for vengeance. His thought process was misguided, but he felt like his wings were clipped and his people were dying. I could only imagine having that sort of responsibility cloaking you at all times. "Why not take everyone to Earth? He went there to get me."

"Food on Earth isn't safe for us, and we lose our memories and our magic if we stay too long. Look at what you're going through. What's compounding our problem here is that because we can't bury our people in our own land, their magic can't return to our roots. If this doesn't get rectified, we will become weaker, especially our future generations."

A bitter laugh built in my chest. "Yet you don't think he'll actually go through with killing me?" Everything he'd said proved that Tavish didn't have a choice. "I believe you're mistaken."

"I'm not." He shook his head. "Tavish losing control validates what I suspected all along. Don't misunderstand— I like you, Lira—but if you make it through the next game and Tavish doesn't kill you, the Unseelie won't understand. So I hope we can count on you to stand beside Tavish and fight for us against your own kind ... or the Unseelie will eventually perish."

The idea of Tavish and me saving his people together sounded way more tempting than it should. For some reason, that sounded *right* ... like that was how it should've been all along. "I don't want your people suffering, so of course I'll do whatever I can to make things right for you as long as my heart continues to beat."

"That would be infinitely more reassuring if you'd said that with your memories and powers reinstated."

"I don't say things carelessly." If aligning with people who'd been wronged and merely wanted their lands back helped them and saved my life, I wouldn't be foolish enough to throw that chance away.

Finnian patted my arm. "I believe you, but when you remember your prior life, your parents, and your people, it may not be so straightforward. I hope your mind doesn't change, or all of the Unseelie, including *myself*, will cease to exist."

Discomfort edged through me, and Nightbane huffed, coming to sit at my feet. He glared at Finnian, his eyes glowing faintly, prepared to attack if the fae made one wrong move.

"This conversation is pointless. Nothing has changed. Tavish has been stressed, and he drank too much. That's all." I couldn't get my hopes up. If I believed there was a chance I could live and that Tavish wouldn't go through with killing me, the wall I'd constructed around my heart to prevent myself from feeling for him would crumble. "I need to focus on healing and resting. They could drag us back into the last game tonight if they wanted."

Nightbane crouched and snarled, reinforcing that Finnian needed to leave.

I wondered if the beast actually understood me. He seemed to sense my mood as soon as it changed.

"You're right." Finnian stood and placed his hands into the pockets of his leather pants. "Get some rest. I'll go find Caelan and help him sober up Tavish."

I kept my gaze on the landscape outside the window, taking in the rising moon that was a faint glow through the darkness. I could see all the way to the ocean and the barren land between here and there.

When the bedchamber door opened, I couldn't stop myself. "Finnian, will he be okay? Are you sure he won't have reached Lorne before Caelan intervened?" I struggled with the idea of Eldrin using another thing against him.

"He'll be fine. I wouldn't have let him out the door if there was a chance we couldn't intervene. We'll take good care of him." The door shut, leaving me in absolute silence.

I lay down on the bed, my muscles twinging from soreness. Even when I'd worked out hard at the gym or after sparring with Dad, I'd never been this sore. Granted, I'd never before been burned to an overdone chicken nugget or injured so badly I couldn't sit.

Still, my emotions churned. I couldn't get Tavish off my mind. I wanted to rip into my chest and yank on the weird tugging sensation to reach him, and that couldn't be natural.

Nightbane jumped onto the bed and settled next to me. I placed an arm around him, enjoying the warmth of his fur. He wasn't Tavish, but he brought me peace.

Eventually, my eyes grew heavy as I clung to the one friend I had in this place.

I WASN'T sure how long I'd been asleep, but the door opening and shutting caused my eyes to flutter open. Nightbane was gone from his spot at the edge of the bed and standing in the middle of the room, glaring at the person who'd entered.

Tavish.

His hair was messier than normal, adding a sexier edge to him, and he had a plate of food in one hand and a glass of water in the other.

I sat up, my muscles protesting, but they'd improved in the short time I'd been asleep. "Are you okay?" I asked, my voice thick with sleep.

He winced. "I'm fine. Sorry about earlier." He walked to the bed and sat on the edge of the mattress in front of me. He avoided my gaze and said, "I brought you something to eat."

Fish and mushrooms.

At least their menu now made sense to me. That was all they had, and I hated how judgmental I'd been when I arrived.

Taking the plate, I took a bite of the fish. I chewed it and swallowed, wishing it were a pizza or something equally more delicious. "Where have you been?"

"Caelan and Finnian took me to my study and sobered me up. Then they forced me to attend dinner with blasting Eldrin for the sake of appearances." His nose wrinkled, and he ran a free hand through his hair, pushing it out of his face. "Sprite, about earlier. I—"

"You don't need to say anything." Though Finnian thought Tavish and I would somehow work things out and be together, this wasn't a fairy tale, and believing it could be would only set me up for disappointment and pain. "I understand why you think killing me is the only option and that what you said while you were drunk isn't true. You don't have to explain."

"But I do." He climbed to his feet and paced. "Lira, *this* was never meant to be our future. From the day you were born until I turned fourteen, I believed you would be my wife and we'd be leading our people together. But your parents changed that the day they allied with the dragons, attacked my people, killed my parents, and forced us to relocate here. They not only betrayed us but also promised you to the dragon prince when you were supposed to be *mine*."

No longer hungry, I put the plate next to me on the bed. My stomach twisted into knots. "What do you mean they promised me to a dragon prince?" The image of the blond-haired man popped into my head again, this time with a smug smile and smoke trickling from one nostril.

He placed the glass on the table, and his wings sagged. "You are supposed to marry him in the next few years."

The thought of marrying someone I didn't know and not Tavish had my heart aching worse than ever before. "But I didn't agree to that."

"It doesn't matter. Your parents gave their word."

The irony of the whole thing stole my breath. "I guess it doesn't matter. I'll be dead soon after all."

Tavish leaned toward me and took my hands. The usual buzz increased to a jolt that thrummed between us, partially filling a void inside me that I'd never noticed before.

"I meant everything I said when I was drunk." His irises lightened to silver. "More than anything in this realm, I wish our future had never changed and we could be together. More, I regret finding you and bringing you here. I wish I had searched harder for another way to break through the veil because I'd give *anything* for you to have the life you deserve. If I could turn back time—"

My heart pounded, and that damn *tug* had me leaning forward. I could see how much he cared and that he felt cornered, trying to do what was best.

This time, I pressed my lips to his. We were opening up to each other, but the course had been set. Everything we said at this point was futile.

"Lira," he whispered. The raspy cadence rolled off his tongue like a song, and he kissed me.

My little bit of self-restraint snapped, and with his mouth molding to mine, logic faded away. His tongue begged for entrance, and I responded happily. Our tongues collided, and his taste reminded me of winter frost and night air.

The jolt between us turned electric as I wrapped my arms around his neck and he tangled his fingers through my hair. A faint burning sensation heated the skin in the center of my chest, but the pressure wasn't awful and thrummed with power. The spot in my chest where the cool, refreshing pulsing came from sparked to life, along with the warmth next to it, coursing through my body in tune with the burn.

Each stroke of his tongue and brush of his fingertips distracted me and had me yearning for more.

I slid my hands up his tunic, feeling the smooth curves of his muscles, and he shuddered at my touch.

He shifted his weight over me, and I gladly lay back, wanting his entire body over mine.

Groaning, he sucked on my tongue and cupped a hand over my breast. I gasped as my body arched; the sensation was overwhelming, and heat exploded throughout my body.

Needing more, I wrapped my legs around his waist, pulling his body against mine. Now he gasped, thrusting against me, allowing me to feel how hard he was. His finger rolled across my nipple, and I pulled back a little to bite his bottom lip.

"Blighted abyss, sprite," he murmured. "You're blasting perfect. I love how you respond to me."

His fingers slipped under the top of my gown, touching me without any barriers. A desperate ache formed between my thighs, and I rubbed against him again, needing the friction.

"Calm down because, if you don't, I won't be able to give you the night you deserve." He chuckled and lifted his head.

His gaze slowly moved down my face toward my breasts, but they stopped when they reached my chest. The smile vanished, and the stony expression he usually wore around me slid back into place.

"What's wrong?" I asked. Had I not touched him correctly or been too eager?

"This was a mistake," he rasped, untangling himself from my body.

My heart seized as my chest yanked so hard I feared my insides would leap from my chest to him. When I thought I'd experienced the worst sort of agony, it was nothing compared to *this*.

Somehow, unguarded kisses and touches I'd never experienced before led me to hand my heart over to my captor ... a man who clearly still hated me.

He frowned and adjusted his shirt. The outline of something that hadn't been there before was visible on his chest. A dark-blue light emanated from it, like the moon glowing through shadows. The tattoo contained thin, delicate branches, with leaves sprouting every few inches and jagged thorns interlocked within.

My breath caught. "When did you get that?" I'd slept next to him for many nights and seen him with thinner shirts on, and I noticed everything about him.

"The same blasted time you did," he answered, his voice low and growly.

"What? I don't—" Something on my chest glowed light blue and gold, and I stared down to find that the same design had formed on me as well. "How is that possible?" I choked. I pulled my top up, hiding my breasts from view now that our intimate moment was over, but the embarrassment stopped registering because all I could do was focus on this magical tattoo that had appeared out of blazing nowhere.

Sitting upright, I moved the dress, my eyes trailing the design as it flowed down my shoulders and arms. The design cut off at my wrists, and part of me knew it was meant to go further, though I couldn't explain how or why I knew that. The magic pulsed steadily, brightening every second or so.

Clenching his jaw, Tavish jumped to his feet, his breathing quickening. So did the pulses of my tattoo.

"I ... I don't understand." My own heart quickened, trying to rationalize what I saw here. Out of everything that had happened since I'd come to Ardanos, this made the least sense of all. "We both got these markings, and neither of us recalls it."

"We were preoccupied." His hands fisted. "Luckily, we ended *this* in time before we completed the bond."

"Bond?" I racked my brain, trying to catch up to the conversation. "Is this what Finnian has been talking about?"

He froze, and the pulsing of my new marks slowed as well.

"What exactly did Finnian tell you?" His jaw twitched, and his face blanched more.

Shit. I'd thrown Finnian into the darkness without

meaning to. "He didn't tell me *anything*. He only said that he believed I wouldn't die if I survived the trials."

"Did he now?" Tavish gritted out and took a few steps back, his wings spreading, making it clear he was leaving.

I needed him to calm down before he confronted Finnian. I hadn't meant to cause problems between them. "Tavish, please don't go." I stood, the bottom of my feet still aching but, thankfully, nothing like before the bath. "I ... I need to understand what's going on." I placed my hands on his shoulders, and his body relaxed.

His face softened before it turned icier than I'd ever seen it. His markings were now covered, which made me feel more vulnerable.

"It's better if you don't because it doesn't change a thing," he replied, pushing my hands off him. "My people are my responsibility, and to save them, you must die. There's no question about it."

The finality of his words was like cold water being splashed all over me. How had I been so stupid as to allow him to kiss me, especially when he'd made it clear that no matter what, I'd die? I'd deluded myself into believing he wouldn't kill me when I should've been focusing on saving myself. By looking for safety from someone other than myself, I'd given a piece of my heart to the person who'd sealed my fate by bringing me here.

I'd been so careless and, worse, stupid.

I couldn't stop myself from asking the one question I needed an answer to before everything between us shattered like glass. "So this meant *nothing*?"

He winced and closed his eyes before opening them again, their color dark like a stormy night. "Sprite, it doesn't matter because, at the end of the night, our circumstances haven't changed." He turned, flying to the door, leaving me in the middle of the night.

And somehow, someway, I knew he wasn't coming back.

When he left and the door shut, I felt more alone than ever. I could've sworn that Tavish had ripped my heart from my chest and taken it with him, leaving me feeling cold and hollow, a shell of myself.

I sobbed, flopped back onto the bed, and stared at the sky, which darkened until not even the moon was visible. The only light I could see was the glow of the tattoo on my chest, which had my heart aching even more.

Nightbane bounded onto the bed and nestled into my side. His warmth eased some of my loneliness, but it couldn't touch the deep, endless void that had been ripped through my chest. Still, I clung to him like a lifeline, needing to not feel alone. I knew Nightbane would always be there for me.

I just wished Tavish felt even a small part of the beast's love for me.

———

THE DOOR to the bedchamber opened, stirring me from my sleep. I jerked my head up and grimaced. Of course, it'd be *him*, the man who'd had me believing that maybe Tavish and I were meant to be together. Maybe that was part of their plan to torture me—make me believe I had a chance to live.

"Hey, Lira." Finnian mashed his lips together and placed a pair of leather pants and a long-sleeve black tunic on the bed while dropping a new pair of boots on the floor.

This particular tunic laced high up to the neck, which

would hide my new tattoo. Something I noted but didn't care enough to correct. Each time, my heart ached worse; my tattoo kept lighting up like it was trying to summon someone.

I didn't respond, but those were the clothes I wore for the gauntlet, which meant one thing.

Round three was here, and Tavish hadn't come back since that night two days ago. Finola had brought me my food and water, and I'd been practicing flying around this room to get a sense of my wings.

It was difficult in here because there wasn't much room to fly high or maneuver.

I untangled from Nightbane and placed my feet on the floor. "I take it the time has come for me to die?" During the past two days, I'd thought a lot about everything, and my remorse for outing Finnian vanished the more I realized it was my future to die ... not *his*.

"Don't say that." He lifted a hand. "I've told you—"

"You better shut your blazing mouth." My blood boiled, and I jabbed a finger at him. "Stop giving me false hope. Tavish made it clear where his loyalties lie, and I won't be a buffoon any longer. I've come to accept this was the plan since I've come here, and I am through letting you mess with my mind."

His jaw dropped. "I've never messed with you. I've seen Tavish's marks. They further validate everything I've been saying."

I wanted to cling to those words, but no. I'd rather die with dignity than the deluded hope that some prince—or, rather, king would save me. *I'd* save my own damn self. "Stop with the bond and mark conversations and comments. If anything, those two things pushed us further apart. My people might have wronged your people, but every single Unseelie wants to murder an innocent whose only sin is who her parents are." Parents I didn't remember, which made this harder for me to understand. They were strangers without faces to me.

I swiped the clothes from the bed and headed into the bathroom. "Nightbane, come with me, please." After two days together, during which he'd been my only companion, he was the one friend I had in this realm.

The beast didn't hesitate, trotting after me while eyeing Finnian the whole while. The fur on his neck rose.

Good. At least Finnian might not be so mouthy. I didn't want him to continue pushing something that was none of his business anyway.

Today, I'd die one way or the other—either at the hands of the prisoners, from the obstacles we faced, or when I tried to escape again. Unlike last time, there was no way I would stop, especially since I had wings. I could now fly high enough to find my way back to Earth and my family. My only hesitation was leaving Nightbane behind, but it wasn't like if I stayed, I'd have a happily ever after.

I removed my dress and tossed it aside as I desperately tried to ignore the glowing marks on my chest and arms. Looking at the magical tattoo caused my heart to throb and the tattoo to pulse harder, as if it were sending out an SOS.

Pushing away the crushing sensation from not being near Tavish, I slipped on the pants and shirt quickly. Despite the clothes covering the tattoo, I could feel it under the material, a stark reminder.

I still wasn't sure what it meant, and I feared that if I learned more, it might make the sting of betrayal worse.

Nightbane whimpered, coming to my side, and I ran my fingers through his fur again. I wasn't sure what I would've done if we hadn't formed this friendship. "Thank you for being here for me."

Someone knocked on the door. "Lira, I hate to rush you, but we need to hurry to the gauntlet. The prison guards are expecting us."

Us.

Tavish wasn't even going to come see me before I entered the last battle. Tears burned my eyes, but I blinked them away. That was for the best. Seeing him would only distract me. I didn't need to struggle more than I already was.

Swallowing past the thickness of my throat, I walked around the bed to reach the boots Finnian left on the floor. I didn't waste any time, almost eager to get out and fight someone to handle the frustration boiling inside me.

I slipped the boots on and bent down to tie them.

Finnian cleared his throat. "I'm sorry if I made things worse. I didn't mean to," he whispered.

I froze on the last loop. "You do realize you just apologized to me?" I straightened, my heart lightening in my chest. "Which means you owe me."

"Oh, I know." He exhaled. "And I do owe you. I fear that maybe whispering in your ear made everything worse for you. That wasn't my intention, and you're right; you've already suffered so much for things you didn't do. It only felt right to say that." He winked, his cocky grin sliding back into place. "But you won't get me to say it again."

Laughter bubbled from my chest, startling me. "I wasn't trying to trick you."

I hated how he managed to make me smile even when I didn't want to. There was just something about him, and he knew it, which made him incorrigible yet charismatic.

"Love, you're about to go into a tournament where you

could die. I'd be disappointed if you weren't trying." He frowned, the twinkle fading from his eyes.

Whether it was right or not didn't matter. "No one deserves this. Not even the prisoners I'm fighting."

"We'll agree to disagree on that." He slowly walked to the door with his head hanging like he was the one about to fight for his life and not me. "Either way, it doesn't change what has to be done."

Nightbane kept pace at my side, and I folded my wings behind me. That was the one thing I'd learned to do without difficulty, and I didn't want to chance anyone harming them as I passed by.

I didn't trust the Unseelie.

When I reached the threshold, I glanced over my shoulder, feeling like I was leaving a large part of myself behind in that room.

Stupid, foolish wildling I'd become.

Torcall and Finola stood tall, their hands on their swords like they were prepared to wield them at any time as the four of us and Nightbane made our way toward the prison.

We walked instead of flying, which was for the best. I didn't want to use my wings before the gauntlet and strain my back muscles any more than I had to. The fall from Earth had been long and fast, which meant my flight upward would take forever ... or feel like it.

Our steps echoed on the smooth floor, informing everyone of our arrival.

Not that they would be afraid.

Soon, the stench of piss and feces hit my nose, and I swallowed a gag. I refused to be weak.

In the hallway, I paused, taking in Dougal, Lorne, Moira, Rona, and Bran with their wings free.

The muscles in my back relaxed. At least, in this fight, we'd have our wings. That would help with whatever obstacles came our way and in my escape.

"Ah, the sunscorched *princess* has finally decided to join us." Rona sneered. "I can't wait to watch her die today."

Today was the last chance the five of them had to kill me. They'd be out for my blood more than ever before, wanting to claim that victory. But I didn't plan on dying.

I had something to prove to them all, including myself.

"Bring out the chains," Struan called excitedly. "Then we'll pass out the weapons for the show."

The show.

My skin crawled.

One guard with hair the color of soil stepped up from the front of the room. The chains were in the shape of wings, and he passed the other five prisoners and came straight to me.

Cold fear knotted my stomach. *No.* This couldn't be.

Two guards stepped around Torcall and Finola and grabbed my arms. I tried to jerk out of their grasp as the one guard with the chains placed them around my wings. The chains pressed against my wings, and my back ached while my wings fluttered, trying to break free. Locks clicked, and the walls closed in on me. I'd never been claustrophobic before, so of course it would happen before heading to war.

"Hand out the swords and shields, and we can let them inside. Eldrin's waiting." Struan rubbed his hands, batting his eyes at me.

My spine stiffened when I realized what was going on.

"What about the others?" Finnian asked and placed a hand on my shoulder, holding me back.

I had no plans to move forward, especially when my

head was getting dizzy. I took in deep, slow breaths to calm myself.

"Last gauntlet, she used her wings, and the others didn't." Struan shrugged. "Eldrin said it was only fair that the other five get to use their wings this time while she's chained up."

"She didn't have wings to chain," Finnian snarled, not sounding like the man I knew. "She got them during the trial. It's not her fault, nor should she be punished."

Bran clucked his tongue. "Interestingly, the princess stays in the royal chambers and one of the king's most trusted is advocating for her against his own kind. I'm sure the Unseelie will be interested to learn that. Right, Lorne?"

"*You* are a traitor. You aren't *my* kind." Finnian's nose wrinkled. "So when you tell this story, please make sure you include that 'by your own kind,' you mean the prisoners who rose against King Tavish by harming the young and ruining limited resources."

The smug expression fell from his face.

"This isn't your decision." Struan grabbed a long sword from behind him. "If you have a problem, take it up with Eldrin."

I suspected that Finnian would do just that, so I took his hand and forced a grin. "I'll be fine." The way he'd stood up for me had made my annoyance with him vanish. Damn Unseelie.

"Let's begin." Struan opened the door and held out the sword and armor to Dougal. "Torcall, leash Nightbane so the beast doesn't follow her inside."

One by one, they handed each of us a weapon, and when I came to him, I almost expected him to pass over me.

But he didn't.

He handed me the same weapon as the others. The

sword was heavy and made of the dark material the guards wore, with matching armor that fit on my forearm.

Still, Struan chuckled. "I can't wait to see you fall."

When I stepped out, Finnian flew beside me.

"Be safe, Lira," he murmured and flew off toward the stands.

I kept my gaze on him as he headed toward Caelan, Eldrin, and Tavish. When I met Tavish's eyes, my heart skipped a beat, and I swore I saw a faint glow under his shirt that my pulse matched.

Strange.

He opened his mouth to say something, so I turned my head, not wanting to know. He didn't get the last word, not like this.

Then I realized the arena was flat, with no obstacle courses that the eye could see. A thick wall of nightmare mist floated on one side. The hairs on my neck rose. Something didn't feel right.

The six of us waited for Eldrin to fly upward and give his usual speech, but then the nightmare gas billowed toward us.

I spun around, trying to figure out how the sword and shield were supposed to protect me, and the gas transformed into the most terrifying creature I'd ever seen.

I raised my sword as the gas formed into some sort of snake. Then the massive snake split into three, each one twice my size.

Three blasting *snakes*.

As an environmentalist, I enjoyed testing water and dirt in the hope of saving the environment and animals, but hanging out with snakes had never been high on my list of priorities.

My chest heaved, and I realized this was the surprise. "Snakes," I rasped, alerting the others who still had their backs to them.

One darted toward me, shadowy tongue slithering out and hissing like I'd angered it by warning the other five.

Maybe that had been foolish, but I'd rather the six of us take them down together. I felt more comfortable going up against fae than shadow snakes.

The three snakes struck before the others had turned around all the way. The one closest to me came for me, and I swung my sword at its neck. Before my sword could hit, the snake dissipated, turning back into mist, and my blade cut through air.

Blighted abyss, how was this possible?

A strangled cry came from my left, and I turned. Another snake had latched onto Dougal's arm while the second one struck at Lorne.

Bran, Rona, and Moira had flown above the snakes.

My stomach roiled. If the snakes didn't kill me, the fae would because they had access to their wings and magic.

Instead of lifting his sword, Lorne raised his hand, and ice shot out of his palm toward the snake. Like mine, the snake evaporated into the dark mist, and the ice shot through the area, hitting the sandy and gritty floor twenty yards away from us, almost halfway across the arena.

My breathing quickened as Dougal and Lorne took flight, leaving my ass alone down here.

Lovely.

A small part of me regretted telling the others about the snakes since it was clear they had no intention of helping me. Four of them beamed and crossed their arms as they settled in to enjoy watching the three snakes take me on. Lorne scowled.

Was this Eldrin's way of demonstrating that even the Unseelie who acted against their king were worthier of life than me?

Quite possibly, but I refused to die that easily.

Dougal screamed and descended to the ground. Startled, I jerked toward him. His body convulsed near me. Sweat beaded on his face as whatever the venom was doing to him took effect and spread throughout his body.

My wings moved, trying to lift me off the ground, but the chains clanked. I wasn't free and probably never would be again.

I swallowed as the wall of mist split into three parts and swirled around me. If I ran through and tried to reach Dougal to save him, the gas would take effect and weaken me for the snakes to kill too. Even though I'd like to help him, I wasn't willing to sacrifice my life for him.

Raising my sword, I felt my tattoo pulse faster, like a heartbeat. I would've thought it was mine—my pulse was rushing in my ears—but it wasn't beating in time.

As the gas condensed again, I prepared and struck. My sword still hit air like the snake wasn't even there.

Could they not be killed? That sounded like something sadistic Eldrin would do. The blazing asshole would stop at nothing to have me killed.

Eiric's voice popped into my head: *Don't waste your energy stabbing at the snakes until they materialize. You can't kill them otherwise. You have to wait until they attack.*

I wanted to stare at Tavish. I had no doubt he was helping me, but the three split sections of air began solidifying again.

They had me surrounded, and I could only hope I found a way out of this. Otherwise, I was breathing my last few breaths.

I turned my head from side to side to keep an eye on them, waiting for the moment. The farthest one on my left seemed to grow denser again.

Without hesitating, I spun toward it and swung my blade where the neck should be. It formed a second before my sword reached it, and its eyes widened as my blade slid through its neck. Though it went against every natural instinct, I continued toward it, hoping my slice had debilitated it—in order to avoid the other two, which could strike at any second.

Black blood squirted from its neck, coating me as I

looked behind me. Another snake surged toward me. Unable to swing my blade fast enough, I lifted the armor a second before the snake clamped down.

Its teeth clanked against the metal, but the force of its momentum propelled me back and slammed me into the dying snake's side, where blood poured from its neck and down my tunic and chest. The blood was cold, and shivers racked me.

The attacking snake released its jaw and was rearing up to attack when Lorne appeared right behind it and lopped off its head.

"Lira, watch out!" he yelled.

I jerked my head toward the injured snake, which bared its teeth as if to attack me, though its head wobbled.

It struck, and I swung toward it, using the hilt of my sword to smack it in the head. Its mouth chomped inches from my face, and my right hand jabbed forward, hitting its eye with the long blade.

The snake's body lurched before it crashed to the ground, sending dirt and sand into my eyes. I blinked to get the particles out since my body was covered in blood. I groaned, but I held up my sword, ready to fight the last snake or anyone else who dared to attack me.

Lorne flew down next to me, scanning me.

My breath caught, and I waited for him to make a move, but he pivoted, so his back was to me.

"The last snake will move quicker now that it's not coordinating an attack with the other two," Lorne said as he pressed his back to mine. "Keep your eyes open."

My body tensed as I prepared for him to turn on me. Before I could call his bluff, through my blurry vision, I saw something black hurtle toward me.

I readied myself to lift my sword, but the snake was already upon me. I thrust my armor toward it, but its head dodged, going for my left side. I wasn't sure what to do, but my feet moved of their own accord, spinning me toward the snake.

Cold terror choked me as I moved *toward* the striking beast, but by me doing so, it didn't have a clear angle to my body. Rotating, I lifted my sword, not wanting it to attack Lorne without him knowing, but the snake dissolved into gas.

"Be ready," Lorne rasped as he landed back on the ground behind me. "It won't wait long. It's trying to tire us out."

"Us?" I hated to ask the question, but he hated my guts. I wasn't sure what he was doing, but I didn't want to fall victim by being too trusting.

Fae couldn't be trusted on either side. That was something my parents had told me multiple times. My brow furrowed, and the world shifted. Mom and Dad had never told me that on Earth. They didn't know anything about fae, yet the memory remained, though the faces and voices weren't clear.

"You saved my wings one too many times," Lorne answered tightly. "I owe you, and that's something I don't take lightly."

My body relaxed marginally, but the snake reformed and streaked around the arena. If Lorne felt like he owed me, I wouldn't argue. I needed every bit of help I could get to survive and fight ... for my life and my freedom.

The snake didn't move like the ones back on Earth. Another random fact jumped into my head. It moved similarly to the ones in the Seelie kingdom that enjoyed playing in the Aelwen River back in Gleann Solas, with more of a glide than a slither because water coated its body. This snake was made of gas and didn't need to move its body from side to side because it was as light as air.

I tightened my hand on the hilt and lifted my sword, ready for the snake to attack. My pulse thudded so hard that I could feel it in my neck. Every cell in my body was alive, and I swore my vision had improved marginally.

The muscles in Lorne's back jerked, and I glanced over my shoulder to see the snake attack him. Lorne swung his sword, but the snake moved to the left, leaving Lorne open for its attack.

Screaming, I jabbed my sword at it. The snake evaporated, and I hit the dirt. My chest heaved from exertion and fear. How the hell were we supposed to kill the damn thing when it kept disappearing into thin air?

"Blighted abyss, Lira. I'm supposed to be paying off my debt to you, not adding more to it." Lorne shook his head, but he placed his back against mine.

I almost wanted to laugh. "Saying *thank you* works just as well."

He scoffed, but we faced away from each other and waited for the snake to reappear. This time, the gas charged toward me, moving faster than I could comprehend until the snake was upon me.

I needed to do something rash, or Lorne and I would die, so as the snake opened its mouth, I thrust the sword and my hand inside while wedging the armor right behind to keep the snake from closing its teeth on me.

A loud hiss gurgled from it, and I jerked my hand out, leaving the sword behind, not wanting to chance getting bitten. I was lucky it hadn't bitten me already, and somehow, I knew the best way to take out these snakes was by handling it just like I had.

I could see the technique being taught to me, but my teacher was blurry.

Why were all these memories coming back to me suddenly? I wasn't sure if they were comforting or not, but I couldn't deny this one had saved me.

The snake rose forward like it was fighting for its life before it dropped toward me. I tried to move, but all I managed to do was turn around and shove Lorne out of the way before its massive body landed right on top of me.

I smacked into the ground with the weight of the snake bearing down on me. I waited for its head to lift so it could bite me before it died, but all I felt was blood trickling from its teeth onto my head and into my hair.

"Lira, hold on," Lorne said.

Then, the sound of several feet hitting the ground caused my heart to leap into my throat.

Now that the three snakes were dead, the other fae had landed, and I didn't have a hard time figuring out their goal.

Me.

I'd survived the snakes to die at the hands of the Unseelie prisoners who had magic and free wings. There was no doubt I'd soon be dead. It had been Eldrin's goal the entire time.

Fear surged through me. There wasn't a damn thing I could do to stay alive. As the blood coated my left side, I lifted my head to see Bran squatting ten feet away, his silver eyes glowing and his smile filled with glee ... as if he could feel my terror.

Like he could very well be causing it.

Emotions could be manipulated as part of illusionary

magic to make someone feel something they didn't truly feel. That had to be his power.

Gritting my teeth, I tried to take deep breaths, but more sand and dirt clogged my throat and filled my lungs, preventing me from calming down. I had to get the snake off me fast.

Blades clanged, no doubt from Lorne and the others fighting. I hoped he could hold them off and wouldn't decide that his debt to me wasn't worth dying for.

I clawed at the ground to free my body from the snake, but my chained wings were stuck. I couldn't flatten them to get out.

"What's wrong, *Princess* Sunscorched?" Bran winked, straightening and stalking toward me. "Having your wings bound and restrained causing you some problems?" he cooed, enjoying the fright on my face.

Even scared, I refused to be a coward.

I curled my feet underneath me and took a deep breath. I tried to stand. If I couldn't crawl out, the next best thing was to shove the beast off me. I groaned, and my legs shook, but eventually, I made progress. My muscles screamed. Strength shot through me, and I stood enough that the snake rolled off my back and landed with a *thud* behind me.

Bran lifted a brow, and his smile spread wider. "This is going to be fun. I get to take the Seelie princess down when she's starting to show signs of actually being a *fae*. So much better than killing you when you seemed mortal."

"Not so fast, *brother*," Rona said from behind me. "You got to have your fun. It's my turn."

She lifted a hand, but I'd had enough. I was done with people seeing me as weak, including Tavish.

I stomped my foot on the snake's head, opening its huge jaws, and reached down. I yanked out my sword. I'd kill them if that's what it took to return home ... wherever that might be.

Suddenly, spiders were everywhere around me, crawling toward me like they were desperate to reach me. I froze, glancing around and seeing more behind me.

Shit. The snakes weren't the only obstacles Eldrin had created.

Lorne and Moira clanked swords, the two of them fighting. Lorne shot ice at Moira's feet, and she fell.

The spiders weren't around them; they were only around me, their target. Fear had my pulse rising and my mouth drying as my mind fogged over. I couldn't hold on to any calm.

When a few of the spiders reached me, I yelled, swinging my sword at them. I spun around, slicing all the ones I could reach in half, but instead of bleeding, they flickered and disappeared like they hadn't been there, and more spiders took their place.

Like they were an illusion.

With every ounce of willpower, I pulled my focus away from the spiders to Rona's face. She wore a smug expression, just like her brother's. Their powers were different but worked perfectly together, and I had to be stronger than them and not fall for their magic.

I stood straight, ignoring the fear that had my heart galloping.

This ended *now*.

Not wanting to leave my mangled armor behind, I bent down and got it. Then I lifted my head, knowing the first person I needed to take out.

Bran.

His fear-inducing powers made me struggle more than the illusions.

I spun and charged him. His smirk disappeared. He lifted his sword just as I reached him, and I swung at his neck.

He blocked me, our swords clanging, but the contact was immediately followed by a loud *crack*.

My world tilted as half of my sword's blade fell to the ground, just as Bran rebounded and jabbed at me.

My world tilted as the sword pierced my side. Sharp torture consumed me. Bran pushed the sword in deeper, and my knees weakened.

Fighting against the urge to collapse, I locked them and jabbed my broken sword into his arm. Though the sword was only half its original size, it could still be used as a weapon. Grunting, he pivoted toward my injury. If I didn't move the sword, he'd keep pushing until it killed me.

My head screamed not to do it, but I clenched my jaw, preparing to feel the most excruciating pain of my life. I stepped away from the sword, freeing myself. It felt as if I were being sliced open again, and bile churned upward from my stomach.

Blood spilled from my wound, and I tried to ignore my concern that an artery might have been severed. At this point, it didn't even matter. Darkness clouded my vision as pain seared through me, but I stood ready to defend myself against the siblings.

"You had your pleasure; now it's my turn." Rona swirled her sword beside her without a care in the world.

In fairness, she probably had none. After all, Moira and Lorne were preoccupied fighting each other—which surprised me—so these two could focus entirely on me. They had their wings and magic, and I had access to *nothing*.

With my weapon broken, I tried raising my armor to block, but lifting it caused the injury to pulse more, and the world spun.

My heart skipped a beat. I couldn't use anything on my left side to help me, leaving that side wide open to more attacks. I had to find a weapon, but what was there in an open arena?

Rona took her time, enjoying the fear on my face. With how uncomfortably warm my body had become and the way my heart pounded, I could feel the fear in every ounce of my blood. I didn't need Bran to increase my dread further.

I stumbled back, causing Rona and Bran to laugh, but I needed to buy time. The only thing I had going for me was that they weren't flying and using their magic anymore, but that also meant they knew they had the advantage. They didn't need to use their fae abilities to take my ass down.

I needed to do something ... and make them irrational. That was the best chance I had of surviving. But how?

I heard the faint rattle of someone breathing like they were moments away from dying.

Dougal.

He had a sword and armor ... which meant I could get a replacement weapon.

I kept my head straight, not wanting to give away my plan to Bran or Rona. If they suspected anything, they wouldn't hesitate to fly over there and take the weapons before I got halfway there, especially with how slow I was. Each breath made me feel closer to death and increased my agony.

If I wanted to get to Dougal's sword, I couldn't make it obvious.

"What's wrong, sunscorched?" Rona quickened her pace. "Are you hurting?"

"Nope, just taking a lovely stroll while bleeding profusely from my side." Luckily, sarcasm worked since I didn't mean the lie.

Still, the answer thrilled her, and she expanded her wings, ready to fly. She cooed, "Oh, that's just the beginning. It'll get worse from here." She flew toward me, her sword pointed straight in front of her chest to stab me in the neck or shoulder.

I dropped so low that my butt hit the ground. Rona flew past me, missing me completely. My side screamed in agony, and I swayed from side to side. I needed to stand, but bile rose in my throat.

Fall to the side. Eiric's voice popped into my head, startling me.

That alone had me toppling over to my injured side as Rona's sword swung where my right shoulder had been. She stumbled forward, leaving her wings open to me.

I jerked to the right, with my broken sword raised high, and stabbed her left wing close to the base. Using my momentum, I brought my feet under my body and stood as she released a bloodcurdling scream. She crashed into the dirt before me.

Adrenaline pumped through me, taking the edge off my pain. I placed my right foot alongside her back and ripped the sword out. Her wing lay limp at her right side.

"You blasted wildling!" Bran screamed.

I balanced on my left leg, preventing myself from falling over, and Bran was on me. He swung his sword at my neck, and I ducked, the sword *swooshing* overhead. As he flew over me, I punched upward, hitting him in the stomach with the hilt of my sword. He grunted and crashed a few feet behind me as his sister stood back up.

Her injured wing hung haphazardly at her side, and her chest heaved. She jabbed forward like her brother had when he'd injured me. This time, I stumbled back, tightening my abs to keep myself steady. Though I'd evaded the sword, it wasn't by much, and fresh pain exploded in my side.

Pushing through the queasiness, I kept my feet moving and spun toward her, jabbing her in the injured wing again since it was closest to me. This time, I cut through the base, and she fell to her knees.

Guilt knotted in my stomach. I hated what I was doing to her, but if I didn't defend myself, I'd die a slow and gruesome death. If I believed I was in pain now, I could only imagine what torment they'd put me through for their own pleasure. At least, this way, they'd likely kill me faster.

"Lira, above you!" Lorne screamed, and the clash of metal meeting metal sounded erupted.

I looked up to see Bran dropping toward me. He held his sword in front of him, aiming for the top of my head. I shuffled backward, the dust billowing around me as he followed me, maybe five feet away.

I flung up my left arm, meeting the tip of his sword and altering the direction of his thrust marginally. Though his sword missed my head, his body crashed on top of me, pressing me down.

My head, wings, and back smacked into the dirt and

sand with his entire body weight on me. My head throbbed and the air whooshed from my lungs. I struggled to breathe. If I didn't get up, I'd die within seconds.

Though my side and ribs screamed, I rolled over, shoving him off me. I straddled him, yanking the sword from his hand, and lifted it, preparing to stab him in the chest. I needed this fight to be over.

Before I could do it, a body crashed into me. I held on to the sword as my side crumpled, and Rona sat upright to do the very thing I'd nearly done to her brother. As she raised the sword, I swung mine upward and smacked hers to the side. I rolled again, causing her to crash to the ground, and jumped to my feet.

Bran flew past me toward Dougal. No doubt he was snagging the sword since I'd taken his, but I couldn't lose focus on Rona. She kicked up her feet, stood, and gripped her sword.

Our blades crashed together, and my body began moving on its own. My feet stepped in a graceful dance as I put distance between Rona and myself. I lifted my weapon over my head, an invitation to attack that she took willingly.

She swung for my chest, and I deflected her blade downward and kicked her in the stomach.

Bran landed behind me, the two of them coordinating an attack. My head throbbed from the earlier injury, and my heart pounded. It was two against one. I had no idea how long this last trial would last since Eldrin hadn't announced it prior to us entering the arena. It could be hours or minutes, but I swore I'd been out here for at least half a day with how much agony I was in.

My hearing enhanced, and the sound of a blade slicing air caught my attention. I ducked and pivoted, not understanding why until Bran's blade moved over my head. I stabbed him in the leg while punching him in the face, my left side burning as if the muscles were tearing apart, and I wobbled on my feet.

From the corner of my eye, I saw Rona drop to her knees and whip her sword at my ankles.

I jumped as my wings strained against the chains to help me balance, but the constricted movement made me tumble onto my injured side.

Rona aimed for my uninjured side.

Awkwardly, I jerked backward, avoiding the blade, but not enough. The edge sliced into my side, cutting a chunk of skin from my body. More agony swarmed through me. The injury felt more superficial on this side, but it was another injury to add to my growing list of issues.

I lifted my hips, focusing on the adrenaline and not the pain, and kicked Rona in the nose. It cracked, and blood poured down her face onto me.

Between the serpents, the Unseelie, and my own blood, I was covered in black and gold.

She took a few hurried steps back as Bran's wings flapped.

I cut my head toward him to find blood dripping from a cut in his prison clothing. His eyes glowed.

My pulse quickened, and my chest tightened, constricting my airways. The blazing night fiend was using his fear-inducing magic on me.

He smirked, confirming my suspicion, then dropped his sword and soared toward me. He held out his hands, and I didn't need to read his thoughts to know his intention.

He planned on strangling me.

Head spinning, I tried to breathe calmly. I wasn't sure if

it was the blood loss, my horrible headache, or my fear making everything swirl around me.

Still, I clutched my heavy sword as his hands met my throat. He forced me onto my back, and my head hit the ground. My vision started to go black from the pain, and his hands tightened on my neck, cutting off my air supply.

Instinct took over, and I kicked him in the nuts. His eyes widened, and his grip slackened. I moved to kick him again, but he crossed his legs, and I shoved him off me.

I stood, swaying, and snagged the sword. The weight seemed to have increased since I'd last held it. I wouldn't last much longer. If I wanted to live, I had to end the threat now.

As I headed toward him, Bran rolled to his side and vomited. That was enough to sober me up. I didn't want to kill him, but I couldn't leave him like this; he'd just rebound and attack me again.

Heart heavy, I decided to do what needed to be done. I stabbed him in the side of the chest, making sure I missed his heart. I refused to kill yet another person.

He whimpered, and footsteps came from behind me, forcing me to glance over my shoulder once more.

Rona stalked toward me, one hand holding her nose and one wing dragging behind her. In her right hand, she held her sword.

I yanked the sword from Bran's chest, the blade making a suctioning noise as it slid free. I didn't bother wiping the blood from the end as I spun around on shaky legs.

My strength kept waning, which meant my time was limited.

Moira and Lorne still battled, and Lorne was merely defending himself despite Moira's gray, angry face as she continued her onslaught.

My vision darkened further, and the pain was almost the only thing I could concentrate on. This had to end quickly.

Rona gripped her sword with both hands, her hands shaking as her own desperation showed through.

She turned and swung the blade at me with her entire body strength. I jumped back, causing my stomach to go concave and my shoulders to curve forward. Her blade sliced my shirt and my stomach, but either I was going numb, or the injury wasn't deep.

Something took me over—something that both felt like me and didn't—and I swiveled my sword and sliced her head from her body. Blood shot from her neck, covering my face and chest, and dripped to the ground.

The world stopped as the realization of what I'd done slammed into me.

I'd killed someone, and not by accident.

I dropped to my knees, a sob building in my chest, and Lorne screamed, "Stop! Moira, no!"

I tried to spin around to see what was going on, but my body responded slowly. It was like a fog had engulfed me, and all I could sense was the agony of my injuries and the guilt from what I'd done.

"This charade ends now," Moira replied. "And the only reason I'm not killing you is due to our years of friendship."

Finally, I turned to find the dusky-haired Moira stalking toward me.

Her body glistened with sweat, but there was a faint smile on her face, like she was enjoying the fight. Something a skilled swordsfae would do.

"Stand up, sunscorched." She waited. "Give me the benefit of not killing a weakling."

"You won't kill me," I slurred as I rose, but I couldn't

stand up straight. I hunched over. Worse, I couldn't lift my sword, no matter how hard I tried.

"I suppose this will have to do," she rasped then lifted her sword.

My heart sank, knowing that my life had only mere seconds remaining.

Something in my chest squeezed tightly until my heart seized and I couldn't breathe. Watching Lira fight ... I wanted to take her place and ruin them all for daring to touch her. But every time I prepared to stand, Caelan's hand landed on my shoulder, keeping me down. That wouldn't have stopped me if not for Lira somehow fighting despite being attacked by two strong Unseelie who could fly and use their magic.

If she didn't kill Bran and Rona, I would, gladly, and enjoy the life leaving their eyes as I got justice for my fated mate.

Fated mate.

Two words I'd been avoiding and definitely not connecting to her, hoping not saying them would dissolve the connection.

All the denial had accomplished was making me lose the few days I could have spent with her, making her mine in all ways.

She couldn't die.

I wouldn't allow it.

"Tavish, we talked about this," Caelan muttered, pressing down on my shoulder harder. "You can't stop the games, especially not for *her*. Your people won't understand or approve. To save them, we need her blood, which means she has to die."

My breathing turned ragged, but the longer I sat here and watched Lira struggle, the more clarity I found.

Rona used both hands to attack Lira, and I jumped to my feet as terror clenched my heart. I shouldn't have waited, and now my fated mate would die because of me.

I was the one who had brought her here.

Blast all my people. Ruling them had changed me into someone I'd never dreamed of becoming, and now I had sacrificed my fated mate for them.

Then Lira surprised me again. Despite her injuries and blood loss, she contorted her body, avoiding the blow, then sliced the wildling's head off.

A few boos came from the crowd, and I scanned around, noting who to punish when this ended. But what I hadn't expected was the number of fae who seemed relieved that Lira hadn't perished.

Strange.

"What a weakling," Eldrin chuckled, pulling my attention back to the arena. "If the Seelie royals could see their daughter now, they'd be ashamed, especially if they knew she mourned the death of an enemy."

My heart ached, and my tattoo warmed and pulsed, causing the yanking in my chest to take control. Lira was on her knees with her head hanging, devastated over the life of someone who'd been trying to harm her.

"How much longer?" I rasped, struggling to keep myself still. I needed to scoop her up and hold her while tending to her wounds. Nothing would come between us anymore, not the Unseelie, the Seelie, and, most definitely, not some *dragon*. She belonged to me and no one else. Forever.

"It's almost over. She's about to die. Don't fret." Eldrin rolled his shoulders and smirked as he watched Moira spin away from Lorne and focus on my mate. "Moira is one of the best swordsfae in our land, and Lorne won't harm her … not really."

I swallowed, knowing it was true. I was surprised that Lorne had fought Moira. If he hadn't, both he and Moira could've killed Lira by now since they were the strongest fighters the Unseelie had, one reason I'd had to imprison them when they'd tried to take the crown before it had ever lain on my head to give to Eldrin. Losing my people would be a travesty. I'd guessed when I created the gauntlet that those two would survive, and I'd have them folded in my wing if I ever needed them to fight against the Seelie again.

Then his words sank in, and I rasped, "Is this not a timed event?"

"Of course *not*." Eldrin's nose wrinkled. "The sunscorched wildling must die."

Moira moved away from Lorne and stalked toward Lira, who still kneeled beside Rona. Bran tried to sit up, but he couldn't. Blood poured from his wound. I'd watched Lira and noticed she'd purposely missed his heart. Still, he was too wounded to move fast enough to get her.

Moira's face twisted with rage, and her nose wrinkled with disgust. She ignored Lorne. He would never hurt her, which meant I would have to intervene. Her eyes glowed, telling me she was tugging at her magic, which was stronger than that of most other Unseelies. She could influence the way someone felt beyond just fear; the strength of her illusions was so great that people couldn't control what they experienced because she could change their emotions before they realized she was manipulating them.

I couldn't hear what was being said with half of the stadium yelling loudly, but I watched as Lira tried to stand.

There was no way she could continue to fight, and I made a decision right then and there.

This ended now. Blast the games and rules, especially when it would last until *she* was dead. I was their king, and I ruled as *I* saw fit. If anyone disagreed with my decisions, I would throw them in the dungeon.

Before I realized what I was doing, I was soaring through the air.

"Tavish!" Caelan yelled, but there was no one holding me back. I flapped my wings harder, and it still didn't seem fast enough.

Lira stood hunched over, unable to lift the sword. I suspected her weakness was partly due to her injuries and blood loss, but that wasn't all. Moira would want her to feel weak and pathetic when she killed her.

Removing my sword from my side, I vowed to end this, no matter what. I swooped down and kicked Moira in the side. She fell to the ground and lost hold of her sword as Lira gasped behind me.

My chest yanked, and I wanted to scoop her into my arms to carry her back to my bedchamber, but not until I'd dealt with the threat. I kicked Moira's sword out of her reach.

"King Tavish," she rasped, raising her hands. "What are you doing?"

"Protecting what's left of my heart." My chest heaved, and my vision turned red. "I won't let anyone hurt Lira again." With that, I stabbed Moira in the chest, digging in slowly. I wanted her and everyone else to understand that I would do whatever it took to protect what belonged to me—Lira. I wouldn't stand aside anymore. Anyone who wanted to harm her had to go through me and my blade.

I lifted my head as I eased it in deeper. She flinched, trying to get away, but I kicked her side, forcing her back completely on the ground. She gripped the blade to remove it, but all that did was cut and bloody her hands.

My eyes connected with the guard who held the horn, and I nodded at him. He'd be a fool if he didn't understand what I meant.

He jerked the horn to his lips and blew, ending the game.

As soon as the last bit of the echo vanished, I removed the sword from Moira's chest, the urge to finish killing her surging through me. However, it wasn't *entirely* her fault. I had declared the gauntlet, knowing Lira would be a target. All three of them would receive grace this time, but one mistake, and I wouldn't hesitate to end them.

"Princess Lira is under my protection," I said loudly, wanting *everyone* to hear it, though my eyes were locked on Moira alone. "Anyone who stands against her stands against the crown and the throne from this point forward."

A collective gasp came from across the stadium, and I stood tall. If they believed they smelled any hesitation or weakness, they would attack, and I'd already put Lira through enough. That ended this instant, and I would grovel for forgiveness for the rest of eternity as long as she allowed me to be part of her life.

Moira shook her head and flapped her wings, getting upright. Her face twisted with rage as she screamed, "*Never!*" She tried to dart past me, but I stepped in front of her, and she hit my armor. She flew back a few feet, her face turning gray. "I would rather *die* than—"

I raised the sword and stabbed her in the heart, killing her. I lifted my chin and bared my teeth, "As you wish, Moira."

Her eyes widened, and her wings slowed as she dropped, dying.

Silence descended, and I stalked past her, not bothering to give her a second glance. She'd acted against me, and I needed my people to see how serious I was about this command.

I strolled toward Bran, knowing I had one more target to deal with until I felt somewhat satiated. When I reached him, his face turned gray from anger, pain, or heartbreak. I didn't give a blast which, as long as he was miserable.

"That Seelie killed my sister," Bran gritted out. "And you just put her under your *protection*."

No, he didn't get to question me. The urge to kill pumped through me and I took in a shaky breath to calm the hatred pulsing through me.

"You don't get to challenge me." My nostrils flared, and I gripped the hilt of my sword, though I wanted it to be his neck instead. "Lira defended herself. That was all. She did nothing unwarranted. The only reason you aren't dead is because you were playing the game. But let me be clear." I squatted so my face was close to his and allowed the darkness to edge around my body, enjoying the coolness of the magic along my molten, hot skin. "If you do *anything* to threaten Lira—and I don't care if it's just blasting staring in her direction that makes her feel uncomfortable—I will kill you and enjoy every moment. Do you understand?"

Bran's lips mashed together.

I stood and placed my foot on his chest as I positioned the sword over his chest, preparing to use it if he didn't agree. "This is your last chance to acknowledge my command."

"I understand," he rasped, hatred lacing each word.

But I didn't care as long as he obeyed.

"Tavish!" Lorne shouted, tugging me back to the present.

My heart lunged into my throat, making me choke as I spun to face him. Fear dug its cold claws into my chest.

The view didn't make sense.

Lorne held Lira in his arms, his forehead lined with worry. Lira's eyes were closed, and her chest rose and fell slowly … like she might be dying.

"Get away from her," I croaked. He must have done something to her. "Did you harm her?"

"No, I'm putting pressure on her wound." His jaw clenched. "She needs more pressure on it to stop the bleeding, like towels or something. She's losing too much blood."

Gold blood slid through his fingers in a steady stream. I hadn't noticed how much she was bleeding because the black blood was easier to see than her gold.

No wonder my tattoos had been glowing nonstop. She'd needed me sooner, and I had been so absorbed in doing what I thought was expected of me instead of listening to my heart. I rushed to them, forcing myself to take her gently from him instead of yanking her out of his arms like I wanted to.

As soon as her body settled into mine, the jolting took over, and my world steadied. For the first time since I'd brought her here, everything made sense to me. She belonged in my arms forever. "Open the door. The gauntlet is officially over."

The guards leaped into action, opening the doors to

allow me through. They tried not to glare at the dying Seelie in my arms, fearing what I may do.

Not bothering to go out with the others, I soared through the doors and headed to my bedchamber. At their posts outside the door, Torcall and Finola glanced at me, and their jaws dropped.

I didn't have time for them to be distracted, so I roared, "Open the doors."

The two guards obeyed, opening them wide enough for Lira and me to fit through.

"Get some towels from the bathroom," I commanded as I laid Lira on my bed.

Finola obeyed while Torcall came to my side and pressed his lips together. "Are you sure you want her on the bed? She's covered in blood."

"That's the least of my worries." I lifted her shirt and saw the large wound in her side.

Between the gaping hole, the thin line cut into her stomach, and a chunk of skin missing on her other side, Lira had taken a worse beating than I'd realized while I'd sat safely in the stands, watching it all.

Blighted abyss, I deserved to be like this ... not *her*.

Finola hurried back into the bedroom with three large towels in her hands. She dropped them beside Lira as Finnian, Eldrin, and Caelan entered the room.

"What in Ardanos are you thinking?" Eldrin snarled. "You almost had me fooled that you cared about the sunscorched more than your people. And where are the bottles? We should be collecting her blood before she dies! She's lost too much as it is."

The memory of the scar on her chest from him attacking her in the tub overtook me. I didn't care if I owed Eldrin—he didn't get to go free after what he'd done to her.

"We need to take the chains off her wings so we can wrap the towel snuggly around her waist." Finnian moved beside me. "Who has keys to unlock them?"

"I do." Finola snatched a set of key rings from her belt. "All of us have keys to those."

"Wait. Why are we trying to stop the bleeding?" Eldrin shoved himself between Finola and me and pointed in my face. "You were going for dramatics back there, correct? Because you wouldn't stop the gauntlet ahead of time to save the Seelie wildling. That can't be possible."

Finnian sighed. "Deal with Eldrin. I'll handle Lira."

In that moment, I realized only one person supported Lira and me and that I trusted Finnian more than anyone.

I gripped Eldrin's tunic and shoved him back.

His wings spread out, offsetting the momentum as his nostrils flared. "Tavish, I knew better than to let you near her. She's messing with your mind. That's what the Seelie do. They—"

Before he could finish, I'd punched him in the jaw. His head jerked to the side, and I shoved the heel of my boot into his stomach. He sailed back several feet into the wall.

"Tavish, you need to remain logical—" Caelan started, but I didn't care to hear anything he had to say.

"I know what you did to her." My blood boiled, thinking of Eldrin seeing her naked ... something meant only for me. "Attacking her in the tub when she was alone with no way of protecting herself."

"What?" Caelan asked with shock. "What is he talking about, Eldrin?"

Eldrin straightened, rubbing his jaw. "It doesn't matter. She's a blasted Seelie. She doesn't deserve comforts. She should've stayed with the prisoners and not been soaking in a bath. She is not one of us, nor will she ever be. She needs to die. That is the only future she should have, and I'll make sure it happens."

Without pause, I took Caelan's sword from its sheath and fluidly stabbed Eldrin in his other shoulder, opposite the wound I'd given him when I was fifteen years old, the last time he'd spoken to me like this as if he were the one in power and not me. I should've known he'd let his ego inflate to this level once more.

Eldrin hissed, and his breathing turned ragged. "This won't change her fate. You'll learn that others will attempt to kill her if you don't handle it yourself."

I understood what he believed; I had too. Until Lira's and my fated-mate connection forced me to think in other ways. "Torcall, take Eldrin to the prison cells. That's where he'll be staying from this point forward."

"You can't do that." Eldrin sneered, though his shirt darkened further in the spot where he bled. "You *owe* me. I saved you from the Seelie."

"And that alone is the reason you aren't dead." If I hadn't owed him the life debt, I would've killed him without an ounce of remorse. I stepped back and gestured to Torcall. "Now."

The area around Torcall's eyes tightened, but he didn't hesitate. He took Eldrin by his injured arm and pulled—a gesture I found interesting since Torcall had been almost as loyal to Eldrin as to me. I had expected him to be gentler, but I wasn't complaining.

"Unhand me," Eldrin commanded and tried to jerk from his grasp, but Torcall held firm. Eldrin lifted his chin as the reality of his situation became clear. "I'm the king's cousin."

"Who disobeyed me." I lifted my chin, wanting him to

see the resolve in them. "And your punishment makes you no different from anyone else."

Torcall forced him to leave, and Eldrin glared at me the entire way until he vanished from sight. Good. He needed to realize he didn't have the right to question me.

"Was that necessary?" Caelan's brows furrowed. "I mean, Lira dying was the plan all along."

My eyes homed in on his face, and I fisted my free hand, needing him to see how serious I was. "It's not anymore, and that *was* necessary. Are you going to begin questioning me and disobeying like *him*?"

"No." Caelan raised his hands. "I'm not, but this wasn't what we agreed on."

"Okay, I'm pressing on the large gash so you can move her to remove the chains without her bleeding worse." Finola sighed loudly. "Let's do this quickly so we can compress all the injuries and sew the larger one up to stop the bleeding."

I spun around to see Finnian kneeling on the couch, his left hand on Lira's arm and the keys in his right. Finola had both hands pressed over Lira's largest wound, nodding for him to move.

When he pushed her to the side, she moaned, and her heart sputtered.

My lungs froze. I couldn't lose her, not after realizing she meant more to me than anything in this realm or any other. She stood for everything I wasn't ... everything that, as a little boy, I'd dreamed we could be together. I wasn't that little boy anymore, but that didn't mean I didn't want her beside me. In fact, she'd made me care in ways I hadn't since the day I lost everything.

Finnian didn't slow, and then I heard the click of the lock.

"Got it. Now I need to unbind her wings." He tossed the keys aside and slowly untangled the chains from her wings. Her breathing weakened, and the pulsing of the tattoos on my chest slowed along with it.

I moved closer, touching her leg ... needing to feel her. But the jolt wasn't as strong as before, and my throat closed and my chest clenched. "Hurry. We need to stop the bleeding, or we'll lose her."

"Just one more lock and her wings are free," Finnian gritted out.

Then, the worst thing in the entire world happened.

Her heart stopped, and pain engulfed my chest. "Lira?" I croaked around my thickened throat.

After her heart still hadn't taken another beat in the next second, the silence confirmed what I suspected. And then my fated-mate mark stopped pulsing and lost its warmth.

I could no longer deny what was happening, and worse, it was all my fault. She'd never deserved any of *this*.

My legs gave out, and I dropped to my knees. A part of my soul tugged harshly, trying to rip away. Someone screamed in complete agony, and I realized it was me.

I'd lost her.

ABOUT THE AUTHOR

Jen L. Grey is a *USA Today* Bestselling Author who writes Paranormal Romance, Urban Fantasy, and Fantasy genres.

Jen lives in Tennessee with her husband, two daughters, and two miniature Australian Shepherds. Before she began writing, she was an avid reader and enjoyed being involved in the indie community. Her love for books eventually led her to writing. For more information, please visit her website and sign up for her newsletter.

Check out her future projects and book signing events at her website.
her website.
www.jenlgrey.com

Hidden Fate

Shadow City: Silver Wolf Trilogy

Broken Mate

Rising Darkness

Silver Moon

Shadow City: Royal Vampire Trilogy

Cursed Mate

Shadow Bitten

Demon Blood

Shadow City: Demon Wolf Trilogy

Ruined Mate

Shattered Curse

Fated Souls

Shadow City: Dark Angel Trilogy

Fallen Mate

Demon Marked

Dark Prince

Fatal Secrets

Shadow City: Silver Mate

Shattered Wolf

Fated Hearts

Ruthless Moon

The Wolf Born Trilogy

Hidden Mate

Blood Secrets

Awakened Magic

The Hidden King Trilogy

Dragon Mate

Dragon Heir

Dragon Queen

The Marked Wolf Trilogy

Moon Kissed

Chosen Wolf

Broken Curse

Wolf Moon Academy Trilogy

Shadow Mate

Blood Legacy

Rising Fate

The Royal Heir Trilogy

Wolves' Queen

Wolf Unleashed

Wolf's Claim

Bloodshed Academy Trilogy

Year One

Year Two

Year Three

The Half-Breed Prison Duology (Same World As Bloodshed Academy)

Hunted

Cursed

The Artifact Reaper Series

Reaper: The Beginning

Reaper of Earth

Reaper of Wings

Reaper of Flames

Reaper of Water

Stones of Amaria (Shared World)

Kingdom of Storms

Kingdom of Shadows

Kingdom of Ruins

Kingdom of Fire

The Pearson Prophecy

Dawning Ascent

Enlightened Ascent

Reigning Ascent

Stand Alones

Death's Angel

Rising Alpha

Made in United States
Troutdale, OR
10/21/2024

23979551R00210